OUT OF LOVE

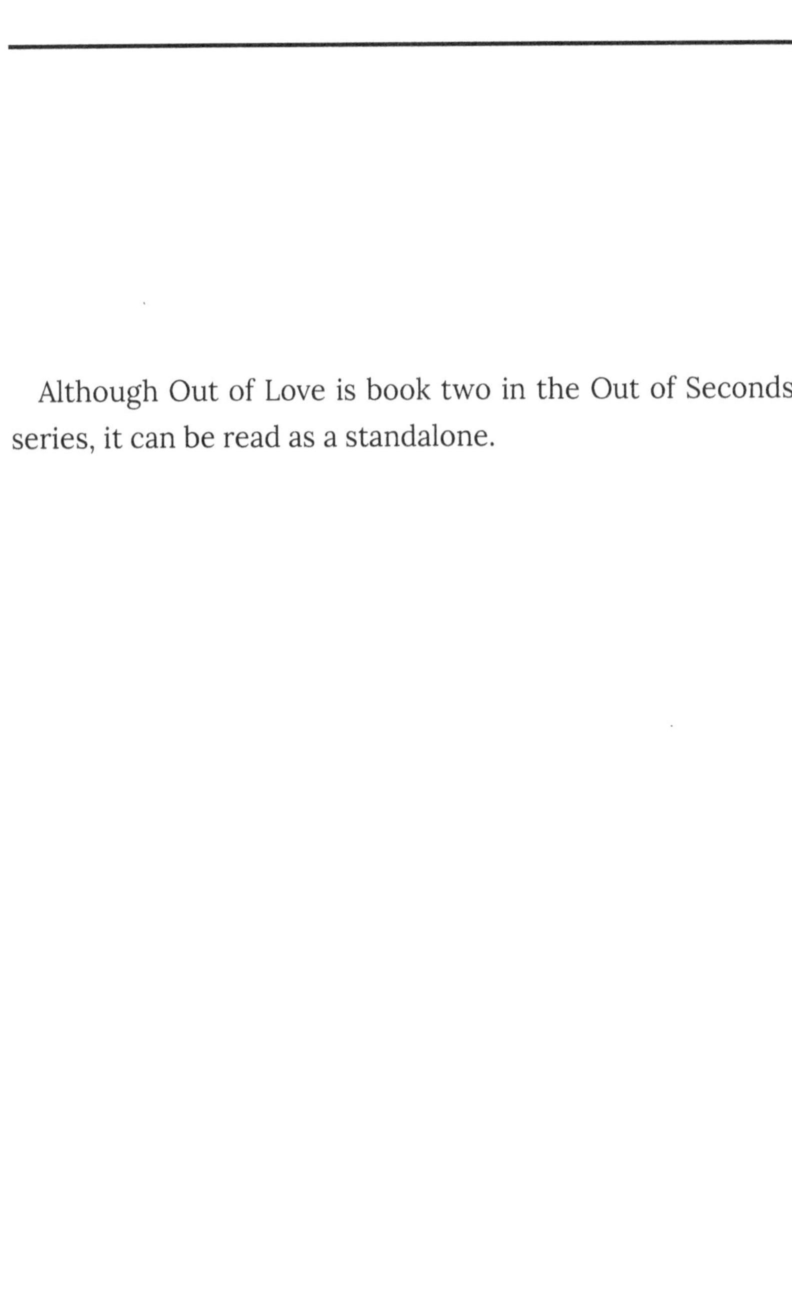

Although Out of Love is book two in the Out of Seconds series, it can be read as a standalone.

To the girl who grew up in a home that broke her heart before the world ever had a chance to.
You were always enough.

Edited by Hilari Cohen

Book cover design by Ever After Cover Design

Chapter One

Scout

I kick my feet up on the dash being the passenger princess I am and fold my arms across my chest. Jameson is driving next to me when I look over my left shoulder to see his soft gaze on me. "Please, just tell me where we are going."

His brow arches when he says, "Scout. Please stop asking questions and let me show you what I've wanted to show you since the day I fell in love with you."

A smile tugs at my lips. "How is a girl supposed to wait quietly on the way to a place like that?"

He shakes his head with a grin. His eyes turn back to the road in front of him before falling back on me.

"James! Don't look at me like that. I hate surprises and you know it."

"Fine. I'm taking you to Wood Lake," he says trying to steady his voice, but I catch the nervous energy in his tone. I don't know why he's nervous to take me to his hometown when we've been there a million times together.

My best friend from college, Harper, also grew up in Wood Lake. She introduced me to her home before she even introduced me to Jameson. I honestly love the small town covered in white pine trees and a lake that somehow makes you feel at home.

"I love Wood Lake! I didn't bring a bathing suit though if we're going swimming. Are we going to that delicious diner with the giant pancakes that taste more like donuts than pancakes? If not, we should definitely go there after."

My head falls to the side as I see Jameson's deep blue eyes are still focused on me. They're always focused on me. After three years being together, he still looks at me like nobody has ever looked at me before. Like I'm the most fascinating thing in this world to him.

"We're not going swimming and we can get pancakes after," he says, giving me a crooked smile. His smile gets me every time.

"Ugh, fine don't tell me exactly where we're going. I'll get back at you though. In fact, I may have a surprise on under these jeans for you. But you won't find out until later."

He cocks an eyebrow at me before his eyes slide down to my jean shorts. Then he grins again, and I know I've already lost this game. "I love surprises Scout. Especially when they have to do with what's underneath your clothes."

I roll my eyes and press my lips together to keep myself from smiling.

Then James says, "I used to hate surprises too."

"When did you start liking them?" I ask, turning the air vents off my chilled legs. The air conditioning was on high and blasting. James sees that I'm cold and turns it off. It's the little things.

"Since I met you, I guess," he answers without an explanation.

"What do you mean?"

"I guess I thought I hated surprises until I figured out that you're full of them."

"I like keeping you on your toes, so you don't get bored of me," I say with a wink.

Then I roll down the passenger side window as we turn down the highway that leads to Wood Lake. The warm June evening breeze flushes against my cheeks and blows through my hair. I stick my hand out the window as we drive slowly by a few houses on the outskirts of town. We pass the large green fields and I admire how open they seem. Nothing out there but the vast crops that help keep the very well populated planet fed. Lines of sprinklers on wheels spray the deep green area and I feel the cool mist sprinkle my hand. I let the pungent, earthy smell of wet grass float inside my nose. And I love it. I haven't always felt this way about small towns. Honestly, I thought I'd always be a city girl, since I grew up in one. I liked the thought of always being hidden within the crowds, nobody caring who you are. But I've changed a lot.

"You really do like it here, don't you?" Jameson asks.

I tilt my head toward him as the wind blows my brown hair straight into my face. I tuck it behind my back and lean into the seat to meet Jameson's hopeful stare. I'd do anything for him. Especially move to Wood Lake with him if that's what he's getting at. Truthfully, I love Wood Lake so much, I'd probably move here on my own. But moving here with James? Yeah, I'd do that in a heartbeat. But honestly, it would surprise me if he wants to.

"I love it here," I tell him. "I could see myself living here. You've never mentioned if you'd ever move back here though. I know it's your hometown and surely there are good memories. But don't the bad ones make you want to stay far from it?"

Jameson grew up in a household that consisted of his deadbeat, drunk dad who would come home to either beat him and his brother or make them beat up each other. He lost his mom to cancer at a young age and even though he's grown and that was many years ago, I can tell he still misses her. His younger brother Will doesn't remember her, but James does.

"That's actually what I wanted to talk to you about," he stammers.

We pull up to an open white house with a wraparound porch and plenty of land surrounding it. I sit up to get a better view and it honestly takes my breath away. It's no mansion but it looks like a house that could be filled with love. It's older but by the looks of fresh paint and cut grass, you can tell it's been taken care of. "This is absolutely beautiful," I say, admiring the house.

"I used to imagine myself living in this house when I was little."

I look over at James as he looks at the house, reliving the memory.

I listen deeply as he tells me the story of how he discovered this house when he delivered newspapers as a boy. He would fantasize that instead of the trailer home he was growing up in with his abusive father, that this was the house he lived in.

He says, "Rather than throwing the paper toward the front door just like every other house, I'd imagine for three minutes each morning that this was my last stop of the day because I pretended it was home. I'd get off my bike and walk it up the driveway and park it right by the garage with the other children's bikes that were there. Then I'd walk toward the door and pretend my family lived here. I imagined running through the yard with my brother Will and a mom that was alive watching us play from the porch. I even imagined having a dad getting home from work with love instead of rage."

A pit grows in my stomach just thinking about what he and his brother went through. "James, I'm so sorry."

He chuckles softly. "Don't be. I loved this place. There even used to be a porch swing to sit on."

I get it. He loved this house because it made him feel safe. "Did anyone ever notice you?"

"If they did, they never said anything."

"Then you'd just leave after a few minutes? Didn't that make you sad?"

He smiles. "No, I knew I'd be back the next day."

He swings his door open to get out of the truck, the positivity radiating off him as my mind is still pondering him as a little abused boy. Thinking about how he wouldn't let reality get the best of him, knowing he'd be there again tomorrow to imagine a better world to live in. James opens the passenger door for me. My heart breaks for that little boy but makes me fall even harder for the vulnerable man in front of me. I wish I could tell him more about my life growing up but I'm too buried down deep in my childhood trauma and heartache to open up the *way I should. I climb out of the truck and look around. James and I have talked about getting married and I know if I agreed, James would marry me in a heartbeat. We've dated for over three years now and I'm completely in love with him. Ever since my best friend Harper introduced us one night in Columbus, I haven't been able to imagine a world without him. But deep down, I can't stop the fear inside me. I'm honestly so scared that if I open up to him about my past that I'll lose him. For lying about who I am and where I'm from. I love him so deeply, it almost hurts. I can't seem to get out of these thoughts.*

"The realtor couldn't be here," James explains. "But I want to show you photos of the inside."

He pulls out his phone and hands it to me. I swipe through the photos with a giddy grin on my face. "Is it newly remodeled? Everything looks new."

"Yeah. New appliances and everything," he answers.

"You want this house, don't you?" I ask full of hope.

"I don't know. Do we want this house?" It's the "we" in that question that has my heart skipping, dropping, cracking. James continues, "I know you're not ready to get married and I know you have so many things locked away in that pretty head of yours. I get that you have heartache, trauma, or mistakes holding you back. But Scout, I want to start our lives together. If this isn't the house you envisioned for us, we can keep our place in the city or sell it and find a place anywhere you want to. I just want to make you happy. And damn, the way your eyes light up when you smile every time we come to Wood Lake to visit and the way you just looked at this house has my head fixating on any possible way I can make this work. Even though

I never envisioned a life back in Wood Lake, something about it feels like you. It feels like us. This house is for sale, and it feels like home."

The vision of the future with James is everything and more. I wrap my arms around him even though I don't deserve him. "I've told you there are things you still need to know and when I'm ready, I'll tell you. I want a life with you, and this feels right. It feels like the next step. So, hell yes I want this house."

His mouth crashes down on mine as my fingers link together behind his neck.

He nibbles on my lip and I smile, our excited breaths out of rhythm as we come apart from the kiss. "I'll call the realtor and make an offer. Although, they told me we're the only ones who have looked at the place in a year so..."

"We're really doing this?" I ask, my hands still wrapped around his neck.

"We're really doing this."

"I'm ready. Let's just hope one of the schools here is hiring teachers because driving to the city every day would not be fun."

Although I loved college and the city, I'm ready to be a teacher in a small town with the man I love by my side. A fresh start. I can't wait to tell Harper I'm moving to her hometown.

"I'm sure getting a teaching job here won't be a problem. The schools are great."

I nod my head, knowing he's right. I feel it. "But what about you? Don't you want to be a US Marshal eventually? Can you even do that here?"

"That's still a way down the road but yeah that won't be a problem. Wood Lake is close enough to city limits and the airport if I have to travel."

"Eek! Let's go celebrate at the diner." I'm turned around to head back to the truck before Jameson pulls me back.

He says, "I want you to know something."

"What?"

"You don't ever have to hide from me, Scout. Ever. There are places in here," he holds my head between his hands, "Dark places that I know you'll never let yourself escape from. And regardless of what you just said, you may never open up and let me help you out of them." I open my mouth to talk but he brushes his finger across my lip to politely shut me up. "And that's okay. I accepted that a long time ago. I don't have to know what those dark places inside your head are but don't hide in them from me. If they invade your day and make you feel devastated, don't cover it up with a smile anymore. Just be you. I don't need you to put on some happy act all the time because I know those places in your head take you from me sometimes. And when they do, I'll tear down their walls and rip you away from them. You don't have to tell me what those places are or what they mean but don't hide from me when you're hurting. I love every little thing about you. I'll always love you no matter what. I don't give a shit what your past is as long as I get your future."

I break into a sob and let the tears fall, since obviously Jameson loves to see me cry. I'm kidding, he just knows I need to sometimes. I bury myself into his chest and grip onto his shirt because he just described me perfectly. He knows me more than

I know myself. He's willing to be my comfort when he doesn't even understand what the hell is going on in my head. He just wants to be here for me, just like Harper. I've never felt so lucky to have found them.

"I love you too." My body shakes as he holds me close. The guilt in my chest subsides after what James just said. I'm not near ready enough for marriage yet but I think we're on the right track.

I feel the sun heating up my dark hair and back. James probably thinks these are sad tears but they're the complete opposite. I've never felt as happy as I do right now.

I sniff, and look up at Jameson. He wipes a tear off my cheek, and I laugh quietly. "It's nice crying here in your chest and all, but I'm really craving those donut pancakes."

He shakes his head and laughs. "Let's get you some then."

I sit up in bed and immediately feel tightness in my chest. I kick the covers off of my feet and stare into the darkness of my hotel room. I'd almost forgotten what the pain felt like. I'm dreaming. Again. And he isn't here with me in bed. Again. I'm thousands of miles away but the memories of James are right here with me. They live in my dreams and waking thoughts, reminding me of the love I cannot have.

Moving into my new home in Wood Lake with Jameson a year ago was the happiest I'd ever felt in my life. Until the day everything turned for the worse and I had to do the hardest thing I've ever had to do. Leave Jameson behind...

I look at the time on the alarm clock. It's four AM and I set it for four-twenty. I might as well get up now to get ready to drive to the Honolulu airport. I have a plane to catch.

Chapter Two

Scout

Breaking up with someone is excruciating when you can't explain the truth. I'll never forget the look on Jameson's face three months ago when I said I can't love him anymore. It was so painful to see, I knew I had to get away. And fast, before I changed my mind. I knew if he begged me a moment longer, I'd stay. But leaving was the only choice I had. It was the biggest heartbreak of my life. And my broken heart is still somehow managing to work as I feel it beating fast in my chest. My hands shake as I make my way through airport security. The feeling I have now reminds me of how I felt three months ago when I was getting ready to take off on a plane to Hawaii as quickly as possible. Only this time, I'm going home, and my feet seem to be moving a lot slower.

I'm hesitating returning to Wood Lake, after everything I put Jameson through. Even though I can't be with him when I get back, I do love my job. I love everything about Ohio. And damn Jameson Karter for taking me back to Wood Lake after graduating from college and making me fall even more in love with him and this small town. It's been embedded into my heart as I discovered who I truly am there. It's everything. It's family. It's love. It's my safe place.

I know it's not forever now, but it's home. At least for one more year while I finish up my contract with the school. I can handle being in the same small town as my ex-boyfriend who probably hates me... right? I have to stay away from him no matter how much I still love him. Maybe him hating me will make that easier.

A service worker at the airport interrupts my thoughts as I stare at the screen in front of me. "Ma'am? If you're not ready to retrieve your boarding pass, I'm going to need you to get in the back of the line. People are waiting."

"Oh right, sorry." I quickly print my boarding pass to Ohio and make my way to the designated gate. No turning back now.

Since all the seats there are filled, I take a seat on the ground by the window. I put my headphones on and close my eyes. I had a lot of time in Hawaii to reflect and really process everything that's happened the past few months and yet my stomach hurts as I hold back the tears and try to figure out how I'm ever supposed to continue living life without Jameson. Going back to Ohio is going to be hard. Going to places Jameson and I went together, being with our friends. In Hawaii, I didn't have to worry about that.

My Bluetooth headphones start making a beeping sound, informing me that they're dying, I sigh. "Dammit." After putting them back into their case, I dig through my bag to find the charger and plug them into the wall outlet -- that way I can at least have them on the flight. I'm aware of all the people around me but I don't mind. That's not why I brought my headphones. It's the quiet that gets too loud. That's when I need my headphones the most.

Leaning my head back against the wall, I glance down at my white cutoff shorts and realize I'm going to miss the tanned skin that Hawaii provided. I know to some people it's hardly a tan at all but on my porcelain white skin, it is. I know it won't last forever, but a girl can dream.

My stomach grumbles, reminding me I haven't eaten anything today. I pull my backpack up onto my lap and start digging through it. I've got to have some candy in here somewhere. When I find my Nerd Clusters, I pop a couple in my mouth.

"Della?" a woman's voice suddenly asks. I about choke on my candy hearing that name again.

I look up and pause to see my old friend from high school. "You seriously don't remember me?" she says.

"Kat?" I stand up. "I'm sorry. I just don't go by that name anymore. I'm Scout."

She pulls me in for a hug. "Oh. Okay, Scout. How's life? I haven't seen you since high school – it was as if you just disappeared. You look so different; I barely recognized you. And you changed your name. It's like you're a whole new person."

"I'm doing good. Are you here on vacation?" I ask, trying to move the conversation along.

"Yes. I'm headed back home to Washington. What a small world. I never thought I'd see you again after you just up and vanished. I'm actually running late, so I better go -- I don't want to miss my flight. You should come visit me sometime in Washington so that we can catch up," she says.

"Sure," I say, knowing that would never happen. "Well, it was nice to see you Kat," I say before she runs off with her bright pink luggage. She's matured a lot. I barely recognized her either.

Since I was living with James before I left Wood Lake, now I need to find somewhere else to stay. I have a property manager showing me a couple places for rent this morning. It's weird being back, but I'm surprisingly okay. I hold my breath as I pull up to the first house that I told her I was interested in seeing. It's on the other side of town from Jameson, even though the town is small enough that I'm bound to run into him at some point.

I can do this.

This little red brick house is old, but I love the look of it. There's a front porch and a large oak tree in the front. It's older but nicely taken care of.

I step out of my ancient car to a friendly woman smiling at me from the house. She's wearing a bright green suit jacket with denim jeans and high heels.

"You must be Scout. I'm Shayna." She holds out her hand when I get to her, and I shake it.

"Hi," I say, "I love your outfit."

Her eyes light up. "Thank you. I like yours too."

I look down at my t-shirt and shorts. Normally I'd probably be dressed nicer than this, but since I've been traveling all day, I chose comfort over style.

"You ready to see the house?" Shayna asks, her hand on the doorknob.

"Let's do it."

She opens the front door and a musty smell drifts out into the air. "It's small. Only one bedroom and one bathroom. But it's just you?"

"Yes. I don't need anything big." *In fact, I kind of like small. Big houses hold too many secrets.*

As I get a tour of the house, I find the kitchen is my favorite part of the place. It has plenty of counter space for me to cook and bake in, two of my favorite things to do next to running. It'll need a good cleaning, but I can see myself living here.

After showing me the inside of the house, Shayna slides the back door open. The backyard is plenty big and it's fully fenced in. Like the front yard, the grass is freshly mowed but looks like it could use some water since the green color has faded to a sickly yellow.

"Somebody from our property management team should reach out to you about mowing your lawn for a small fee. Unless that's something you'll want to do yourself, because that's fine too."

"Thanks. That would be great," I say. I'm relieved since I don't own a lawn mower.

"Do you have any pets?" Shayna asks.

"I don't. Is it pet friendly?"

"It is."

"I really like it. I assume it's ready to move in?"

Shayna smiles. "Yes. Nobody has lived here in years since it's an older home, but I've always thought it was charming."

Even though I miss my home with Jameson more than anything, this feels right. "I love a house with character. I'll take this one," I say.

Shayna gives me an amused expression. "You've got it honey." A smile crosses her face. "I like you."

I smile back as I take another look at my new place. The dust swirls around, illuminating the air, the hardwood floors need a good scrubbing, the walls need some decoration, and the windows are so dirty you can barely see out of them. I could use some distraction over the next week before school starts, putting this place together. It will take both time and effort. I need that. It's perfect.

"Thank you."

I'm lucky the little house is mostly furnished so I won't have to make any big purchases.

"You'll need to put a deposit down today, but the first month's rent is free," she says.

"A deposit won't be a problem."

"Let me go get the paperwork from my car so you can start moving in."

After filling out the paperwork, I hand the clipboard back to Shayna. She reads through it and says, "I see you teach at the elementary school. What grade?"

"First."

"That's amazing. I don't know how you teachers do it, but bless you," she says.

I smile. "Thanks."

After getting my key from Shayna, I'm all smiles knowing I've found a place to live. Luckily, I was able to get most of my things out of Jameson's house and into a storage unit right after our breakup. I figured I wouldn't want to go get it from him later since that would be torture. Rafe, an old college friend from the city, didn't hesitate when I called for help to move my stuff out quickly that day. I push the thought of how difficult that was away and climb into my car.

Waves of nostalgia roll over me as I drive through town, but I try not to let it make me sad. Everything here seems so different, yet it's exactly the same. It's only been three months since I was here, but it feels worlds away somehow. I park at the supply store downtown and take a breath before walking in. Luckily nobody seems to notice me as I gather the things I need. I don't recognize anyone in the store either, since James was always the one to shop here.

After checking out, I walk out of the store and my stomach grumbles when I smell something fried and delicious. It must be the bar across the street where I also hear music playing. After putting all my cleaning supplies inside my car, I walk into the new bar called Bourbon Bros.

An actual band is behind the great country music I heard from outside, and I take a seat in a booth so I can watch them. Some familiar faces are seated at the bar, but I don't know them well enough to get up and greet them. A woman named Katrina who did my hair once is with Theo, who works at the grocery store. They look like they're flirting. Hmm, I never would have guessed the two of them would hit it off. Good for them.

"What can I get you?" the waiter asks.

"Whatever it is that smells so good."

"That'd be the curly fries. Can I get you anything else?"

"A grilled cheese on the side. Does this band play here often?"

"Every Thursday."

"They're amazing."

"Them and the curly fries are keeping us in business. Drink?"

"Just water, thank you."

As soon as I'm done eating and I settle my tab, I'm out the door, although I hope next time I can stay longer. I'm relieved I found somewhere new to go by myself. Every other bar and restaurant in town will remind me of Jameson because we went everywhere together.

When I get back to the old house, I unpack my suitcase and boxes before doing some cleaning. It's already getting dark, but I'm not tired anyway since I slept so much on the plane.

After deep cleaning the whole house, it already looks much better. And it smells good in here now with the candles I bought at the store lit and scattered around. Something as simple as a clean home and burning a candle in my own place feels really nice. I don't start work for another week, so I have some time to get settled in. I'll go to the school tomorrow to get my classroom ready. It feels weird being back here when I haven't even told Harper yet. She doesn't know where I've been over the summer. I texted her a month ago and told her

I just needed space to clear my head. I'll call my best friend soon. But considering she's dating Jameson's brother Will, I'm taking my time. I'm not ready for James to know I'm back yet. I assume Harper and Will are still living together in Columbus while Will goes to school. As excited as I am to see Harper again, I'm dreading what's to come.

I lay in bed, and of course, I think of Jameson. I try to stop myself from wondering what he's doing right now. And what he'll do when he finds out I'm back.

⚬

I found myself here, sitting outside our house like a creeper. The house that's not mine anymore. It's dark inside but his truck is in the driveway. He's probably asleep. The memory of us when we decided to move in here together creeps in. We were so excited to start our lives in Wood Lake and we did for a whole year. I wish I could go back in time and change things so that I could still be in there with him, but I can't.

This is too much. Being near him and not being able to be with him is killing me. Living here will be much harder than I thought, but it won't be forever. For now, I've got to learn to let him go.

I finally let myself cry on the way back to my new house, alone.

Chapter Three

Scout

The best feeling in the world to me is when my lungs ache, I lose feeling in my legs, and my chest burns with each quickening breath. My shoes thud against the pavement and I'm shut off from the world at this moment. Nobody can take running from me. It's who I am. They may be able to take away the one person I love most, but they can't take this. My therapy session is corrupted when I think about Jameson.

I miss him.

I run harder. It hurts more. The pain is my favorite part. I need the pain of running to overtake the pain in my heart. I glance over my shoulder to look behind me, which is something I never used to do, but I do now.

I realized at the last-minute last night that I needed a few extra supplies for my classroom. Since there is only one grocery store in Wood Lake and it doesn't have the things I need, I drove to Columbus before the sunrise to knock out a run in my favorite park before my Target splurge. I wouldn't normally run this early in the morning, but when I couldn't sleep at three am, I decided to head out an hour later. It was still pretty dark when I started my run just after five.

"Scout!" another runner yells as I'm about to run past them. The morning sun is just light enough to recognize a fellow track teammate from college.

"Hey Matt," I say. "How are you?"

"I'm good. The coaching job at Copper Hill has been keeping me busy."

I smile. "You're the new track coach at Copper Hill?"

He nods.

"That's amazing. I heard about Coach Rem retiring."

"Yeah, you missed the party." Matt laughs.

"I was on vacation. In Hawaii."

"Really? You and Jameson? We need to get together sometime. I miss the college days when we all used to hang."

I take a deep breath after hearing Jameson's name. "That would be fun."

"How is Jameson anyway? I heard he's quite the badass US Marshal."

I look down and kick a rock across the pavement. "Oh, we broke up before the summer. I went to Hawaii alone."

Matt looks shocked with his eyes wide open. "Shit, really?"

"Yeah. It just didn't work out." I change the subject. "Do you like coaching the track team?"

He shakes off his surprised expression and nods. "I do. We haven't done much training yet though, so ask me again in the spring." He chuckles. "Hey, maybe you could come to track practice sometime. Show the distance runners how it's done. Give them some advice."

"Yeah. I'd like that."

Although I miss track sometimes, I'm happy that part of my life is over. The pressure of being the star in track really got to me my senior year of college. I always thought maybe I'd run professionally and pick up some sponsors and train hard enough to make a living doing what I love, but the more I thought about it becoming a job, the more I realized I just wanted to keep my relationship with running simple. Running could never be my career or I'd end up hating it. I knew then that once track was over, I'd just keep running for myself, so I'd fall in love with it again. And it worked. Maybe eventually I'll run races again but at the time being, I like what I'm doing. Just simply waking up every day to run for me. Nothing else.

"Well, I'll let you get back to it. See you around Scout."

"Yeah, see ya, Matt!"

After running six miles, I sprint to my car, quickly jump in and head to Target so I'm able to get to work and start preparing for the school year starting next week.

Back at home, I feel the heat on my scalp as I tilt my head back and let the hot water stream down my long hair. I finally texted Harper this morning and told her the news that I'm back in Wood Lake. She couldn't believe I had been here for days and hadn't told her. But I was worried she or Will would tell James, and I've already hurt him enough.

I called Harper on my way to work, as promised.

"Hey!" she said when she answered the phone.

"Hey! Miss me?" I ask.

"Of course! I can't wait to see you! I can't wait to see your new house! How does it feel, Miss Independent?"

"Like I'm finally a grown-up." We both laugh. This is the first time I've ever truly lived on my own, unless you count the time I lived in my car for a few weeks when I ran away from home. "But I'm just renting."

"Still, I think it's great. I really do miss you, Scout. Can you meet up for dinner at Allessios? Then afterward I can come see your house?"

Allessios is our favorite Italian restaurant in Wood Lake, and I really want to show her my new place too. So instead of meeting her in the city I say, "I'd love to. Seven, okay?"

"Of course. Can't wait to see you."

"I look forward to it. See you there."

We hang up just as I'm pulling into the elementary school five minutes later.

I walk up the stairway with anticipation to get my classroom ready for the school year.

⚘ ⚘

As I'm waiting for Harper at a booth inside Allessio's, I mindlessly tap my foot up against the wall. I don't know why I'm so nervous. I guess I'm just worried about what Harper might say about Jameson. And bring up what I did to him. I'm sure she heard an earful of James' side of the story since she's dating his younger brother Will. Dating the two hot Karter brothers together was a dream come true for two best friends. The four of us were always together. Since James and Will had a dead-beat dad and their mother passed away when they were little, they didn't have a lot of family besides each other. Since I don't talk to any of my family anymore, I guess you could say it felt like the four of us were each other's family. Well and of course Harper's amazing parents who also live in Wood Lake. Harper walks into the restaurant and I stand up. When she spots me, we run together for a big hug. I didn't get to say goodbye before I left in a rush to O'ahu. Harper is all smiles as she sits back down, and I take the seat across from her.

"I ordered you some wine. Okay tell me everything," I say. "How are you and Will?" I look around. "You haven't seen blue eyes lurking around since I've been gone, have you?"

Harper spits out her wine when I bring up her obsessive ex-boyfriend. "Only you would joke about that. And no, I haven't. Will and I are doing great. In fact..." She holds up her left hand, showing me the perfect diamond ring.

"Holy shit!" I yell. I cringe at myself and duck my head for swearing so loudly in a nice restaurant. Harper laughs as I grab her hand. "Will did such a good job. It's perfect. It's so you."

"Thanks. I love it," she says, sliding her hand back as the waiter comes to our table. I haven't even had a chance to look at the menu yet, but I know exactly what I want because I always get the same thing here. After ordering my extra cheese ravioli with alfredo sauce, Harper orders her usual margherita pizza, and we get right back to chattering away.

"When did this proposal happen? How did it happen?"

"A couple weeks after you left. I wanted to tell you in person. The day he proposed he wore the ring on his dog tags and said he was going to wait until he took me to dinner that night to ask me to marry him. He had a whole date planned out. But I got a flat tire on the way home from work and when he came to my rescue and started changing the tire, his dog tags came untucked from his shirt, and I instantly saw the ring. He gave me a confused look when I gasped but as soon as he realized what I saw, he got down on one knee and proposed on the side of the road right then and there." I laugh because it sounds exactly like Will.

"Before he even changed my tire! There were literally cars driving by honking at us. It was perfect."

"That's so sweet."

"Do you want to hear the best part?"

"What?"

Excitement radiates off her as she smiles. "We're moving to Wood Lake after the wedding."

My jaw drops followed by a huge grin. "Are you serious?" I couldn't be more excited to live in the same town as Harper. It'd be nice to have a friend besides the other teachers from work.

"Yes!" she says excitedly.

"I can't wait. When is the big day?"

"We were planning on waiting for Will to finish medical school, but he still has two years. He talked me into getting married on October fifth."

"What?!" I yell a bit too loudly again. I try to keep my voice down when I say, "Like next month, October?"

She nods excitedly and I squeal.

"I know it's soon," she says looking down at her ring. "But we just can't wait."

The waiter fills my glass of wine and I take a sip. "I'm so happy for you, Harp."

If Will and Harper are getting married next month that means I'm going to have to see James... I knew I'd see him eventually but just the thought puts a pit in my stomach.

Harper can read my brain like nobody's business. Her smile fades away as she grabs my hand. "Do you want to talk about what happened? With you and Jameson?"

I shake my head. "I'm sure you've already heard all the gritty details."

Harper sighs. "Not really. He hasn't talked much about it."

"How is he?" I instantly regret asking that question when I see the hesitant look on Harper's face.

"I know you've been through a lot, Scout. I won't ever make you tell me why you did it. But you hurt him." Harper's words punch me hard in the gut, but I needed to hear it. "He's okay now but the first two months were rough when you left. Will was worried about him. I was worried about you. You never answered your calls or hardly ever texted me back."

"I'm sorry. I was hurting too. I just needed space."

"I would believe you, but I remember you telling me that you hate being alone when you're hurting. I would have flown to you in a heartbeat if I had known where you were. I was worried about you. You were with me when I needed you. Why couldn't you let me be there for you?"

I feel bad Harper feels this way. "I was afraid if I had told you where I was, Jameson would have found me and made me change my mind."

"Scout," Harper whispers.

"I'm fine," I lie.

"I know how much you loved him, Scout. It's okay to not be okay."

"I'm doing way better now than I was those first couple months in Hawaii, okay? I drank way too many margaritas and cried every day on the beach. But I'll never forget the beauty of the island on my morning runs, how beautiful and green it was. The yummy pineapple dole whip I ate way too much of. I even danced in the rain with some old lady once. Marty. Man, she was a hoot." Harper smiles again. "I made memories I'll never forget."

Hawaii tried to heal my broken heart, but I've realized nothing can. I'll never find love like that again. I fell too hard, too fast, too deep. And I don't know if I'll ever recover but I have to try.

I swallow back the tears as I feel that heaviness in my chest again. Deep breaths.

But before I have a mental breakdown, our food arrives, saving the day.

I quickly eat every last bite of my pasta since I didn't have time to eat lunch.

There are two types of people when it comes to food: Those who scarf it down and those who savor it. I've always finished eating before Harper. She's a food savorer, and I'm definitely the food scarfer.

Harper is still chewing her pizza when she says, "I thought maybe you went back to Tennessee. I was worried I'd never see you again."

Guilt still eats at me when she says Tennessee. Because that's where she believes I'm from since I've always told her that. I've almost told her the truth many times. That I'm actually from Washington and I used to go by my first name, Della. I know I can trust Harper with everything. It's the people who I ran away from that I'm scared of. The less people who I love that know about my past, the better.

"Of course not. That would never happen," I tell her.

When Harper finishes eating, we hop in our cars and drive to my new house. And my best friend is as happy for me, just as I knew she would be.

Chapter Four

Jameson

On my way to work this morning, I happened to see Scout running down Oakville Boulevard as if she didn't have a care in the world. As if she didn't rip my goddamn heart out before she left to go who knows where. We all assumed we'd never hear from her again and yet there she was. I don't know when she came back, but I'm fuming at my brother for not telling me. I almost called him but decided I'd rather ask him about it when we meet at the gym. We meet here in Wood Lake every once in a while since he says he misses this gym. I think it's me he misses, but he can call it the gym. I'm sure he'll get a membership when he and Harper move here after their wedding. He'll have to commute to work and school for a while, but he's fine with it. I look at the time. He texted that he's running a little late after some medical emergency at the hospital in Columbus, so I start on the punching bag without him. It's probably better to get some anger out on it before Will gets here anyway.

I picture Scout dancing alone the night that I met her at the bar. *Punch.* I picture us on that stupid rooftop we weren't allowed to be on that same night. A *harder punch*. I picture our first kiss at the apartment she shared with Harper. *Punch, punch*. I picture us moving to Wood Lake together, talking about marriage, and about how hard I let myself fall for her. Punching the bag over and over again, I think about that day she destroyed me. I'll never understand why she did what she did. Why was I not more guarded? Like she was? I let her inside my heart like an open fucking book and she ripped me to shreds. The fact that I still let her make me feel this way pisses me off. This woman steals all my time. I'll probably never be the same again. I feel my anger peaking, and I let out a heaving grunt as I kick the bag hard.

"Shit," I hear Will say behind me. "You heard."

I turn around to face him. "When the fuck were you planning on telling me that she's back?"

He scratches his head. "I was meaning to tell you. Soon. Before the wedding at least."

Shit. The wedding. She'll be there.

I turn back around. "I saw her running this morning," I say, punching the bag again.

"I'm sorry. I should've told you," Will says as he puts on his boxing gloves.

A couple walks in to use the other two bags. I nod at the familiar faces. I know most of the other members from being here so much over the summer. Two men have already been boxing in the ring at the far east corner of the large gym. Will and I prefer the bags since we have that option. I think getting into the ring together would bring up too many traumatic memories. I know boxing is different with the gloves and rules and everything. But to be honest, I never want to hit my brother again. Not since my dad made me do it while he made some money off it. Last I heard, my father was in Harvey County Jail. I don't give him the time or energy to look him up anymore. I don't think Will does either. Neither one of us has seen him in years. We'd like to keep it that way.

I punch the bag over and over until I'm drenched with sweat. Will is still doing his workout on the bag while I walk over to where the weightlifting equipment is kept.

After an hour workout, Will and I walk out of the gym together.

"Are you going to talk to her?" Will asks.

I play stupid. "Who?"

"Scout."

My heart drops at the sound even though I knew what he was going to say. I wish that name didn't hold so much meaning to me.

"No, why would I?"

"I don't know. Figure out why she left, I guess."

I lean up against my truck. "I already know why. I don't need her to tell me she doesn't love me again. In case you forgot, that wasn't exactly the best day for me."

Instead of going to my last day of work at the Sheriff's Department after Scout decided to walk out on everything we had, I made the mistake of going to the bar to get wasted off my ass. Luckily, Will was there to help me get my shit together in time for me to start my job as a U.S Marshal. Scout dumped me at the worst time possible, just as my career was taking off.

"Harper met up with her. She seems to be doing well. She's renting her own place," Will says, as if I care.

I change the subject. "You ready for the big day in... three days?"

Damn, my chest hurts thinking about seeing Scout in just three days.

"Yeah, we're ready. Harper was stressed about the reception venue after the last one called and canceled on us. But we got it all figured out. As long as she's happy, I'm happy."

My brother may be getting married young but he's definitely marrying the right woman for him. I've never seen him love anything or anyone as much as he loves Harper. "I'm happy for you brother."

"Thanks. I'll see you tomorrow," he says, walking off to where he's parked as I climb into my truck.

As hard as I try to keep Scout out of my mind, she's literally all I can think about. The unwanted memories of her live inside my head as they continue to invade me.

This girl almost doesn't even seem real. I only just met Harper's roommate at the bar and grill two hours ago and I want to know everything there is about her. She's got this mysteriousness about her that's driving me crazy in a good way. Most women I can read like a book and have them figured out by a simple conversation. I usually get bored. But not this girl. She's different. We climb up the ladder to the rooftop and Scout laughs. I love the fuck out of her laugh.

"Are we allowed to be up here? I am a police officer, you know."

"In that case, yeah officer we are definitely allowed to be up here," she says with those flirty green eyes. She does a little spin before she plops herself down on the ground. "Sit," she says. So, I sit.

This girl is dangerous, and I'd probably do anything she tells me to do. Why do I want to keep her?

"Where are you from?" I ask.

"W- Tennessee."

"Nice. Do you like it here?"

"I love it." She scoots closer to me, and I don't think I've ever felt this nervous with a girl before. She says, "I've changed a lot since I've been here. I'm a girl who now loves Target, beer, and bonfires."

"What did you used to love?" I ask.

She bites the inside of her cheek as she thinks. She almost looks a little sad and I want to punch whatever hurt her. "Honestly, I don't know. I've always loved running, I guess."

"You run?"

"Yes. I'm on the track team at Copper Hill."

"Wow. That's really cool. Tell me more, I really like listening to you talk."

Her smile lights up my whole goddamn world. How do girls like her actually exist?

"Honestly Jameson, I'm still trying to figure life out. I want to be a teacher, I can be too loud sometimes, I love to party, but I also like having nights in watching movies and eating too many snacks. And I'm probably going to break your heart."

Her honesty is intriguing. She's worth the risk. "Then break it," is all I can say.

Chapter Five

Scout

I needed September to move slowly because I needed time. But instead, it flew by and in a blink of an eye it was already October.

It was Harper and Will's wedding day and I had to face Jameson. To say I'm feeling terrified would be an understatement. I'm the maid of honor and he's the best man. *Of course.*

I'm worried that as soon as I see him, I'll say something stupid. Seeing him is going to hurt. But I've got to be strong.

We're at Harper's parents' house in her old room getting ready for the big day.

"White is definitely your color," I tell Harper after she puts on the elegant wedding gown that fits her body perfectly. I've always admired Harper's natural beauty. She has a tan skin tone, bright hazel eyes, and naturally curly, long brown hair.

I appreciate the little spin she does so I can get the full effect of the dress. I can't help but admire the small yet important details like the opening of the back, the way the train flows down onto the floor, the long sleeves, and scooped neckline. Gosh, this dress was made for her. I feel a little sad I wasn't here to help her pick it out. Instead, I was on a tropical island, feeling sorry for myself, and trying to forget.

Don't go there. Today isn't about you.

"You look beautiful, Harper. You do realize that dress is coming off as soon as you and Will are alone, right?"

She laughs as she sits in front of the mirror to touch up her make up. "Will and I are being so non-traditional for this wedding. I mean, I was supposed to stay in here last night, but I ended up in the guest bedroom with him. We're ridiculous, we can't even go a night without each other." She giggles. "We even made breakfast and had coffee this morning together before getting ready."

"I love that so much." I smile at her and pull out my *something new* because who wants anything borrowed?

When I hand her the box she says, "You didn't have to get me anything!" She opens it up and smiles brightly. "They're beautiful." She puts the dainty diamond earrings in as she looks at her reflection in the vanity mirror.

I smile behind her. "Of course, I did."

She turns around to hug me. "You look pretty, too."

I glance down at my silky low cut mauve bridesmaid dress that splits up my thigh and flows down my legs. Harper is the world's best bride for picking me out such a flattering dress. Then I look in the mirror at the beautiful flower arrangement on my head. Harper's mom talked me into getting the flower crown and now I'm hoping it's not too much. But I do love the delicacy of it.

"Aren't bridesmaids' dresses supposed to be ugly?" I ask.

She laughs but when she looks at me her smile fades. "Are you okay?"

I try and force my best fake smile. Today I won't get to dance with the man I love. "Don't worry about me. Today is your day. I'm so happy for you."

"Is it going to be weird? Walking down the aisle with Jameson?"

Just the thought of it makes my stomach flip. "Harper. Today. Is. Not. About. Me." I help her put on her veil. "Now get your pretty ass out to the car so we can get you to Boulder Beach to marry you to your best friend."

My stomach is in knots when we get to the lake not too far from Harper's parent's house. I don't see James yet as we line up by the trees to get ready to walk down the trail. It's a sunny October day, and I couldn't be happier for Harper and Will. Their relationship is so real, and I love seeing them both so truly happy. Harper was so worried the weather wouldn't hold up and they'd have to do the wedding ceremony somewhere indoors. It was very important to her that they do it here, at Boulder Beach. I honestly think she would have changed the date of the wedding if they couldn't get married here. That, or we would all be standing out in the rain freezing to death as they exchanged vows.

Thank you, weather Gods.

The pine trees stand tall, giving the wedding a rustic outdoor vibe that I love. The leaves on the maple trees standing next to the pine trees are vibrant and colorful as they shine in the sun and fall to the ground, forming a natural but colorful carpet. It's decorated so simply and perfectly with white roses and brown accents. The colors complement the changing leaves as the sun shines out on the water, radiating glittery light.

Harper and her dad are up the trail further, hiding in the thick trees so the groom can't see her yet. They didn't have a rehearsal although maybe they should have. Maybe Jameson doesn't know where to line up to walk down the "aisle." I look out toward the guests seated in front of the lake. My nervous energy spirals out of control as I chew on my bottom lip and play with a strand of hair. *He's not here.* A little girl with a tight bun in her hair, wearing a pink dress with flowers walks up to me nervously. I recognize Harper's aunt pointing her in my direction.

"You must be the flower girl," I tell her. "You're in the right place, this is where we line up."

She doesn't look nervous anymore, just excited. "Are you a princess?" she asks sweetly.

I smile. I don't want to break her spirit. "It's sort of a secret but I have been crowned a princess before."

"Really?" she asks.

"Yes, but don't tell anyone okay? And you look like a princess too. Do you want to be a princess?"

"Yes!" she shouts.

"Then I crown you princess now." I take off my flower crown and put it on her head. It's a little big but it balances on her hair beautifully. "Perfect."

She smiles brightly and says, "Thanks." Then she turns around with her basket, waiting for the start, clearly taking her job very seriously.

My eyes are looking for Jameson in the crowd when I hear him clear his throat behind me. I don't know how long he's been standing here but I whip around to his tall build and feel weak in my knees when I look up to see his handsome, rugged face. Jameson looks at me with slightly furrowed brows, like it's painful for him to see me. He's changed since I saw him four months ago. The suit he has on is tight around his strong arms, making it visibly noticeable that he's gotten bigger. All summer long, I was wondering what he was doing. Now I can see that he was obviously living at the gym, lifting weights the entire time. *Dammit, why does he have to look so good?*

The music fills the air, I *think*. I'm a little distracted as Jameson's eyes painfully roam down to my feet strapped in black high heels then back up to my face.

"Turn around," he says.

My breath catches at the domination in his voice, reminding me of how good he is in bed. "Let's get this over with."

Definitely not something he's ever said in bed. For the love of God Scout, get your head on straight.

We both turn around to get ready to walk when he slides his hand around my bare arm to link us together. His familiar touch makes my stomach drop as it sends a surge of energy to the beating of my heart. I hate what it's doing to me. Stumbling over a rock in my heels as we step forward together, James catches my fall.

"Careful princess, you don't want to trip and fall over all the lies you tell," he whispers in my ear.

Ouch. I deserved that. And he doesn't even know half of them.

When we get up to Will waiting at the altar for his bride, I do the hardest thing I'll have to do all day and pull apart from him. Harper makes her way down the aisle with her dad and the look on Will's face is my favorite part. I glance over at James, and he doesn't look back at me. His eyes used to always be on me, but I guess that tells you how much can change over time.

I lied. The hardest part of today is seeing James with the blonde he brought with him to the indoor wedding reception in town. I roll my eyes. I can't believe he brought a date. She's gorgeous and must be funny considering James can't seem to stop laughing with her. I gulp my champagne and slam the glass down a little harder on the table than I meant to. Jameson glances my way and I quickly look away. Will and Harper are dancing together, and I've got to remember that today is about them. I'm happy for my friends. I go to get another drink when a hand reaches behind me and takes what I so desperately need away from me.

"The last thing we need is a drunk maid of honor," my friend Rafe says. Harper and I became good friends with Rafe in college when we all lived in the same apartment complex.

"Is she prettier than me?" My eyes are back on the blonde who continues flirting with James as they dance. The champagne rushes to my head, giving me a buzz.

"Come here," he says with open arms. I bury my head into his chest, and he rubs my back.

Then he stands me up straight and hands me back my drink. "I changed my mind. You do need this. But as soon as it's gone, we're dancing."

My drink is down in a matter of seconds, and I follow Rafe to the dance floor. Harper comes up next to us and we all laugh and dance to the music as I pretend my heart isn't completely ripped in half.

When I spot James alone, I somehow have the audacity to walk up to him. I think I have the champagne to thank for that. "Did you lose your blonde puppy?" *Shit, I drank too much, and I probably shouldn't have said that.*

His glare sends chills down my arms. "Did you lose your champagne glass?" he bites back.

I roll my eyes just as his date steps up next to him. She has no idea who I am.

I'm sure I have a bitchy look on my face when I say, "I'm Scout."

She looks at Jameson then back at me. She *does* know who I am. I smile at that.

"I'm Ava," she says.

"How long have you two been dating?" I ask.

Ava goes to say something when Jameson says, "Can we talk?"

I stare into those blue eyes that creep into my dreams every night as they scold me like I'm their worst nightmare. "Sure."

Jameson drags me to an empty corner of the large room. "What are you doing Scout?"

"I'm celebrating my best friend's wedding. What are you doing Jameson?"

"You don't get to ask questions that you don't deserve to know. Not after what you did," he says through gritted teeth. "Let's get one thing clear. Stay out of my business."

"Got it," I whisper. "I'm sorry. It's just hard. Seeing you with someone else. But as rude as I've been tonight, I am happy for you James. I'm glad you're moving on." *I don't want him to move on, but I have to let him go.*

"I've never been happier," he says coldly, shattering my heart on the floor.

As he goes to walk away, I grab his arm, "Wait James. We were happy. Don't ever forget how that felt. Please."

He keeps his back to me as he says, "You're right. We were happy. Until you destroyed everything we had." He turns to me, and I see hurt all over his face again, just like that day. "I'll never forget how *that* felt."

I hate that I hurt him. The look he's giving me hurts worse than his words. It's written all over his disgusted face. He hates me. Jameson hates me. The man who used to tell me he didn't know love existed before he met me now hates *me.*

But the longer he stares, the more the hate from his eyes starts to fade. He's looking at me like he used to. He looks at me like he knows how much my heart is still racing for him.

I need this. I need it so much I want to capture it forever. He may hate me but right here in this moment, he doesn't. Before I can stop myself, I touch his scruffy cheek and his eyes flutter. My heart is spiraling out of control when he grips my wrist *hard*. The hate is back in his eyes. *He's so mad.* But he doesn't move my hand, he keeps it on his face and my wrist is on fire at the hard hold he has on me. *He doesn't want to let go either.*

"James," I whisper.

Then he instantly drops my wrist and says, "But like I said, never been happier."

As he walks away, I feel a tear stream down my cheek.

"I'm so sorry," I whisper.

After watching Harper and Will drive off to their honeymoon hours later, Rafe offers to drive me home and I quickly agree since I've been drinking. I'll call an uber to get my car tomorrow.

Once at the passenger door, I freeze when I get a glimpse of Jameson opening Ava's door to his truck. He shuts it behind her and glances over his shoulder to see me standing and watching. He pauses for a moment; our eyes meet with sadness. But then he turns away to get into his truck.

"He's still in love with you," Rafe says, who's already in the car when I slam the door shut.

"No actually, he hates me. I don't want to talk about it. What about Kevin? Why didn't you bring him?"

"I don't want to talk about him either," Rafe says.

I sigh. "Relationships suck."

My phone vibrates and I look down to see a text that causes my chest to grow heavy with worry when I see who it's from. Clicking on it, I see a screenshotted photo of Rafe and me at the wedding I had posted on social media tonight.

Happy to see you took a date to the wedding. And here I thought you'd take me, since I'm the one he caught you with.

I read it over twice before placing my phone back in my purse. I never should have signed up on social media. But my account is private -- how did he even get this photo? Today has been hard enough without texts that I know are a whole lot more threatening than they seem.

I flashback to the dark place that changed me forever. I can see it just like a movie, all the parts that haunt me. I can feel him dragging me by my hair. I'm trying to get them off me but they're too strong. Their laughter is evil and rings in my ears. "Do you know what we do to snitches Della?"

I haven't had a flashback like this before. I'm shaking so badly I think about jumping out of the car to get away from it.

"Scout? You're shaking. What's wrong with you?" Rafe says.

I can't control my breathing anymore. "Can you pull over?" I ask him.

He immediately pulls over on the side of the road. I jump out and hold my chest. I can hardly breathe. Rafe slams his door and hurries over to where I'm sitting on the side of the road. "Scout, you need to breathe." He grabs my hands. "Breathe with me. In and out," he says.

It's helping. Tears are rolling down my face. I don't know what's happening to me.

"Scout, you just had a panic attack. Has that ever happened to you before?"

I wipe my face. "No. Maybe in dreams," I admit.

Rafe looks worried.

"I'm okay," I tell him. "Sorry about that."

Rafe grabs me and pulls me in for a tight hug. "Don't you dare be sorry Scout. I don't know what you're going through but I'm right here."

I let him hold me. He has no idea.

Chapter Six

Jameson

It's nearly two in the morning when I get home from taking Ava back to the city after the wedding. I met Ava just over a month ago at a baseball game in the city. She was sitting in front of me in a baseball cap over her short blonde hair, cheering for the other team. Things got heated between us on the bleachers that day and even more heated when we got to her apartment in Columbus that night. We're not together, I'm not ready for that kind of commitment again. And she's recently divorced so she wants to take things slow too. We've been more of a comfort to one another than anything. Not sure how healthy that is but we're in a good place being friends with benefits. But I kind of like Scout thinking we're more than that. Ava wasn't expecting to see her at the wedding, and I feel bad I didn't give her a warning. Now she thinks the reason I didn't stay at her house is because of Scout. She's right, but not in the way that she thinks. I just want to be alone after today, after seeing Scout again. I take off my suit jacket and unbutton my white shirt. Now she's all I can think about. Why did she come back? After taking off my belt, I sit on the side of my bed and stare at my nightstand. I haven't opened it since the night Scout left but I know what's in there. Feeling even more frustrated at myself, I hit the top of the table before throwing the drawer open. I eventually pick up the fabric Scout left. The scent of her makes me miss her. God, I hate that I miss her. She probably left the tank top on purpose just so I wouldn't forget about her. Sounds like something she would do. I try to stop, but as I stare down at the shirt, the memory is forced back into my head.

Scout found out last year that Captain America was my favorite superhero and made fun of me for it.

She laughed. "I didn't know you were a Marvel nerd."

"Marvel is not at all nerdy," I said defensively. "I'll prove it to you."

After watching Captain America and Avengers, Scout realized she was a "Marvel nerd" too.

We binged all the Marvel movies in a week.

A few weeks later, I was out back, grilling us steaks for dinner when she came up behind me and said, "Hey Cap." I turned around to see her wearing a Captain America cropped tank top and matching underwear. I groaned, threw her over my shoulder and said, "This is for calling me a nerd," before I spanked her ass. I about lost it when I heard the light gasp of a moan that escaped her mouth.

I took her to my room right then and there and ended up burning our steaks.

The Captain America tank top was something Scout loved to sleep in. I can't believe she left it. I told her whatever she left would be put in the trash, but I can't find it in me to throw the damn thing away. I put it back in my nightstand drawer and hope one day I'll be able to get rid of it.

Chapter Seven

Jameson

Our team got called to action in Cincinnati. We went undercover and found a fugitive we'd been looking for months now. He played a big part inside a dangerous drug gang we'd been looking into, so this case was important to us.

Angela, Bond, and I are headed home with a victory.

"I can't believe how easily that guy actually believed the two of you were engaged."

Angela laughs. "I'm drinking this bottle of wine tonight if you guys want to join me."

Bond looks at the bottle. He tries to read the name of the wine out loud but fails. "Shit, this stuff sounds expensive. I'm in."

Tonight was too easy. We deserve a celebration. "Sure."

After an hour of driving, Angela is passed out in the backseat.

"How was the wedding with the ex?" Bond asks.

Bond and I have become good friends. He's been a U.S Marshal longer than me and I've learned more from him than any training. I only met him two months ago when he joined our team in Ohio. His real name is Bronson but since he and I became friends, they call us James and Bond. At first, we hated it, but the nickname Bond has grown on him.

"Terrible," I say.

"How'd she look?"

Fucking perfect. Scout's image is burned inside my head as I picture her long legs and the way her dress showed off every curve of her body. Her dark eyelashes framed her bright green eyes, the ones that used to get anything they wanted from me. Those eyes stripped me raw of my vulnerability. They never changed color, they're always the same emerald green no matter what she's wearing. Scout's eyes became my favorite color.

"I don't want to talk about it."

I tell Bond way more than I tell anyone else. Even more than Will since Scout is practically family to him and Harper. Bond is just easy to vent to.

"You didn't fuck her, did you?" he asks.

"Never again."

"Just making sure you didn't screw up."

I'm thankful Angela is sleeping, or else she'd be in on this conversation. She likes to give me more shit than Bond does.

"How's Ivy?" I ask. Bond had been away for a couple days to visit his niece who was diagnosed with cancer.

"She's hanging in there. Those treatments are extremely hard on her, but her doctor is one of the best."

I look over at him to see his heavy, worried eyes.

Angela sits up when her phone rings as we hit the city lights. When she gets off the call, she explains the bad news.

The fugitive we caught tonight already got out on bail. These high-end drug traffickers have too much money and get away with way too much shit. I'm definitely not in a party mood now, so after I drop them off at Angela's place, I drive home to Wood Lake.

Most of the time I can leave the shit I feel on the job where it belongs. I don't usually bring it home with me. But tonight, I do. I feel like everything we did today was for nothing.

The first thing I notice when I turn onto my street is Scout's car in my driveway. What the hell is she doing here?

Just as I'm pulling next to her car, she comes walking out of the house like she still owns the fucking place. She's not welcome here anymore. Scout looks up to see me and her eyes widen with shock before she runs toward her car. I jump out just as she starts her engine and speeds off. *What the fuck?* Getting back into my car, I pull out my phone and dial her number. She doesn't answer. Figures. Now I'm getting pissed off.

I turn on my flashing lights as I drive up behind her.

Chapter Eight

Scout

I can't believe he is pulling me over. I throw my car in park and roll down my window as Jameson walks up.

"Are you seriously rolling your eyes at me right now when you're the one that just broke into my house?" he asks.

I sigh. "It used to be my house too, James. And I left something there that I wanted back. I figured you wouldn't want to see me, so I got it myself."

I'm pretty sure I just saw Jameson Karter roll his eyes. "Are you going to tell me what it is that you took? Or am I going to have to figure it out myself?"

"It's mine. Don't worry, I didn't touch any of your girlfriend's things."

It hurt to see Ava's red bra hanging on the towel rack in the bathroom. Honestly, I kind of wanted to shred it up into pieces.

"You better watch your sassy mouth," he demands.

"Or what?"

"Get out of your vehicle."

Is he for real? "You can't be serious James."

"You heard me, Scout. Do you know what happens when you don't obey a U.S Marshal's command?"

I throw my door open and James steps back. "This is ridiculous."

"You can think about that the next time you want to break into my house. Turn around and put your hands on your car."

"You're unbelievable," I say as I turn around and touch my car.

"I'm unbelievable?" he comes up behind me and whispers into my ear. "You're the intruder." Then he slides his big hands down my sides and grabs my hips, causing me to yelp.

He's frisking me.

"Spread your feet apart," he demands as he drops down to grab my ankles.

If he's going to play this game, I'm going to play back. I step apart a little further than necessary and arch my back, sticking my ass in his face. "Is this good officer?"

His hands slowly slide up my legs until he reaches the top of my thighs, his fingers digging at the crease of my backside. Then he says, "Yes." The deepness in his voice causes me to gasp. He slides his hands to the front of my legs, causing the ache between my thighs to become even more intense. I can tell he senses my arousal as he takes his time touching me. But I honestly never want him to stop.

His hands go up each side of my ribs before he slides them over my breasts.

"James," I whimper.

His hands grip my body tighter, the sexual tension between us bursting into flames.

"Do you hate me?" I whisper.

"I wish I had never met you," he whispers directly into my ear as I feel his hands grip my hips even tighter. "So yeah, I guess you could say that I hate you. But somehow you still make me feel like this." He presses his erection up against my ass. I feel my wetness soak my panties. He reaches into the front pockets of my jeans, and I lean back into him, wanting more. Then he pulls the key out of my pocket and dangles it in front of my face. "This belongs to me. Don't sneak into my house again."

He lets me go, catching me off guard as I stumble forward. Feeling completely pissed off and sexually frustrated, I glare at him over my shoulder before getting back into my car.

I'm about to shut the driver's door when James holds it open. "Hang on. That's what you snuck into the house for?" He points to the Captain America tank top laying on the passenger seat.

"Yes."

The look on his face is ripping me apart. He shuts his eyes tight, like it's too painful for him to look at the shirt and relive the memory of the first time I wore it for him. It took me a lot longer than I thought it would to find my tank top. I figured James must have thrown it out when I decided to check one last spot. His nightstand. I wonder how often he's pulled it out of his drawer to think of me.

"James," I say. Seeing the pain in his eyes when he opens them again makes me want to wrap my arms around him and never let go. But all I can do is say, "I'm sorry."

"It's your shirt."

"Not about the shirt. About *everything*. You're not wrong to hate me."

He pushes himself off my car and nods. "Goodnight Scout."

Chapter Nine

Jameson

When I get home the first thing I do is shower. I've got to get rid of this hard-on. I'm frustrated as I stroke myself knowing that Scout is the only thing on my mind. The feel of her body on my hands again, the rhythm of her breathing when I touched her, the way she said my name and leaned into me for more. God, the way I had to hold myself back from spanking her ass when she shoved it in my face. I could tell she was turned on. I imagine her pulling me into the backseat of her car and begging me to give her what she desperately wanted. Just remembering the way Scout feels is enough to make me finish.

Anger comes crashing down on me.

"Fuck!" I punch the stone wall in front of me as water streams down my face. Even after everything that's happened, Scout can still wreck me. I lean my head up against the wall as hot angry tears flood from my eyes. I have doubts that I'll ever heal. My fist hits the wall again and again. Scout has no idea what she's done to me. Life was a lot easier when she was across the ocean on an island.

My phone rings on the bathroom counter so I turn off the shower and grab a towel. It's Ava. *Shit, Ava.*

I pick up. "Hello?"

"Hey. How was your day?" she asks.

"Fine. How was yours?"

"Good. The barbershop was crazy busy today."

"Speaking of which, I need a haircut."

"Will you be in the city tomorrow?" she asks.

"Yeah, unfortunately." I drive to Columbus almost daily now that work has been keeping me so busy. I considered moving back but after all the chaotic shit that happens at work, coming home to a quiet small town is a comfort I've come to love.

"I have an opening at three tomorrow if you want to swing by. Then maybe we can get coffee after?"

"Sounds great. See you tomorrow."

"See ya."

We hang up and I turn on the game as I eat the leftovers from my fridge for dinner.

I try and meal prep on Sundays so that I don't have to worry about cooking during the week. And, I'm trying to stay in shape.

⋙ ⋘

I like to pretend it's my job that keeps me up at night. And not the girl that used to sleep next to me in this bed every night. The day Scout left, I had to wash the bed sheets three times before I was finally able to get the scent of her off them. I look over at my empty nightstand, hating that she found her shirt there. I don't want her to know how much she still gets to me. She doesn't deserve whatever the hell kind of sick satisfaction she gets out of messing with my head.

Chapter Ten

Della

Eight years ago...

Curiosity has eaten at me for the past two hours as I listen to my brother and his guests downstairs. Some kind of "business meeting," he called it. And I'm not allowed to attend, considering I'm only fifteen. Almost sixteen. But there is something about it that seems so mysterious, and I want to know what it's about. He's worked for my father's company, the Whitlock Corporation for years now. My dad has tried pushing my brother to move him up the ladder so he can be business partner material someday. My dad is always telling him that if he wants to take over one day, he'd have to work hard. I know my dad thinks Ethan hangs out with his friends too much. I've even heard them fighting about Ethan not showing up for work. He doesn't take it as seriously as my father. My dad works hard every day. His business is the most important thing in the world to him. I've seen the way my father's employees respect him. All he must do to get someone to do something is look at them a certain way, and they'll do it. What would it feel like to have that kind of power? Ethan desperately wants that. He just doesn't put much effort. I find that kind of mentality isn't unusual here in Bordersville, Washington. Our rich neighborhood just outside of Seattle is loaded with entitled young adults. Even most of the kids I go to my private high school with seem to take advantage of the life we have here. I think Ethan assumes that one day, Whitlock Corporation will just be handed to him. He has the last name after all. I find it a little strange that he's always having meetings while my father is out of town on a business trip.

My dad was married to someone else before my mom, but it ended badly when Ethan chose to stay with his dad. Now he sees his mom maybe twice a year, and I've never even met the woman. But Ethan seems to hate her for some reason.

When my dad isn't away for business, he's working late at the office in the city. He's hardly ever home anymore. My mom's in bed all the time now. I hardly see her. She's gotten worse over this past year. Or maybe it's that I've gotten older and understand now that she cares a lot more about her next drug fix than anything else, including me. And Ethan is having a lot of "meetings" downstairs lately and has made it clear that I'm not allowed. I've never felt so lonely. I want to know what's going on down there.

After I hear glass shatter, everything gets quiet. I slowly open my bedroom door located on the top floor of the house and creep down to the basement, where Ethan's meeting is. I know he'll be mad if I get caught but curiosity and loneliness are getting the best of me. There are cocktail glasses every-where down here and I'm pretty sure I smell weed. This looks more like a party than a meeting. *I knew it.* I roll my eyes at the mess. Figures. A couple of guys are down on the marble tile cleaning up some glass. Of course, he hired people to clean up after him.

Luckily the workers are too busy to notice me creeping past them. I take a deep breath and slowly make my way into the living room area of the basement. There are about five guys and a couple of pretty women plopped on the sofa laughing together. All of them are dressed nicely and I wonder if they all work at Whitlock Corporation. I stand back where no one can notice me. The muffled voices get louder, but I still can't make out what they're saying. Ethan isn't in the living room, so I walk over to his office to see if he's in there. I still roll my eyes at the fact that he has his own office at home at the age of twenty-five. Not making a sound, I lean my ear up against the office door and listen.

A man is speaking to my brother in a hushed tone, but he seems excited. "I can't believe you were able to talk Helix into the partnership deal. Do you realize what this means? We won't have to go through Whitlock Corporation to launder our drug money anymore, which means we don't have to worry about getting caught. Strip clubs make so much money, nobody will ever question where the influx of cash comes from." The gasp somehow stays lodged in my throat. *Drugs?* My heart races inside my chest.

"I know," Ethan whispers, "now I don't have to lie to my dad anymore."

I hear pacing across the floor and can feel the nervous energy from outside the door. Then the other guy says, "Hell, you don't even have to work there anymore. This opportunity is better than his boring business. Aren't you sick of being his little bitch?"

I don't like the way this sounds.

"I'm nobody's bitch," Ethan says. "My father never suspected that I was washing cash through the company. If anything, he's my bitch." Ethan laughs like this is all a joke.

The guy says, "Act like a businessman and set up another meeting with Helix to get the ball rolling. But this time an actual meeting, not a fucking party," he says to Ethan.

"This was a meeting and Helix loved it," Ethan says.

The man says, "You may be right, but we need to show him how serious we are about it. Tell him to bring all the paperwork."

Loud laughter from the guests in the other room startles me, and my knee hits the door. *Shit.* I back away, hoping like hell they didn't hear the thud. My heart is racing in my chest.

Silence.

Just as I'm about to tip toe back up the stairs, the office door bursts open. Ethan walks out alone and says, "Della, what are you doing down here?"

I shake my head furiously and like an idiot I say, "I didn't hear anything."

He stares at me for a moment, and I think I see a hint of guilt. "Go to your room," he says.

"I'm not a child, Ethan."

The look he gives me is annoying, but I do as I'm told and turn around to go straight to my room.

It's clear to me now why he doesn't want me coming down here for his "meetings." He's obviously involved in something bad. Drug money? Strip clubs? Using our father's business to cover it up? I wonder if my dad has any idea about this.

An hour later, I'm still wide awake in my bed thinking about what I heard downstairs when Ethan walks in my room without knocking.

"What do you want, Ethan?" I sit up, turn on the lamp next to me on my nightstand to see him glaring at me through bloodshot eyes.

"I can't believe you're such a fucking snoop. You know you're not allowed down there at that hour. If you tell any-one..."

"I'm sorry. I just.... Dad's gone and mom's always in bed. I was lonely," I say.

He almost looks like he feels sorry for me. My brother is ten years older than me, but he still looks young.

"But Ethan, drugs? I think you should get out of this while you can. The man I heard you talking to is clearly dangerous and eventually he's going to get caught and bring you down with him. And it's wrong."

I'm startled as Ethan lunges toward me, and before I have time to do anything he grips my neck, making it impossible to scream. I can't even muster a sound with his big hands wrapped tightly around my throat, closing off my airway. Then, thankfully, I see the guilt in his eyes, and he lets go.

"I'm so sorry Della. I didn't mean to do that. I'm just stressed about this business."

"What the hell is wrong with you?" I try and yell, but my voice comes out small and raspy.

He sits down on my bed. I'm too stunned to move at the way Ethan just acted. "If you tell anyone what you heard tonight, next time…" he pauses.

"Next time what? You'll keep your hands wrapped around my throat until I'm dead?" I snap.

He puts his hand on mine. A pathetic apology.

"Don't touch me," I say, pulling away. I feel tears coming and turn my head from him so he can't see me cry.

He sighs. "Look, I'm sorry. Just please keep your mouth shut."

"Okay," I whisper.

He stands up and steps toward the door. "Good. Glad we cleared things up, sis." Then he's gone.

I've never wanted a lock on my door until now. My body is overtaken by an uncontrollable sob as I bury myself underneath the covers. My shaky hand touches my tender neck again, where my brother's hands were wrapped tight. It's sore and he may even have left a mark. I'll have to cover it up with makeup, so nobody asks questions. But he looked like he felt remorseful about it, and he apologized. I take a deep breath to stop myself from crying. I remind myself that he apologized. It was *nothing*, I lie to myself over and over again.

❦

My friend Kat is sitting at the bar stool in the kitchen as I make us popcorn with extra butter.

"This summer is going to be the best," Kat says. "I'm so ready to chill on the beach in Hawaii. Della, you have to come!"

Kat invited Savanna and me to her family's beach house in Hawaii.

"My dad said he's thinking about it."

Loud music comes from downstairs when I pull three sodas out from the refrigerator.

"When will Savanna be here?" I ask.

Kat shrugs. "Soon I'm sure. Is Ethan having another party downstairs?"

I sigh. "Probably."

She grins mischievously. "We should go."

"To the party? No way."

Kat pouts as I walk out of the kitchen to shut the basement door since the sound of distant party music is tempting her.

"You know it's lame to be the first one to show up to the party, right?" I hear a male voice behind me before I get to the door.

I whip around to see one of Ethan's friends, a guy I've always thought was cute. He's never talked to me before. He's hot, with his dark hair and prominent cheekbones. He seems younger than my brother and I'm sure Ethan is a bad influence on him.

"Considering that I live here, are you referring to yourself being the first lame person to show up?" I ask jokingly.

He smiles sheepishly, a dimple appearing on his right cheek. On the same side, a small hoop earring dangles from his ear lobe. He's just the right amount of sweet and *a bad boy.*

"You are as fiery as Ethan says. We have never officially met. My name's JC."

I gulp. "I'm Della."

I turn to see Kat still sitting on the barstool staring at us.

"I'm Kat," Kat says.

He arches his brow and walks past me. "Nice to meet you both," he mumbles.

"Okay, JC practically just invited us to the party. We have to go now," Kat says after JC leaves.

"You can't be serious. Ethan will kill me if we step foot down there," I say.

"Come on. He'll be too busy to even notice us," she says.

"What happened to getting snacks and watching a scary movie?" I ask.

"We're sixteen now, Della. Let's party," she pouts.

I glare at her. We've been friends since we were kids. And she always knows how to talk me into things I don't want to do. Maybe that's why I like her so much.

"Fine," I give in to the peer pressure hoping it doesn't get me into trouble with Ethan.

She grins excitedly. "Yay, I'll text Savanna and make sure she doesn't come over in her PJ's."

⚜

"You guys ready?" I ask, taking one last look at my reflection in the mirror. I'm wearing my favorite pink skirt and a white crop top with brand new white sneakers.

I run my fingers through my straightened hair as Savanna says, "Yeah girl. Doesn't your brother hang out with the wrong crowd? I've seen him with Ace from the old alternative high school, and he's been to prison."

Kat rolls her eyes. "Who cares. We get to go to an actual party. Bad boys are sexy."

I laugh. "Let's go. Ethan has no idea we're coming so he might kick us out."

Ten minutes later, I spot Ethan eyeing my friends on the sofa. Savanna is talking to Ace while Kat is coughing up smoke from taking a hit from some other girl's joint. I nervously make my way over to Ethan to explain when he notices me. His face reddens, "What the fuck? What are you doing Della? Get out of here! I told you not to come down here again."

Before I can say anything, JC walks over and whispers something in Ethan's ear, but I can't hear what he's saying.

"Fine. You can stay but only this once," Ethan says to me. Someone calls JC and he walks away. I wonder what he said to Ethan to let me stay.

"Do our parents not even care that you throw these parties?"

Ethan glares at me. Clearly, he's still annoyed I'm here. "Dad cares but I'm twenty-five so he can't say shit. And I always have them when he's out of town anyway."

"And what about my mom? Does she ever even try and shut it down?"

Ethan laughs. "Why would she try and shut it down? She's too involved in her own crap."

I look down at the floor and can't help the sadness that comes over me at how different she is. She used to make dinner and we'd sit down as a family, and she'd ask and care about my day. Now I look at her and it's like her soul has been taken right out of her. I don't even remember the last normal conversation I had with her. But dad just ignores it when I bring it up to him and blames it on her being depressed since my grandma passed away. But that was years ago. I stopped trying to talk about it with him.

Ethan has already walked off when I spot JC sitting in the corner of the room with his back against the wall, smoking. Feeling a little caught off guard with his eyes on me, I wave like the child I am. He smiles slightly, like I'm amusing to him before he stands up off the floor. *Oh gosh, I think he's coming to talk to me. Does he like me?* That's when he walks up to another girl with a tattoo sleeve and bleached blonde hair. When he catches me watching him, his eyes stay glued to mine as he talks to her. The girl says something before they start making out. A twinge of jealousy bites at me but I feel more embarrassed than anything. I sit down next to Kat and a few others as they talk about how they get the munchies when they're high.

"Is that why I'm so hungry?" Kat startles me with a yell.

"You're high?" I ask.

She giggles. "Maybe a little."

A popular song comes on and I pull Kat up with me. "Let's dance!"

Others are already dancing, and we join them. A tall, slim guy comes up behind me. "Hey, I'm Jason," he says.

"Hey Jason! I'm Della," I yell over the music. I look behind him to see JC still talking with the blonde. "Dance with me?" I ask.

Jason smiles. "Okay." His palms lightly touch my hips as I sway them to the party music.

When the song stops, I hear a girl yell, "Body shots!"

What the hell are those?

More music comes on as I stand back and watch a girl lay on the coffee table while some dude pours a shot of alcohol on her stomach. Then he quickly licks it out of her belly button, and I'm taken aback. *Kinda gross, but okay...*

A few more girls take turns getting licked and sucked on and I continue standing back. Kat hands me a shot and I feel the vodka burn my throat. "Having fun?" I ask.

"Hell yeah!" she yells. "Let's go try body shots!"

I shrug and follow her to the table. We both lay down and Jason takes the full shot glass from some guy. Jason asks if I'm ready before pouring the liquid into my belly button. Feeling buzzed and entertained just as Jason is about to lick the vodka up off me, JC pushes Jason over to Kat and quickly licks my stomach himself. But takes his time sucking while I feel his tongue roll over me. I feel an excitement I've never felt before but then I hear someone call my name. "Della Whitlock!"

It's *my dad.*

Chapter Eleven

Della

Ethan and my dad haven't spoken to each other in weeks, not since I was caught at the party. I tried to explain to my dad that my friends and I snuck downstairs without my brother's knowledge, but he still blames Ethan. Now I get a death glare from my brother every time I look his way.

By the way my dad yelled my name at the party, I expected a bigger punishment. Embarrassment still tortures me at the thought of him sending me to my room in front of everyone. But it could have been worse. Savanna and Kat told me my father sent everyone home and then I heard him and Ethan yelling at each other. I heard my dad tell Ethan that he had no right jeopardizing the company with his unethical practices. But when I asked Ethan about it, he just ignored me. Clearly, he's still mad at me, but at least he hasn't hurt me again. My dad never fired him or said another word about it in front of me, but they're still not talking. That's why I'm surprised to see him and Ethan in the kitchen at the same time when I get back after my run. My dad says something to me that I'm not sure I even understand.

"I'm sorry. Did you just say I'm going to summer camp? Do I get a choice?" I ask my father.

Ethan takes a gulp from his coffee cup and says, "I think summer camp is a great idea."

"Do you want to join your sister, Ethan?" my dad scolds.

But Ethan just smiles.

"Dad, I don't want to go," I beg.

"You're young. You should be going to summer camp and not to parties," he says, glaring back at Ethan.

Ethan rolls his eyes and walks out. I know he's happy my dad is finally speaking to him.

"You'd better get packing. You leave in two days," my dad tells me.

⋘⋙ ⋘⋙

This summer I was planning on doing a lot of things. I had a whole running schedule planned to start training for high school track. And I can kiss the possibility of going to Hawaii with my friends goodbye because I lost the argument with my dad. I overheard my mom telling my dad that they shouldn't make me go if I didn't want to and that she knows I'm a good girl. But my mom doesn't know me. Not anymore. The fact that she called me a good girl makes me not want to be one at all. I cringed at the way she was trying to stick up for me, but I didn't say a word because I still wanted out of camp. It didn't matter. My dad got his way. Plus, I'm annoyed that Ethan is somehow mad at me when he's the one that got us both in trouble. I can't believe that I have to be here for six freaking weeks. I can kiss my track training and Hawaiian vacation goodbye because I won't get out of this place until the beginning of August. Then I'm right back to school to start my sophomore year.

My school's track team is very competitive. They don't let freshmen on the team so last year I watched from the stands, studying each track practice and home meet so that I'd be ready to make the team this year. Now I'm worried I won't get the training I need. I'll be six weeks behind everyone else. I'll just have to train hard this fall and when winter hits, I'll run on the treadmill when I need to. I'm nervous just thinking about tryouts next spring, but I'm excited.

"You've got to be kidding me," I mumble to myself as our family's driver Fred drops me at Camp Lotsa Fun. Even the name makes me cringe. But what makes me cringe even more is seeing all the kids who are getting off the buses. I'm easily the oldest person here. I hope nobody from school ever finds out about this. My reputation will be garbage.

"Fred. Please take me home, this is a kids' camp," I tell the driver.

"You are a kid, Miss Della."

Fred opens the back door of the car for me as he stands next to my duffle bag.

"Your father told me you would try and get out of this camp, and it was important to him that you stay here and have fun."

Right. Camp Lotsa Fun.

I take my duffle bag and sigh. "It's not your fault."

"Six weeks will fly by and by the time it's over, you'll be sad to leave. Do you want me to walk you in?"

"No, I'm a big girl. See you in six weeks, Fred."

The camp director shows me to my cabin where there are ten bunk beds lined up against the wall with girls sitting on them. It turns out I was right; I really am the oldest person here. I'm spending my summer with a bunch of middle schoolers.

"Find a bunk partner," the camp director says before walking out.

I glance around the room, wondering how I'm going to survive this camp when someone says, "Della Whitlock?" I turn around to see a girl I don't recognize.

"Do I know you?" I ask the girl with long sandy blonde hair and freckles skimming her nose.

She adjusts her glasses. "Yes. Well, no but I know you. We went to the same middle school. I'm Bailey."

"Okay."

Bailey continues, "It makes sense though that you don't know me. I'm two years younger than you."

Ugh. This is going to be a long six weeks.

I look around for an empty bed to claim.

"You can bunk with me if you want," Bailey suggests.

I nod. "Okay but I get the bottom."

She smiles cheerfully. "Okay."

"They're doing a craft in thirty minutes. Do you want to go together?" she asks.

Just the thought of doing a craft with a bunch of twelve-year-olds makes me want to rip my hair out.

I smile at the girl. "I have a better idea."

Bailey and I hike up the trail with our water bottles and snacks we snuck from the camp kitchen.

"This is such a thrill!" Bailey squeals behind me. "I'm so happy you talked me into this. I feel so rebellious."

"Way better than arts and crafts, that's for sure," I mumble.

I'm looking at my feet as I hike up the rocky trail when I almost step on a butterfly. It's not very pretty and I don't know how it's even alive. I kneel to pick it up to examine its white tattered wings, wondering why it's so damaged.

Bailey says, "I've never seen someone so fascinated with a butterfly before."

She's right. It may be the ugliest butterfly I've ever seen but for some reason I feel infatuated by it. The butterfly is somehow able to find the strength to flap its broken wings and fly away.

When we get up to the top, we are surrounded by a beautiful nature scene as we look down to see more rolling mountains, trees, and wildflowers.

It takes my breath away and I know that I should try to remember this moment.

Bailey asks, "Do you ever wonder why we ever have a worry in the world when there are places like this that exist?"

I take in the beauty of my surroundings one more time and that's when I realize that Bailey isn't so bad.

Bailey and I skipped Arts and Crafts every day. Sometimes we would sneak snacks from the kitchen and hide out behind the cabins. Sometimes we would go hiking. And eventually we just stayed at our bunks since nobody really expected us to be there anyway. The camp directors gave up on me, which was exactly what I wanted them to do.

Now there's only one week left at Camp Lotsa Fun and I'll never admit out loud that I'm not ready to leave. I don't want to go home. I feel safe here. Happy even. And having Bailey look up to me the way she does warms my heart. She's become a friend. There is only one thing I miss.

"I miss boys," I tell Bailey as I pout while I sit on the bunk.

She sits on the other side of me and combs her hair with her fingers.

"There are lots of boys here," she points out.

"Yeah. Little boys. I miss *real* boys."

"Like the kind you kiss?" she asks nervously.

I sit up straight. "Wait, have you ever kissed a boy before?" I ask.

She shakes her head furiously. "No."

I get a very mischievous idea. "I think it's time to change that. Tonight."

Her eyes widen. "Tonight?"

I pull her forward so we both sit facing each other. "I've seen the way you look at that boy Nash. And I've seen him looking at you too."

She turns beet red. "Are you serious?"

"Yes. Let's write him a note and have him meet us behind the boys' cabin. It must be late though, when everyone else is asleep. Then you can lay one on him."

"Lay one on him? You think I should be the one to kiss him?"

"Yes. Never wait for a boy to kiss you first. They are way too slow and nervous. You'll figure that out soon enough."

She nods her head. She hesitates for a moment and I can tell she's waging an internal battle. "Come on Bailey. You could have your first kiss tonight. With a cute boy. You say the word and I'll help you. But if you're too uncomfortable—"

"Get a pen and paper," she practically yells.

I squeal with excitement as I jump up to retrieve the supplies to write Nash a note.

⚜ ⚜

"Are you sure he saw the note?" Bailey whispers as we wait for Nash to show up behind the boys' cabin.

"Yes. And he was grinning when he read it. He likes you," I assure her.

"Here. Have my tropical ChapStick, he'll love it."

"Della, I'm nervous," she says, her eyes filled with doubt.

"Don't focus on the kiss. Just talk to him. Get to know him. Then if you want to kiss him, go for it. But you don't have to do anything you don't want to do. If you decide you don't like him and you want out, give me the signal and I'll rescue you."

She nods her head. "Okay get lost for now. I have a boy to kiss," she says nervously. I think she was hoping that would come out more confident than it did.

"You've got this." I run away from the cabins and hide behind a tree as I watch my friend waiting for Nash. She paces back and forth, and I can feel her nervous energy from here.

Nash finally shows up ten minutes later. He probably gave poor Bailey a heart attack, thinking he wouldn't appear.

I watch her laugh and flirt with this boy and they're clearly hitting it off. He takes her by the hand, and she leans into him after tucking her hair behind her ear. She's nervous but she's going for it. *Go Bailey!* I'm cheering her on in my head as she kisses him. She's doing it and I couldn't be prouder. But there is a flashlight headed their way and they can't see it because they are clearly busy. I go running out of the trees and toward the flashlight. As I expected, it's the camp director. Luckily, he believes me when I say I'm the only one who snuck out of the bunk.

I ruined my last week at Camp Lotsa Fun. They're sending me home tonight. Apparently, they've had enough of me. But I smile the whole drive back home, knowing Bailey got her first kiss.

Chapter Twelve

"**C**ome on Ethan. Answer your damn phone," I mumble. This is my third time calling and I can't get him or my mom to pick up. My dad is away on business again, so I don't bother calling him. I'm relieved when Ethan answers with a "Jesus, Della, what?"

"It's about time you answered. I ran off the road and now I'm stuck. Can you come help me?" I've only had my driver's license for a few months now and I'm still trying to get used to driving in the snow. Clearly, I'm bad at it.

He groans, obviously annoyed with me. "Where are you?"

I squint my eyes, trying to figure out exactly where I am with all the snow coming down in the dark. "I think I'm on Belaine Drive. It's hard to see."

He hangs up and that better mean he's on his way. I'm worried if I keep spinning my tires, I'll just keep getting more stuck. So instead of trying to get out, I crank up the heat and sit back and wait. I'm relieved when headlights pull up behind me ten minutes later. Ethan walks up to my driver's window except it's not Ethan, it's JC. My heart races like it always does when he's around. I almost thought he was interested in me at the party but after seeing him a few times since that night, he's made it clear to me he's not. It's only been awkward hellos when I see him come into the house with Ethan. And the fact that I haven't heard them downstairs anymore has me assume they have moved their parties elsewhere.

"Where's Ethan?" I ask.

Ignoring my question, he says, "I'm going to shovel around you a bit then you're going to have to get out and help me push. I'll tell you when I'm ready to have you shift the car into neutral."

"Okay," I say, trying not to sound as nervous as I feel. I'm almost as bad as Bailey was the last time I saw her.

After JC is done shoveling, he yells to put the car in neutral and I get out to help him push.

My damn Ugg boots have hardly any traction and I try not to slip while we push. Luckily, after the fifth try, my car rolls free from the snowbank.

I shout with excitement, "We did it!" But my feet ungracefully slip out from under me, and I fall straight on my back. Luckily, the snow was thick enough to soften the impact.

With an embarrassed laugh, I say, "I'm okay!"

"You sure?" he asks, reaching a hand out to help me up.

"Yeah," I whisper as he pulls me up close to his face. I try to pull away but he holds me tight, not letting go. My heart races at the way he stares into my eyes. "JC, what are you doing?"

He ignores my question again and leans in closer, kissing me gently on the lips. My eyes fall shut as I kiss him back.

And when he swipes his tongue against mine, my stomach flutters.

We step apart and he says, "Do us both a favor and don't tell your brother I did that." Then he smiles at me before walking away to his car.

I've kissed a few boys this year but none of them have felt like that before. I've almost forgotten what a terrible night it was getting stuck in the snow. On my drive back home, I replay our kiss repeatedly in my head knowing my face is flushed. I'll blame it on the cold if Ethan is home when I get there.

I'm sitting on the window seat in the living area, looking out at distant city lights, stirring some tea since my cramps decided to wake me up early this morning. My friends all started their periods years ago. This is my first one and I was relieved it was finally here. But then I cried because I was too embarrassed to tell anyone I had just started, and I'm not about to ask my mom for help. Most likely it's the hormones, but I've never felt more alone than I have the last few days. And all I can think about is JC and the fact that I never heard from him after our kiss last week. My mom's voice startles me. "Hi darling girl. What are you doing up so early?"

What am I doing up? What about you? You're never up.

"I'm not feeling well. I couldn't sleep," I tell the woman I haven't talked to in weeks. Right now, she almost feels like my mother as she hugs me from behind.

"Oh no. It's that time of year. Everyone seems to be getting the cold or the flu. Let me get you some medicine." She lets go of me and moves to the kitchen cupboard. She hands me some over the counter medicine and some water. *My mom is taking care of me. Something rare. Something I want to hold onto and pretend like this is how it always is.*

I'm not actually sick so I don't take the medicine, but my mom doesn't seem to notice. I want to tell her I started my period, but something is holding me back. It's as though I feel like she doesn't deserve to know anything about me.

"How's school?" she asks.

"Good I guess."

"Are you involved with any boys? You're so beautiful. Surely they're chasing after you."

I think about the kiss with JC and feel a smile tug at my lips. I try and wipe it off but my mom saw it.

"I take that smile as a yes? Who is he?"

"Just someone from school," I lie.

I get a glimmer of satisfaction that my mom seems interested in my life, but I try to swallow it down because I know this won't last.

"I was thinking," she says in front of me as she reaches her hand out and places it on top of mine. "Maybe you and I can go to that ice skating rink you used to love. Just the two of us. And go for a drive around the city. You used to love all the Christmas lights. You'll make time for your mom, won't you?"

"Sure," I say, pulling my hand away from her.

"If you weren't feeling sick, we'd go today. Or maybe over Christmas break. How does that sound?"

I nod my head as I take another sip of tea.

"Oh dear, you're even losing your voice. Let's get you to bed."

As my mom helps me to my room, I flashback to the memory of when she was herself and sober. I think I was only six or seven the last time she took me ice skating. Just the two of us.

We're holding hands laughing as we quickly get the hang of ice skating again.

When I get brave enough to let go of my mom and do a little twirl, she says, "You're an ice queen, ready to rule the world."

I giggle and do it again and again until I'm so dizzy everything is spinning.

My mom catches my fall as I laugh even harder. We're so happy.

"We were so happy," I accidentally say out loud as my mom helps me into bed.

She wipes my hair out of my face. "What do you mean?"

I pause awkwardly because we've never had this conversation before. I don't know how to confront her about the drugs. About how she makes me feel.

"Della? What do you mean?" My mom interrupts my thoughts.

"Sometimes I just wish things were how they used to be. I wish you'd get help."

She looks taken back. "Get help for what?"

My dad steps into my room. "What are you two doing up so early?" he interrupts.

"Della was just about to tell me what she thinks I need help with," my mom snaps.

She's angry.

My dad looks at me then back at my mom and says, "She's a teenager. We parents can't do anything right." He laughs nervously before he holds my mom by the hand and leads her toward the door. "It's nothing important right now. Right Della?" my dad says, giving me an unfamiliar look.

"Right," I lie.

I can't talk to her. I've never been able to talk to her. Or my dad. He knew exactly what I was about to say because every time I bring it up to *him*, he instantly shuts me down. I don't understand why he doesn't want her to get clean. I was too young at first to understand what was going on. I just knew my mom was slipping away from me. It was gradual and little things she would do started to hurt me. Like when she forgot me at school or when she started losing interest in me. Or any other time I needed her. My mom is never here and when she is, she's *not*. I can't remember the day she changed but I do remember the day I realized that she did. I've never looked at her the same.

"You really should be more grateful. I don't know why you're upset," my mom says. "You have everything. Look at this big house you live in. Look at this room. Look at the closet filled with more clothes and shoes than most teenagers ever dream of." My dad tugs on her and mumbles something. Anger stirs inside of me, but I don't allow myself to cry. My mom shuts my bedroom door behind her.

And we never went ice skating.

Chapter Thirteen

Della

"This feels like our spot," I say to JC. We're four miles from my house and surrounded by trees in a secluded area. It's starting to feel warmer outside as spring takes over, melting the snow.

"It is," JC says with a crooked smile.

"Am I the only girl you're doing this with?" I ask JC shyly, as we scramble for our clothes in the backseat of his car.

He looks me sweetly in the eye. "Of course, you are Della." He looks me over. "God, you're perfect."

"Shouldn't we like make things official then?" I ask before slipping my shirt back on.

JC, the guy I've given everything to, sighs and my heart drops. "You're only sixteen. I could get in a lot of trouble. Imagine what would happen to me if your brother found out. Shit, or even worse, your father."

"I'll be seventeen in two months. And my brother loves you. But yeah, we should keep this from my father, which will be easy since he's never home." I mumble the last part.

He touches my knee. "Della, more than anything I want you to be my girl. But time isn't in our favor right now. You're too young."

I really don't want to cry in front of him.

"How about I promise you that you're the only girl I'm having fun with? Will that be enough for now? I can't lose you."

The sincerity in his eyes breaks me. He seems genuine.

His phone vibrates and he opens it without giving me a chance to answer. His phone is important to him. I glance down at the text, and it makes no sense to me.

"What does *the Devil's not listening, but I've got the bread* mean?" I laugh.

"It means duty calls babe," he answers, getting into the front seat to drive.

"Duty? What exactly is that anyway?" I feel nervous bringing this up since he's friends with my brother, who is very clearly involved in illicit drug dealing. I just hope JC isn't.

"Haven't I told you what I do for work?" he asks with a smile.

I shake my head no and buckle my seat belt as he speeds off.

"I'm in sales," he answers.

I practically yell. "Drugs?"

He looks surprised and hurt. "What? No, of course not. Well, maybe a little weed sometimes, but mostly I sell home security systems. I make a good living from it."

I'm relieved he's not involved with whatever the crap my brother is. "Oh. That's great," I say.

"There's some stashed in the back if you want some. I don't charge cute girls," he says with a smirk.

I laugh. "Weed? No thanks. It makes me feel lousy, and track is too important to me to risk failing a drug test."

"Another thing I love about you," he says, making my heart race.

"You love me?" I ask.

He puts his hand on my thigh. "Yes. I love you. I'd do anything for you. I guess that's why I can't stay away."

I was not expecting him to tell me he loves me. JC loves me. A smile tugs at my lips.

"You look happy," he says.

"You make me happy. I think I love you too," I tell him.

I've never really known what love is, but this is the closest I've ever felt to anyone. And I can't wait until I'm eighteen and JC and I can finally be official.

"Shit, there's your brother. I'm out," JC says before leaving the booth.

The diner is packed with Bordersville locals like it is every Sunday morning, but by the look on Ethan's face, he saw us together. I turn around just in time to see JC exiting out the back door of the diner on the opposite side of Ethan. JC asked me to stay over last night and promised to take me to breakfast this morning. It felt like an actual date. He's never taken me out in public before. Now my brother is ruining it. I thought JC and I could handle Ethan together, and I'm a little hurt he ran out so quickly. It was only a matter of time before

Ethan found out about us. I sigh as Ethan sits down in front of me. Then keeping my head down, I stir my coffee.

He just stares at me, and when I finally make eye contact with him, he asks, "How long have you been sleeping with my business partner?"

"Business partner?" I ask, feeling myself tremble.

"Yes. JC's the one that got me into the drug trade in the first place." He's staring at me as I process all of this. "Don't give me those judgemental eyes Della. You're just as involved as I am now that you're screwing him."

My heart shatters. I knew Ethan was obviously involved with drugs, but JC lied to me. He told me he sold security systems. How did I not realize that JC was the one I heard speaking with Ethan in his office the night I found out about the drugs?

"I- I had no idea. I just thought it was you involved with dealing drugs here and there and keeping it from dad. But it all makes sense now. You need to get out, Ethan. This is serious."

He arches his eyebrow. "I need to get out? What about you? I know JC brings his girls to this diner after fucking them, so don't deny that you're sleeping with him."

My heart races in my chest. "I didn't know."

"Just stop sleeping with him," he says. "I'll tell him I don't want you to be a part of all this."

I nod.

"Good. I'll give you a ride home."

JC tried calling me after the diner incident, but I didn't pick up. I needed time to process all of this. This is not something I want to be involved with, especially the man who controls it all. But I want to talk to him about it first. Maybe he'll leave this bad business behind for me. He loves me. He's the one person in my life who seems to care about me. I sprint up the hill in my running shoes toward our spot. The trees get thicker and thicker the further I go up. My pace quickens when I see what feels like fate. JC's car parked in our spot. He knows I run when I'm upset, and he probably hoped I'd end up here. I should've answered my phone. He cares about me. I need him. I smile as I sprint toward his car, hoping with everything in me that he listens to me. If not, I'll have to do the hardest thing I've ever had to do and leave him. But I don't want to think about that right now. He'll do anything for me. I walk to his window and stop in my tracks. JC is on top of another *girl*, kissing her the way he kisses me. I back away from the car because I can't look anymore. Everything was a lie. I swallow back my tears and run back home. And as soon as my bedroom door shuts behind me, I cry. I cry all night long. Until I wake up the next day, then I let anger take over when I pick up my phone to dial a number.

I'll never let myself feel this hurt again, that's for damn sure. JC doesn't deserve my broken heart. Luckily, I didn't have to end my non-exclusive relationship with JC. I laugh that I felt the need to end anything at all. We were *nothing*. Even when I thought we were something, it was all a lie. I pretended like I didn't even know what JC was arrested for when Ethan told me he went to jail. JC has tried reaching out to me by phone but every time I see that the jail is calling, I ignore it. Eventually, a month later, he's finally given up. And I'm still sick to my stomach that I gave him my virginity and let myself think I loved him. And I'm more than ready to move on and put JC in my past. I just hope he or Ethan never figure out I was the one who called the police and told them about the stash of weed in his car. It probably wasn't the best decision, but I let anger get the best of me. And I don't regret it. He's lucky that's all I snitched on him for. I could get him in a whole lot more trouble but that means taking my brother down too.

Since I'm not going to let myself cry over a guy again, I've decided it's best not to get attached. I guess that's probably why I've kissed four different guys since JC. I'm planning on having a truly fun summer without any moping. After slipping on my mini skirt and lip gloss, I head out the door to make it five.

Chapter Fourteen

Della

As I'm sitting at my desk in junior English, I find myself staring at Rhett Frayer again. There is something just so sexy about the way he's always drawing these weird nerdy superheroes in his notebook. And plus, he pays attention in class, gets good grades by working hard, and comes from an intelligent family instead of a wealthy one. His dad is known to be a smart science guy. I'm sure he's right behind his father, because Rhett actually tries, I can tell. He's not being handed anything and it's intriguing. Especially since I'm spoiled rotten. I'm grateful for all that I have but I'll admit it hurts when my parents use our money as an out for how they treat me sometimes. I wish they knew they can't buy my love.

Nobody knows that I fantasize about Rhett on a daily basis, including him. He's sort of shy, and I know that if he knew the things I imagine in my head, he'd be beet red with embarrassment.

"What are you drawing?" I whisper to him. Talking to him for the first time feels secretive and I like it. For some reason I like that he's such a good boy. I've tried the bad boy thing, and we all know how that turned out.

He covers the drawing up with his hand, clearly afraid I'm going to make fun of him for it.

"I don't bite," I whisper with a wink.

He smirks. "I've heard otherwise."

I frown. "You've heard I'm not nice?"

He chuckles and shakes his head. "You're the heart breaker of the junior class Della. And honestly, I'm a little scared that you're even talking to me."

Even though his words sting a little, I realize that Rhett is even cuter when he talks.

"You should be scared," I whisper with a flirty smirk.

By the pathetically sad smile I see on his face, I can tell he feels bad for me. It offends me a little. Why does he feel bad for me? He's cute but he knows nothing about me besides what he's heard from other people.

"You don't know me, Rhett."

The bell rings and I gather my things. I wish I could be lucky enough to be with a guy like Rhett Frayer. Maybe one day I'll get to marry a guy like him.

Kat is waiting for me right out the door, probably ready to gossip about the latest rumor.

"Hey," I say as she looks down at her phone.

When she finally looks up, she says, "Ew, Oh my God, look at Rhett Frayer."

"Ew?" I ask, feeling offended that's what she thinks of my crush.

"He's just such a nerd. Anyway, I want to tell you all about my date last night." I tune out Kat as she blabbers her story. I look in Rhett's direction, watching him walk away. If only he didn't feel bad for girls like me.

"Hello? Earth to Della! Are you in there?" Kat asks.

I shake off the fact that Rhett can't happen. "Oh yes, sorry. Just tired. What did you say?"

"I said Ryan Bradley has been asking about you. The most popular male junior at this school? The star player of the baseball team?"

"Wow," I say, trying my best to act enthused as I open my locker.

Kat looks at me like I'm stupid. "He's been asking about *you!*"

"That's cool I guess."

"No, Della you don't understand. I'm pretty sure he's going to ask you to Homecoming. Don't mess this up. Especially after everything that happened last year."

I assume she's talking about JC. "What is that supposed to mean?"

Her familiar smile is all too fake. I'm getting sick of it if I'm being honest. "Oh, hun. I just mean you're kind of getting a bad rep. Everyone knows you were having sex with JC and that he ended up in jail. He's a bad guy and now people are a little scared of you by association, I think."

I've heard.

"And after JC, rumor has it you got around a lot. I mean *I* know you're not a slut. But that's what *they* are calling you. Honestly, Ryan will be the best thing for you right now."

The word slut stings. *People really think of me that way? I like boys, but I care about my reputation. I wish I didn't* care what people thought of me. Now I'm going to be calling myself a slut in my own head all day when I know I'm not. *I'm not. Right?*

"You're in your own little world today." Kat snaps her fingers at me. "Let me know when you hear from Ryan. I can't wait to see the two of you together."

I let out a breath when Kat walks away and lean my back against my locker.

Anxiety crushes me as I wonder if Coach Evelyn will hear that I was dating a guy who ended up in jail. Will she kick me off the track team? I cannot let that happen. Kat may be right. I have to fix this.

"Hey, Della," I hear a masculine voice to my right. I turn to face Ryan Bradley. "Are you alright?" he asks.

I let out a breath. "Yeah, just a lot on my mind, Ryan."

He smiles and then laughs. His face is a little red and I find it cute that he's a bit bashful. "I know it's a month away, but I figured I'd better be quick before someone else asks you. Would you want to go to the Homecoming dance with me?"

I didn't expect to be asked so soon. Especially since everyone is supposedly afraid of me these days. "I'd like that."

"Cool," he says grinning ear to ear. I appreciate how happy he seems.

I'm about to walk off when he says, "Hey Della wait, do you want to hang out this weekend too?"

"Sure, that sounds fun."

He smiles. "Okay I'll pick you up Saturday then. Text me your address."

As we exchange numbers, I realize that Ryan really is cute. He has golden brown hair and a tall athletic build. But I've never paid attention to him, or at least not like I've noticed Rhett Frayer. I wonder if he's going to the Homecoming dance. I brush that thought away and tell Ryan goodbye.

Chapter Fifteen

Della

What if we let people see what was truly going through our minds? Could we let them know our thoughts? We assume we know someone from the outside by the way they smile, or by how many followers they have on social media. We judge people on how popular they are or how good they are at sports. We assume just because they are prettier or have a nice car that they're happy. The truth is, we can never know what someone is going through. Everyone is fighting some type of battle of their own. Most of the kids at my high school think I have it all. Even though I started to have a bad rep after JC, I'm still the pretty track star with rich parents, and I'm dating the most popular guy in school. I honestly probably have Ryan to thank for turning things around for me. Kat really was right. As a junior in high school, I stand up here on the stage at the dance wearing the home-coming princess crown. I'm all smiles. Nobody understands how bad it hurts that my mom didn't even help me pick out this dress or help me get ready for tonight. That I've given up all hope for her to want anything to do with me. She probably won't even realize that I may not come home tonight. But here I stand. Faking it. Smiling like the perfect homecoming princess that I'm pretending to be. Ryan is whistling at me from the crowd of other students cheering. Some of the others think I'm the luckiest girl ever to come here with him. We're young. We're having fun. I would be lying if I said I didn't love parts of my life, because I do. I have a lot of friends. I've set state records for track and I'm passionate about that. I shouldn't be sad, right? But I am. I'm sad a lot of the time. Ryan stands up and takes my hand to lead me to the dance floor. His smile is so bright in the dark and he looks so good in a tux. I feel his warm hands around my waist as we dance to a slow song.

"Are you having fun?" he asks.

"I am. Are you having fun?"

"Of course. You look pretty tonight," Ryan says.

I smile. "Thanks."

The song ends and I pull out my phone to get a selfie of us and then notice I have a bunch of missed calls from Ethan. *What the hell?* I quickly open a text from him, and it knocks the wind out of me.

"Everything okay?" Ryan asks, looking down at me.

"My mom is in the hospital. I have to go."

He grabs my hand. "I'll drive you."

I don't say much in the car because I'm worried about my mom. Ryan speeds through a yellow light and I'm thankful that he's getting us to the hospital quickly.

"Thanks so much for taking me to the dance, I'm so sorry about this," I tell him.

As he's parking his car he asks, "Do you want me to come with you?"

"No, go have fun with your friends." I give him a kiss before getting out and rushing into the hospital. Ethan is sitting in the waiting room right as I walk in.

"What's going on?" I ask my brother.

"Mom overdosed. I found her having a seizure on the kitchen floor and brought her straight here. They have her hooked up to a ventilator now."

"She stopped breathing?" I panic.

"She's breathing now, Della. She's going to be okay."

"We need to get her help. She has to go to rehab."

"Della, she's an addict. She won't get help unless she wants to."

I could punch him for the lack of sympathy he has for my mom.

Then I realize something. I don't know how I didn't notice before. "Wait a minute. You're the one giving her the drugs, aren't you?" I ask.

He looks ashamed as he looks down.

"How could you do this? This is all your fault!"

"Della, please. If she stopped getting them from me, she would just get them somewhere else."

I ignore his last comment because if I don't, I'm definitely going to punch him. "Does dad know she's in the hospital?" I ask.

"Yes. He's on his flight home," he says.

"When can we see her?" I ask.

"Go ahead. Room C6." I glare at him before walking away and he looks at me like he feels bad, which he should.

My mom is asleep and hooked up to a bunch of machines when I walk in her room. I pull a chair up next to her and grab her hand. I whisper as I sob, "You're hurting yourself mom. Please stop doing this."

When I wake up the next morning and look in the mirror, I see my messy brown hair that lost all its perfect shiny curl from the night before, and the mascara that's smudged underneath my eyes.

I'm a mess.

Ethan drove us home from the hospital around midnight to get some sleep, but I stayed up looking for the perfect rehab for my mom to check into when she gets released from the hospital.

I strip out of my pajamas and get in the hot shower to wash it all off. After putting on my matching gray oversized soft hoodie and shorts, I climb back into bed and check my phone for any updates from my dad. He went straight to the hospital when he flew in from his business trip. I'll head back over there later to show him the rehabs I found. I have a couple of texts from Ryan asking if I'm okay.

Music is playing in my ears through my headphones as I make blueberry muffins in the kitchen. The lyrics are a distraction for me since I'm getting tired of being alone with my own thoughts. As I go to put the muffins in the oven, I'm startled to see my dad standing in the dining room. I almost drop the muffins but luckily I catch them just as the pan hits the rack. I'm probably being loud, but I wouldn't know since NF is rapping in my ears. After shutting the oven and setting the timer, I take out my headphones.

"How's mom?" I ask.

"She's doing great. Being released at noon."

His choice of words annoys me a bit. "I wouldn't say she's doing great considering she's in the hospital from an overdose. I have a list of rehabs. Have you decided which one she's going to?"

He scratches his head. "Your mom said this was all just a misunderstanding. Said she accidentally got into the wrong medication for her headache. It was an accident."

I slam my hand down onto the counter. "You and the doctors really believe that?"

My dad reaches out to touch my arm, but I pull away. Then he sighs and says, "Look, you're too young to be worrying about all of this. I promise I'll investigate it. For now, let's welcome your mom home when she gets here–"

I interrupt, "And pretend like everything is fine? You're just enabling her. No, it's more than that. You and Ethan are supporting her, and I want nothing to do with it. No thanks!"

I sprint past my dad toward the door, get into my car, and drive to Ryan's.

Chapter Sixteen

Della

My alarm blares for the fourth time before I drag myself out of bed to get ready for my morning run. After putting on my shorts, sports bra, tank top, and running shoes, I fasten my hair up into a ponytail and head downstairs. Deciding I need a boost of energy before my legs can work, I start up the coffee pot. The sound of the machine brewing warms my insides. *I'm coming for you caffeine.* Last night was a restless night of tossing and turning. I'm nervous about all the athletic scouts Coach said will be watching at track state this weekend. Apparently, they liked what they saw before, but this year as a senior is the most important. I'm especially focused on impressing the coach from Wallington. The thought of going there on a track scholarship sounds too good to be true. As I'm drinking my coffee at the kitchen table, Ethan comes in alone. He's talking loudly on his phone. I'm immediately uncomfortable when he says, "JC come on. You've only been out for a week. I don't think it's smart—" he pauses, and I can hear JC's voice on the other end. I can't make out what he's saying. I'm kind of surprised I haven't heard from him, although I'm relieved, since I'm the reason he was put in jail in the first place.

Ethan hangs up his phone and steps into the kitchen.

"JC is out of jail?" I ask.

Ethan glares at me. "What's it to you? He's not your business. Not anymore. Stay out of it."

I run my fingertip around the rim of my mug, feeling a sense of paranoia for some reason. Even though I know that JC doesn't realize that I was the one who turned him in. "He hasn't asked about me or anything has he?" I ask.

Ethan's back is to me when he huffs out a pathetic laugh. "Quit flattering yourself Della. It's been over a year since you guys hooked up. He's already been with three different women just since he's been out of jail. You mean nothing to him."

The last sentence hurts a little. Not that he means much to me, but he was my first time, so I guess he does more than I want to admit. But if I don't mean anything to him then why did he try calling while he was in jail? *Did he suspect it was me?* I leave that question out just as Ethan says, "Don't you have a boyfriend anyway? Jesus."

I chug the hot coffee down my throat as if the liquid gold isn't meant to be savored and slam the empty mug down. I'm more than ready to go on a run and I don't need to be standing around fighting about absolutely nothing with my brother.

Ignoring him, I'm about to head out the door when I bump into my dad who is standing in the doorway. "Whoa, sorry dad."

"No going out of the five-block range we talked about," my dad says sternly. What does he think will possibly hurt me? I don't understand why he's always so worried for my safety but it's annoying.

"I won't." I will, but he doesn't need to know that.

"I'll walk you out," he says following behind me as I dart for the door. I haven't talked to him much since the incident with my mom and the fact that he still hasn't gotten her into a rehab.

The front door shuts behind my dad and me. I'm about to take off when he says, "You have a track meet this weekend?"

"Yes. It's a big one. College scouts will be there."

My dad smiles, clearly pleased. I know if he has time to show up to the meet he will. But he usually can't. "Ah, will Wallington be there?"

The thought of disappointing my dad if I don't get into Wallington brings a terrible pressure in my chest. "That's what I've been told, yes."

"Well, if they don't offer you the track scholarship, I'll fund your schooling myself. You know that." His words irritate me. He doesn't know how good I am at my chosen sport.

"I'm hoping for Wallington, but I'd love to run track at any school really."

He raises an eyebrow. "Any school?"

"Any proper school that I think I'd like, yes."

He holds a confused expression. "Are you saying if Wallington doesn't offer you a track scholarship, you'll accept a less prestigious school? To run laps?"

Now he's starting to make me mad. "Come on dad, you know track is more to me than anything. It's more than running laps. I'm just saying there may be other options to consider. Wallington will always be my first choice."

He looks calmer. "Good. Wallington will always be your best option, Della. With everything going on with your mom and with the business booming this year, I could really use you around here."

I'm left speechless that the reason he wants me to go to Wallington is to stay here to babysit my mom and... help with Whitlock Corporation?

My dad studies me then looks around. "I'd love to hire you as an intern your first year, while you go to school, then build up from there. Look, I know your brother believes he'll take over the family business someday, but I don't know if he'll ever have what it takes. If you come out on top with a college degree from Wallington, you can join the family business."

Suddenly Ethan bursts past my dad. I don't know how much of that he heard, but it's obvious he's not happy. Awesome. Another reason for my brother to hate me. I don't even know if this is what I want anyway.

My dad stares at Ethan who is climbing into his car, then looks back at me. "Think about it sweetheart."

"That's what running helps me do. Think," I say walking back, trying to escape.

He nods with a manicured hand on his chin. "Good. Well, enjoy your run."

"Bye." I throw my headphones in my ears, start my watch, and begin my much-needed therapy session.

After my run, I have a text from my friend Kat.

You coming to the party tonight?

Of course, I text back.

∾∾∾∾ ∾∾∾∾

"You and Ryan are so cute together," Savanna says at the loud house party.

I glance up at my boyfriend who is playing beer pong with his guy friends. I wonder if his parents are home tonight. Sometimes they're away on business and I can sleep over. He's an only child golden boy who gets anything he wants. Exactly the kind of man I never want to settle down with. We're together because we look good together. And he's not a bad kisser so that helps.

"Thanks." I smile.

Kat comes up behind Savanna and me, giving us a hug. "Guess who just showed up," she shouts so we can hear her over the loud music.

"Who?" Savannah asks. Honestly, I couldn't care less.

"Wylie Hemmings," she shouts with excitement.

I don't know who that is, but I smile and pretend I do. I pretend a lot.

"Oh my gosh, Della!" I hear a girl shout behind me.

I turn around to see a familiar face. It's Bailey, two years older now. I haven't seen her since summer camp, but I've heard the rumors about how she tries way too hard to fit in. She's desperate to be popular when she's supposedly unpopular. I've heard she's tried out for every sport and failed to make the team. I also heard a rumor that she stole expensive makeup from a girl in the locker room, but I doubt that's true. I could have told people that they are wrong about her. That she is kind, smart, funny, and honest. She's even fun to hang out with and easier to talk to than any of the friends I have now. We had so many laughs together at Camp Lotsa Fun. I could have helped her out by telling everyone that they have her all wrong. But I didn't. Instead, I pretend that I have no idea who she is.

I'm about to smile and hug her but then I realize where I am and who's watching.

"Um... Do I know you?" I ask Bailey, feeling as snotty as I sound.

"It's Bailey. From Camp Lotsa Fun. You don't remember me?" She sounds so hurt but all I can focus on is getting out of how she just announced that I went to the most embarrassing camp I've ever been to.

"I have never been to Camp... what did you call it? You have me mistaken for someone else," I tell her, feeling like the liar that I am.

Guilt consumes me as I feel like Bailey looks into my soul. "That was one of the best summers of my life. And now you just ruined those memories. I thought we were friends. I've seen you around school but I've never had the nerve to come up and talk to you. I was afraid this is exactly what would happen. I was right about you the whole time."

The truth hurts. She knows exactly the type of person I am. She knew as soon as we left that camp that we'd never be friends again. I'm too shallow, too worried about my own popularity and big fat ego to care about anybody else. And the fact that she can see that covers me in shame.

Kat says, "Clearly, she doesn't know you so get lost, Bailey."

I'm too ashamed to look Bailey in the eyes. But when I do finally look up, she's already gone.

"How did that girl even get into this party? Did you hear that she stole Charlotte's contour set?" Kat asks.

"We don't know if that's true," I say, although it feels too late to stand up for her now. I'm the worst.

Kat rolls her eyes.

"Enough about her," Savanna says. "Let's celebrate tonight. Five more months, girlfriends, and we're out of here!" She takes a sip from her fruity cocktail.

"Wallington, here we come!" Kat shouts.

Both of their dads also helped get them into that school. If I stay, things will basically be the same. My stomach churns at the thought. Both of my friends are staring at me, like they're waiting for me to do something. They want me to be excited with them.

"Wallington!" I yell, doing my best to sound happy.

Chapter Seventeen

Della

Wanna hang tonight?

This is the second text I've gotten in the past week from JC. The first time I didn't respond, and I don't plan on responding to this one either. I set my phone down on my bed and open the letter from Copper Hill University in Ohio. *Again.* A sense of confusion overcomes me thinking about how I'll have to turn down the full ride scholarship for track and why that makes me a little sad. I never imagined myself going anywhere but Wallington. It's all I've ever wanted. Everyone knows all the pro runners are made at that school and Coach would kill me to turn down an opportunity like that. Everyone has been pushing me to accept the offer and I know it's a no brainer.

Suddenly my phone starts ringing, and I hesitate swiping to answer when I see who it is, but for some stupid reason I do.

"Hello?"

JC says, "Hey. I'm out front. Can you come out and talk?"

I'm surprised that he's at my house. "Is Ethan with you?"

He chuckles. "No. I'm here to see *you*. I have something I want to tell you."

I pause. "I'll be out in a sec."

Feeling slightly nervous to hear what JC has to say, I drag my feet out the door to see him sitting in his car. He must be scared at the thought of having Ethan or my dad see him with me. I hop in the passenger seat.

"Hi," I say awkwardly. I haven't seen him in two years, yet he acts like it was yesterday. And he looks the same.

"Are you avoiding me?" he asks.

Feeling uncomfortable, I tuck a strand of hair back behind my ear. "I've been busy with graduation and figuring out what college to go to." I'm having a hard time looking into his eyes as I speak but I feel him looking at me.

"College," he says. "Where?"

"Wallington," I answer.

He smiles. "Good. You're staying close."

I nod, not knowing what else to say.

He adjusts in his seat and says, "I've been thinking about you a lot."

"Why?" I ask. "I'm nothing to you. You proved that when I caught you with another girl in the backseat of your car."

He doesn't even seem surprised. "You were too young back then. Now that you've graduated, I want you to be my girl."

I sigh. "JC. That's not a good idea."

"Why not? Because I went to jail? I want you, Della."

I roll my eyes. "You went to jail for having a little weed, but I know exactly what you do *professionally*. And no, you don't want me JC. You want the challenge and I'm not going to be a part of your game ever again. You're right, I have grown up and I'm no longer interested."

Suddenly my phone starts vibrating on my lap, and I look down to see that Ryan is calling. I look up at JC to see him glaring at my phone. Clearly, he's not happy about the phone call. I open the door to get out and I'm surprised when he grabs my arm.

"Let go," I say angrily. He immediately does, and raises his hands up. He hasn't even seen how feisty I can be. Then I say, "Do yourself a favor and find someone else. But before you tell the next girl you love her, you better make damn sure you mean it. Stop calling me."

I stand up and slam the passenger door behind me. JC doesn't deserve my time anymore.

Ryan snuck over tonight after JC left since my dad is out of town on a "business trip." We usually do this at his house, but his parents are home tonight. Besides, I'm sure my mom is passed out downstairs. I'm not sure where Ethan is but he never gets home early on Saturday nights. He's probably out committing another crime like it's no big deal.

Ryan and I sneak into my room and before I can kiss him, he says, "I'm so stoked for the party tomorrow night on Hemsworth. You're still planning on coming with me, right?"

I smile. "Of course."

We've already talked about how things will most likely end between us when summer ends. And we're both okay with it. He wants his own college experience and I want mine. Ryan is leaving for Los Angeles to play baseball for California State. I'm suddenly jealous that he gets to go far away from here.

I go to kiss him again, but Ryan asks, "Did you accept Wallington's offer yet?"

"Planning on it tomorrow." I don't know why I've procrastinated for so long. Not wanting to talk or think about life anymore, I kiss Ryan hard on the mouth, happy to shut him up.

We fall onto my bed and continue to make out when I tell him about the fantasy I have. It has to do with us in the shower.

"You're on fire tonight," he says.

He instantly agrees to the shower, and we tip toe to my bathroom and strip down. Ryan cries out when the water is too hot, and we laugh.

"Shhh, be quiet." I bring my finger over his lips and then kiss him. I'm kissing him wildly when I hear my bathroom door burst open. A scream escapes my throat as Ethan jerks the shower curtain open.

"Dude, what the fuck?" Ryan says.

"Ethan! Get out!" Feeling humiliated and exposed, I cover myself as best as I can with my arms.

Ethan grabs my wet hair and drags me out of the shower when I notice he has a friend with him. JC.

"Ow, Ethan stop!" I beg as I try and get his hands off me and fail. I've never felt so mortified in my life. "At least let me get a towel."

I catch Ethan look up at JC who shakes his head to the towel. *Looks like he's the one giving orders.*

"Ethan please," my voice shakes. "You don't need to listen to him. I'm your sister."

Ethan ignores me as he yanks my hair even harder and continues dragging me out of the bathroom completely soaked and uncovered. I have never felt more betrayed by my own brother.

"Stop! You're hurting her!" Ryan yells out as he tries to stop Ethan but JC punches Ryan in the face and tells him to get out.

I cry out for Ryan as he scrambles for his clothes. My knees hit the carpet and Ethan still has me held by the hair as my head is jerked up to watch Ryan grab his things.

JC looks down at me and laughs. "He's leaving you because he's done with you, you stupid slut."

Ryan charges at Ethan but JC is already grabbing him and pulling him away.

"Don't hurt her," Ryan says.

Then JC looks at Ryan as he continues to push him back. "If you don't leave right fucking now, I'll personally make sure you'll never be able to walk again, let alone play baseball, Ryan Bradley."

The color from Ryan's face drains as he looks at me through such frightened eyes, I almost don't recognize him. "Della, I'm sorry," he says. He can't help me. But I'm relieved when he leaves so that they won't hurt him.

I'm left alone in the room with Ethan and JC, feeling afraid and humiliated. "Let me go," I beg Ethan again. "I'll expose you guys to the police and dad if you don't let me go."

Ethan begins screaming in my face. "You and dad think you're so much better and smarter than me. I've worked my ass off to take over the company someday and as soon as perfect Della graduates, he's already wanting to hand it over to her. If only dad could see you now!"

"Ethan please," I whimper. "I don't want anything to do with the company anyway. Why are you doing this?"

He slams his fist down by my head, causing me to jump. "You're the one to blame for this. You got yourself involved."

Now JC plays the good guy and steps in and says, "Ethan let go of her."

Ethan let's go of my hair, and I slowly start to stand when JC says, "We're not upset that you got involved, we're upset that you thought you could get away so easily."

I practically laugh. "We slept together over a year ago. You're just sad that I don't want you anymore."

Anger floods JC's eyes before he grabs me and shoves me down on the bed face down. Then he says, "No. I'm mad because you're a liar. I'm mad because you didn't tell me you have a pretty boy boyfriend. Because you ignored me when I called from jail. And I'm mad because you're the one who fucking put me in there in the first place."

I'm shocked. With the side of my face pressed into the mattress I say, "Wh-what are you talking about? How did you–?"

"How did I find out? You told me today when you said the police found weed in my car. I never told anyone why I was even in jail. Not even your brother. And I'm hurt you felt the need to do that. Was it because you thought I'd never let you be with anyone else? Because by the sounds of it, you really have gotten around. What number was this boy we caught you with in the shower anyway? You're a slut. But not only are you a slut, you're a fucking snitch. Do you know what we do to snitches Della? Tell her what we do Ethan."

"We beat them until we know they'll never dare betray us again," Ethan says.

"You're lucky if that's all we'll do," JC says.

"You're evil! Don't touch me," I scream then kick him to get his weight off me. I'm able to roll onto my back.

Then I'm shocked when his fist hits me in the face so hard that I feel blood rushing out my nose and my eyes water. Ethan does nothing to stop it. "Help!" I scream in hopes anyone can hear me.

"Nobody can hear you Della." When I try to stand up JC slaps me hard across the face, making me dizzy. Then he grabs a pillow off my bed and shoves it on my face. I can't scream for help now and I can't breathe. My brother is going to let his friend murder me. My chest tightens at the terror. I don't want to die. I try kicking him with my legs and hitting him with my arms, but I feel my body getting weak.

Suddenly, JC jerks my head up by grabbing me by the hair and I'm relieved I can breathe again. "You disgust me," he says.

I feel my body tense up and cringe at his words. Tears are streaming down my face as I lay pinned down, naked on my bed. He gets closer to my face, and I realize I've never hated someone so much in my life.

Then he whispers, "I love that fear in your eyes. I knew you were weak."

He licks my cheek, and I headbutt him hard in the face. He jerks but doesn't let go of my arms. Then his tongue swipes his bloody lip, and he smiles. But it quickly fades, and he says, "If you ever betray me again, I'll kill you."

Suddenly I hear my bedroom door burst open. JC jumps back and stares at the intruder. I'm shocked when I sit up to see my mom standing in my bedroom.

"What's going on here?" she asks.

My mom stares at Ethan in disbelief and her face reddens when she looks me over. Immediately, I'm reminded that I'm naked and feel humiliated all over again.

"Get out!" my mom yells at Ethan and JC.

I'm instantly flooded with relief as they both move faster than I can blink. My mom stops Ethan as he walks past. I can't hear what she whispers and by the look on her face, she's not done with him. My mom runs to me after JC and Ethan leave.

"I'm here baby," she says, covering me in a blanket.

I throw my arms around her and sob. After I calm down, I explain everything.

She rubs my back and says, "I just really wish you wouldn't have gotten yourself into this mess. What were you think-ing?"

My mom's words are painful to hear. She thinks this is my fault.

"I was thinking *I didn't feel alone for once*. When I got myself involved with JC, I was thinking *someone loved me for once*. I was thinking I had no one else to turn to because you're never here for me!"

My mom shocks me as she slaps me across the face.

I quickly run to my bathroom and throw up in the toilet. Then locking myself in, I lay on the bathroom floor and cry. My mom knocks. "Della, I'm so sorry. I felt like you were blaming me."

I ignore her.

She sighs. I almost want her to offer to sleep upstairs with me but at the same time I don't. I need my mom. But I don't want to need her. Especially since she just slapped me after I was almost killed. "I'll be downstairs if you need me."

I have to get out of here. I can't live like this anymore. These people aren't my family. I bet I can still get into Copper Hill. I never thought I'd go through with it and move away from home, but it's time. My decision is easy now. I'm leaving, tomorrow.

After I pull myself up off the floor, I look in the mirror at the girl who's ready to take on the world herself. No addict mother to ignore her, no powerful dad to control her, no brother to hurt her. Just me. Della. *Scout.*

⚜

It's late. Really late. But Coach said I could always come to her for anything. So that's exactly what I'm doing. No matter how hard it is to ask for help, sometimes you have no other choice. I'm sitting in her driveway at three am, hoping she'll wake up to the text I just sent her.

Della? What is it? Are you okay? She texts back.

I'm parked in your driveway. Not okay. I delete the **Not okay** and hit send.

Coach comes out her front door in a matter of seconds, wearing a state track hoodie with the words **Coach** on the sleeve. I know how badly she wanted the words **1st place Champions** on the sleeve too. Our team won 2nd place at States, and I think she's still a little beat up about it.

When she reaches my car, she opens the passenger door and gets in. "Hey, what's going on? Are you alright?"

My chest hurts at the thought of what happened tonight. What almost happened. Before I realize I'm doing it, I burst into uncontrollable sobs. My coach pulls me into her, letting me cry on her shoulder as she tries to comfort me.

"Do you want to tell me what happened?" she asks when I finally calm down.

I tell her everything and she listens carefully.

"I can't stay here."

"Shhh. I know," she whispers.

"What am I going to do?" I ask, desperate for my coach's advice.

"What do *you* want to do?" she asks.

It feels good to hear someone ask me that.

"I kind of want to go to Ohio and attend Copper Hill."

She touches my hand. "Then go and don't look back. I'll contact the principal and let him know your situation. I promise I'll make sure your records are secure, so they can't find you."

After talking to Coach last night, she let me crash at her house, but I only got a few hours of sleep. I'm anxious to run away from home. There is still so much I must do before I can leave, so I need to get moving. I head toward the car dealership.

I found the most affordable car there that looked like it could drive all the way to Ohio and hold me over for a few years.

The car salesman looked at me like I'm crazy. Then he glanced at my Genesis luxury sports car.

"So, let me get this right. You're telling me that you want to trade this in for that?" He points to the yellow Volkswagen.

I press my lips together tightly. "Yup. That's right."

He chuckles and shakes his head. "Alright. Let's figure out the paperwork and get you on your way."

I leave the car dealership with $40,000 in my pocket and drive my yellow bug to my house which I know will be quiet. I write my parents a letter telling them I'm moving away to California with Ryan. I don't feel that guilty about lying. They don't deserve a goodbye and I know my dad would never let me leave.

The house is quiet as I throw some of my things together in my bedroom. I hurry out fast and head downstairs to find my mom asleep in her bed. I know better than to try and wake her so instead, I kiss her on the cheek and whisper, "Bye, mom."

After loading up my car, I drive to the thrift shop. I've heard that they buy high-end clothing for resale. I didn't bring everything I own with me, but I've bagged most of the expensive stuff I've gotten over the years. The clothes have been very loved, but now it's time to let them go. Time to start fresh -- and I could really use the extra cash. I don't even have a job yet and I still have to pay rent and buy books when I get to Copper Hill. Coach already has an apartment set up for me when the semester starts in August, but I'll have to find a hotel to stay at until then, and that won't be cheap either. Unless I stay in my car. Thirty-eight days. I can do that until my apartment is available.

When I walk into Greta's Closet, I see row after row of designer clothing. People are rummaging through the items. Wow. Why have I never come in here before? Checking out the prices of the clothing, they are still way too expensive for me to buy.

I speak to the lady at the desk upfront and she's thrilled when I hand her a huge garbage bag full of clothing. After going through it, she hands me a surprising amount of money.

"Wow, thank you. I'll go get the other bag."

The woman smiles. "You have a whole other bag?"

"Yes."

"That's amazing. Thanks!" she says.

As I'm headed out, Bailey is walking in alone. I hate how horrible I was to her that night at the party. I acted like I didn't even know her just so my friends wouldn't give me crap about it. I'll regret how I treated her for the rest of my life. She doesn't give me the time of day when I smile at her. She barges past me as if I don't exist. It's the payback that I deserve.

"Bailey, wait," I say.

She turns around slowly, looking at me with sad eyes. She's always been so desperate to fit in. But I want to tell her not to fit in. She doesn't want that. Not at all. Because if "fitting in" means having to change who you are, then "fitting in" can suck it.

I step toward her. "I'm so sorry. About the party. I didn't treat you right in front of the people I thought were my friends. It wasn't fair. If I could go back and change it, I would."

She nods and looks around. "Well, nobody is around to hear you say that, so you're off the hook. I don't need your apology Della, just leave me alone. What are you doing in a second- hand clothing store anyway? Daddy cut you off for five minutes?"

I bite the inside of my cheek and take a deep breath. "I deserve that." Tucking a strand of hair back, I clear my throat to say what Bailey needs to know. "Don't change who you are, Bailey."

"What?" she asks with a glare on her face that looks like I'm the last person she wants advice from.

"Don't change who you are for them. You're going to be popular. How could you not be? You're a beautiful and intelligent girl. And clearly you have style." I point around to the clothing and I'm relieved when she smiles. But it fades and she sighs.

"I can't even afford this stuff. Sometimes I come in to see if anything is marked down. They do that here sometimes."

"Bailey, do you actually like these clothes?"

The look on her face suddenly brightens up. "Oh, I love clothes. It's my dream to work in fashion one day."

I smile. "Really?"

"Absolutely." She looks down at her leggings and oversized button-up blouse. "But it seems silly."

I clear my throat. "I have something for you. Don't move."

"Um… okay," she says.

I quickly walk back outside to the Volkswagen and pull out the full bag of clothing that probably costs more than the car I just bought. I'm pleased to see Bailey is standing there waiting for me.

I hand her the bag. "Take these clothes. I was just going to give them up anyway. Whatever you don't want, go ahead and sell. The saleswoman was looking forward to selling them, but you want them more. I can tell." I smile at her in hopes that one day she'll forgive me.

She looks at me with disbelief as she takes the heavy bag from me. "Wait, are you serious?" When she looks around as if she's being punked, it makes me a little sad she thinks I would hurt her again.

"I'm serious. Maybe it will help you feel a little closer to your dream job." I wink and I'm surprised when she pulls me in for a hug.

"Della, thank you. This is unreal. I'm so excited to rip through this bag when I get home."

"Of course. But what I was trying to say before is when you get popular and start making way more friends than you can keep up with, don't forget your old friends. They matter. Those will be the ones that you remember." I wink. I'm happy to see her smile as she realizes what I'm talking about. "And when you find yourself changing how you act and treat people, just know it will wear you down and break you in the end. If you don't like any of the clothes in the bags I gave you, don't wear them to please anybody but yourself. If you like the boy in English class everyone else makes fun of, kiss him in front of them. Don't make the same mistakes I did. Just don't change yourself for them Bailey, okay?"

"Okay. I won't, I promise."

As I'm about to walk away she says, "You may have let them change you, Della. But in the end, you came back. That's all that matters. I forgive you."

I smile at my old friend and will treasure the memory of our time together.

Chapter Eighteen

Scout

It's only been a few weeks since I last saw Jameson and he decided to frisk me. He left me so turned on that I'm still trying to forget about it. I'm surrounded by dogs barking as I walk through the shelter just outside of Wood Lake.

"This one here about bit my hand off when we took her puppies away. She's an aggressive one. There's a cute Maltese over here that you will love."

"I'll take her," I tell the volunteer as I kneel next to the Australian Shepherd. Her fur is a beautiful mix of black, white, and brown. Her brown eyes look into mine and I can already tell that we're friends.

"I know how it feels to have something important taken from you," I tell her.

The dog stares back at me like she wants me to rescue her.

⚬⚬⚬

"I didn't know you liked dogs," Harper says after I introduce her to Sickem. She runs around like a maniac out back while Harper and I sit on the lawn.

"I wasn't really planning on getting one so soon. But she's perfect."

I tilt my head up toward the sky. It's a sunny, fall day and the weather feels perfect. But as soon as the sun goes down, I know I'll need a jacket.

I continue, "I'm glad I have a fenced yard for her to play in. She loves it here."

When I first brought her home, I gave her a bath. It wasn't fun trying to calm her down in the bathtub while she splashed and whined. I told her she was going to be okay and tried to convince her she needed to be washed. After getting her tame enough to clean her up, I was drenched in the bath water myself. She pouted for a while afterward, but I think she finally forgave me. Especially after seeing the yard.

"You named her Sickem? Like sic 'em? The term they use for dogs to attack someone?" she asks.

I laugh. "I thought it was cute. She doesn't understand the term and I can't wait to see the worried looks I get when I call her name."

Harper laughs. "You are crazy. She really is a beautiful dog."

"Thanks. I think so too."

"You should come over tomorrow to our new house. I still have quite a few boxes to unpack but I want you to see it. We'll make dinner," Harper suggests.

"I'd love to help. I can't wait," I say.

I may have to accept the fact that Jameson will be there. But Will is his brother and Harper is my best friend. We can handle being in the same room from time to time. I *think*.

"Tell me more about Ava. When did Jameson start seeing her?" I ask.

"You seriously want to know that?" Harper asks.

No but I have to know. "Does he love her?"

Harper shakes her head. "I don't think it's anything serious. He really doesn't talk about her much. But she is nice when he brings her around."

I sigh. "I know. And pretty. And funny."

Harper sighs. "You're jealous."

"Of course, I am. She gets to be with him, and I don't," I accidentally say.

Harper is confused with my words, her eyebrows pulled down. "What do you mean?"

"I just mean I don't deserve him. That's all."

"That's why you left? That's why you did all of that?"

The pit in my stomach painfully reminds me that it's still there. "No. I left because of *what* I did. He deserves someone who wouldn't hurt him. I always kind of knew that I would. I'm not good at love. At relationships."

Harper tucks her hair behind her ear. "You were madly in love with him for four years. What changed?"

I shake my head. "I don't know. I'm messed up." I bury my head into my knees and groan.

"Scout, you're not messed up. You're human." Harper rubs my back, trying to comfort me even though I broke her brother-in-law's heart.

I half laugh. "A very messed up human who isn't capable of having love." *I had it. I was happy.*

I sit back up, running my fingers through my hair next to my scalp. "Are you still in the honeymoon phase? Or are you starting to feel like an old married couple already?"

Harper smiles slowly and wickedly.

"I'll take that as the honeymoon phase," I say, and we both laugh.

She lays her head down on my shoulder. "I'm so happy you came back."

"Me too."

"You can bring Sickem over for dinner. Please come, Scout," she begs.

"I'll be there."

Chapter Nineteen

Scout

My students are my miniature best friends. I love seeing them learn and grow. It makes me especially happy to see their faces light up when they solve a problem, or how excited they get over the simplest things like recess. After that panic attack I had the night of the wedding, I hope I never have that happen here in the classroom. The kids are having quiet reading time for twenty minutes, something I have them do every day. To make it more exciting I let them choose anywhere in the classroom to read besides just sitting at their desks. Reading is so important for their little brains. I can hear girls whispering a little too loudly on the bean bag chairs in the corner. Skiley is quietly trying to read, but the girls are trying to get her attention. Skiley is a sweet girl in my class who doesn't talk much. She doesn't have many friends, so I like to keep a close eye on her to make sure no one is bullying her.

"You're always just reading. Don't you ever talk? We know you have a crush on McKray," I hear one of them say.

I quickly walk over to the girls on the bean bags and plop down next to Skiley, who looks like she's reading about sea creatures.

"Did you know crabs taste buds are on their feet?" I ask, sitting in-between them.

I know I can't force all my kids to be friends, but I don't allow bullying.

They all giggle at my fact about crabs. Except for Skiley. Skiley is wearing a yellow dress, and her bangs are growing out, getting in her eyes.

"Skiley, I love your yellow dress. Yellow is my favorite color; I even have a hair barrette that would be so pretty with it. Would you like to wear it?" I ask her.

She looks up from her book. "Sure," she says, still frowning.

I go back to my desk and reach in my purse to find the hair barrettes I bought from the dollar store. When I saw them, I thought of Skiley and a solution to her hair being in her face.

"Here," I say, pulling her hair to the side and clipping the yellow barrette with sparkles and pink flowers. "Now you'll be able to see better with those beautiful big brown eyes."

She smiles. "Thanks Miss Addison," she says.

"That's so pretty," Sarah says to Skiley.

"Can I have one Miss Addison?" Sarah asks.

"Of course," I hand them out to Sarah and two other girls she's sitting with. The bell rings and it's time for recess. The girls include Skiley today on the swings.

I move through the small grocery store in town and decide on a green salad kit that's easy to throw together, some diet Pepsi to stash in my fridge, and more dog treats for Sickem.

When I get home from the store I shower and get dressed before freshening up my make-up and start curling my hair in loose waves. Harper already texted me and asked if I was still coming. I think she's excited to be living in the same town again. I am too. When I met her in college, I knew she was going to be my best friend. She has been ever since and always will be.

Like always I start thinking about Jameson. I wonder if he loves Ava like he loved me. Does she know how lucky she is?

When I'm done with my hair, I try to get that pit out of my stomach and go get Sickem in the car to head to Harper's.

Chapter Twenty

Jameson

I 'm a little more than unnerved to see her car here. I never would have agreed to help Will move his furniture today if I knew Scout was going to be here too. I think about leaving Will to carry all of this into the house himself but instead, without saying a word, I grab the other end of the couch.

"Hi to you too brother," Will says, walking backward with the other end of the couch into their new house. I hear Scout and Harper in the kitchen as we walk in.

After Will and I set the couch down in the living room, Will says, "Thanks for your help."

The four of us always used to get together like this. We're acting as if nothing has changed. As if the woman standing in the kitchen making a salad didn't fucking rip my heart in two. *Everything* has changed. I don't want to look at her. It's painful to see how good she looks in her mini skirt and yellow sweater. She knows how much I love her little skirts. *Why does she do this to me?*

Scout is talking to Harper about some of her students. She's always been passionate about her job and I'm glad that hasn't changed. And as much as I want to, I can't look away. She looks nervous and clears her throat when she sees me. I finally turn around because I hate that she caught me giving her the time of day. She doesn't deserve my attention anymore.

"Take a break and let's eat before you guys get the rest," Harper says.

"I'll go start the grill," Will says.

"Hi James," Harper says.

I look at her and nod before I step out back to where my brother stands at the grill. He must feel my anger radiating off me because he says, "This was Harper's idea. I told her it wouldn't be smart to invite both of you. She just misses it when we all used to hang out."

"You could have at least warned me," I say, grabbing a beer from the cooler.

"I didn't want to make a big deal out of it," he says.

I groan as I watch the gorgeous woman I despise through the window. Couldn't the outside of her become as ugly as the inside of her did? Or has she always been ugly on the inside, and I was just too blinded by her beauty to see it? She turns toward the window just as her finger goes to her mouth. Her eyes are on me as she sucks off whatever sauce was left on her finger. Her perfectly pink, plump lips sliding off her wet finger as she looks me dead in the eyes. Rage courses through me at the same time as all the blood flows to my cock. I close my eyes because I can't watch anymore. She wasn't trying to turn me on, she licked her finger just as she was looking outside and happened to catch my stupid, sorry ass staring again. *Quit fucking looking. She's not yours to look at anymore. She's ugly. Picture her ugly insides so that you can quit letting her pretty outside get the best of you.*

"How's the job going?" Will thankfully interrupts my thoughts.

"It's stressful. But you know I wouldn't like it if it were easy," I tell him. Just like Scout. She's never been easy. Why am I like this? I've always liked a challenge, I guess.

"How's work for you?" I ask.

"It's alright. The staff I work with is great. But I'd be lying if I said I wasn't ready to move on. Just a couple more years of following doctors around. Then I'll get to be one."

It's still surreal to me that my little brother has been so successful at his young age. He started medical school before he turned twenty-three and will be a doctor by the time he's twenty-seven. Not to mention he served in Afghanistan for a year before that.

"I know I always say it, but I'm proud of you," I tell him.

I'm only older by eighteen months but growing up I felt like his parent sometimes. Even though I was pretty shitty at protecting him from our own father.

"I know man. Thanks." He clears his throat before taking a sip of his beer. "You could invite Ava here you know," he says.

"I'll bring her next time." I take a big mouthful of beer and point toward the house with the bottle. "This is a nice place."

"Thanks, I love being back here," Will says.

"Will Harper still have to drive into the city for work?"

Will nods. "Sometimes. But most of her clients aren't too far." Like Scout, Harper also works with children, but as a social worker.

A dog comes sprinting out the door and leaps into the grass. Where the hell did that thing come from?

"You got a dog?" I ask Will as he takes the cooked meat off the grill.

"She's mine," Scout says, standing next to me. *Don't look at her.* "Her name is Sickem."

"Sickem?" *Only Scout...*

The Australian Shepherd runs up to me and I reach down to offer my hand to the dog with the weird but cool ass name. She licks my hand. And dammit, I realize I just said a word to Scout. I didn't mean to. I always wanted her to get a dog to run with. To protect her. She runs with her little pink pepper spray, but a dog is even better.

"I rescued her from the shelter."

Scout kneels next to her dog and Sickem licks her face, causing Scout to laugh.

She laughs.

I haven't heard it since we broke up. I hate to admit that the throaty sound of it is music to my ears. Making her laugh used to be one of my favorite things to do. Now it just hurts that it's not mine to listen to anymore.

I groan. "What are you doing Scout?"

"What do you mean? I'm just being friendly. I don't want things to be awkward between us." She stands up and leans in closer.

I step back. "Well, I'm not interested in being your friend."

Then from the back door, Harper yells, "Jameson! Will you help me in the kitchen? Please."

Shit, she probably heard me. I don't care though. I'm not going to pretend to be friends when we mean nothing to each other anymore. She means nothing.

I follow Harper to the kitchen, leaving Scout outside.

"You don't have to be so mean," Harper says, leaning up against the counter with her arms folded.

"I'm not being mean, I'm being honest. Someone's gotta be."

Harper presses her lips together. "You're hurt. I get it, believe me. But you have no idea what Scout's been through. None of us do. I'm really worried about her James. She's been acting... different."

Different? Different how? I want to know everything, but I know it's not a good idea to get involved.

Feeling frustrated, I run a hand through my hair. "Fine. I won't be mean. But I'm not going to pretend to be her friend either."

"Okay, thank you. Let's eat."

<hr>

Harper and Will do a lot of the talking at dinner. Scout and I are quiet. It's awkward as hell.

As I'm trying to keep down my hamburger, Harper says, "Scout, you should come to the farmers' market with me this week. I heard there's amazing produce there this year."

Scout lights up. "Oh, I love a farmers' market! There were so many in Hawaii. The fresh mango was my favorite. It tasted the best on the beach after a hike."

"Did you happen to go to Pearl Harbor while you were there?" Will asks.

"I did. It was interesting."

The loud screech of my chair scooting away from the table stops the conversation as everyone looks at me when I stand up.

"Glad you had a fan-fucking-tastic vacation," I tell Scout before dumping the contents of my plate into the trash and head toward the door.

I can't be here anymore and listen to what a great time Scout had while I was here trying like hell to survive. "Thanks for dinner."

"You're leaving?" Harper asks.

I'm sure everyone is relieved even though she acts as if she wants me to stay. The tension had to be making everyone uncomfortable anyway.

Will clears his throat. I don't care if he needs my help with his damn furniture. I'll come help tomorrow when Scout's not here.

My feet can't move toward the front door fast enough. "Yeah. I have some stuff to do. I'll see you guys later."

I step outside the door and as soon as it's shut, it flies open again. Scout steps outside with me. Her expression is soft and full of sympathy. I turn my head because I don't want anything to do with her pity.

"You don't have to be the one to leave. I'll go," she says.

"You stay," I say.

Her voice cracks. "You're their family, James. You're Will's brother. I should be the one to go."

Does she not realize she's just as much family to them as I am?

I glance over my shoulder. "I'm meeting Ava anyway," I say, hoping my words sting but also wanting to take the words back as soon as I see the look on her face.

"Oh." Her green eyes glaze over like this is the first she's heard Ava's name. She knew I was seeing someone. *If you can call it that.* I meant to hurt her but I kind of hate myself now for doing it.

Scout looks down at her new companion. The dog follows her every move and Sickem brushes up against her. It's as if she can sense that Scout is upset and she's trying to comfort her.

Scout has changed so much over the last few years. I remember the first night I met her. She had short black hair and wore way more makeup back then. But her energy was just as wild and fun. I loved it. Now she's let her natural, silky brown hair grow out, usually wearing it in loose curls and wears little makeup. She's matured a lot and she's gotten even more attractive to me over time. Of course, she changed over the years when we were still together. Everyone does. But right now, I can't help but notice how different she seems. Do I even know her? Did I ever even know her at all?

Frustration builds inside my chest. God, I can't look at her anymore. When I turn to walk away, she says, "James. Hawaii wasn't always a vacation. I was grieving the loss of us too."

I should apologize for what I said inside about her being on vacation, but I can't find it in me to do it. She doesn't deserve anything from me. I should want her to hurt the same way she hurt me. But for some fucking reason I hope she doesn't feel this way too, feel the pain I do since losing her.

I climb into my truck and drive off, leaving her behind without another word.

⁓⁓⁓ ⁓⁓⁓

"Do you think we'll ever be exclusive?" Ava takes me by surprise while watching a movie at my place. I usually meet her in the city, but she insisted on driving over here tonight. I thought we were on the same page. I'm not anywhere close to getting serious right now. I don't know that I ever even want to get as close to anyone as I did Scout. I thought I knew what love was. I thought it was equal. Now I just believe two people fall in love and one falls harder than the other and that person ends up broken in the end. It's depressing, but that's the way I see it now. I don't want to hurt Ava. She's been there for me, and I care about her.

"I didn't think you wanted anything exclusive," I answer.

I'm a little afraid she might hit me with the look she just gave me.

"Ava, you said so yourself that you're not ready for anything serious anytime soon. And you know I'm not either. We both made that clear the first night we met."

"We've been seeing each other for months. I kind of just thought you would want more now."

I'm such an asshole. I should have known this was coming.

"And you do? Want more?" I ask her.

She shrugs. I take that as a yes and say, "Listen Ava. I'm going to be honest because I don't want to hurt you. I'm really fucked up right now. I'm not even halfway over what Scout did. And I know you're going through something similar, so you get it. I don't want to lose what we have but I'll have to let you go if you ever want anything more from me."

She sighs. "As soon as you laid your eyes on Scout again, you've been using me like a comfort toy. I thought I was more to you than that."

"You've never been a toy to me, Ava. I respect you. You've become one of my closest friends. I love spending time with you." *Fuck, am I using her?*

"Listen to yourself."

Shame runs through me. "I'm so sorry. I never meant to use you like that."

Suddenly, Ava throws her leg over me on the couch and sits on my lap. I'm a little taken back since I thought she was mad at me. "Use me one more time."

I feel so shitty for doing this to her. She deserves better. "You don't deserve to be used. You deserve to be loved."

Her expression is sad and confused. "And you'll never be able to love again?" she asks.

I've never felt like such an ass. "No." I hate that I can't give this woman what she deserves. She's incredible and any man would be lucky to have her.

She sighs. "I knew what this was from the start. I didn't expect to start having actual feelings for you." She continues to straddle me as she takes off her shirt. What is she doing?

"No, this isn't your fault. We can't do this again."

"Stop. I want to do this. Then you'll never hear from me again. I know you can't love me but the least you can do is use me one last time."

Use me one last time. Her words hit me and the guilt I feel intensifies as she takes off my shirt and I let her. Her mouth crashes down on mine and I kiss her back. All I've given her in the past was sex because that's all I was capable of giving. I can't do this to her again. I pull away and grab her wrist to stop her from unbuttoning my jeans.

"I'm sorry. I can't do this."

She looks up at me with so much sadness. It hurts knowing I'm the one that caused it. I brush my finger across her cheek. "Someday someone is going to give you what you deserve. They'll love you more than you've ever thought could be possible. I'm sorry that can't be me." *And I hope the guy comes back and kicks my ass for doing this to her.*

She painfully stands up and puts her shirt back on. "Someday I hope you'll have that again too."

I won't.

"Bye Jameson."

Chapter Twenty-One

Scout

Halloween has always been my favorite holiday. Being able to dress up as anything I want has always made me feel happy, and walking around in the dark at night, knocking on strangers' doors for candy as a kid was always really fun. Today, my class is really excited for the Halloween party at the school tonight before they go trick or treating. I'm dressed as Velma from Scooby Doo. The kids love my costume. We've played musical chairs, have eaten donuts, drank apple cider, and now I'm reading a ghost story.

Ben, the school's counselor, stands in the doorway of the classroom and studies me while I read. He's been working at the school longer than I have and has become a friendly co-worker since I started working here.

"Everyone say hi to Mr. Dallis," I say to the kids when I finish the story.

He smiles a toothy grin and waves. I tell the kids to quietly read by themselves for twenty minutes while I grade some papers.

Ben walks over to my desk. "Velma?" he asks.

"Yeah, the students love Scooby Doo."

"Aren't you more of a Daphne though?"

Is he hitting on me?

I must look as surprised as I feel because he says, "Sorry that was lame."

I glance up at his tall striped hat and realize who he's dressed as. "What can I do for you Dr. Seuss?"

"Are you still available to help at the school Halloween party tonight?"

"Of course. Whatever you need me to do."

"I know it's last minute, but Mrs. Gardener called in sick with the flu. She's not able to help with the cake walk anymore and her cakes are the community's favorite. Her red velvet is my personal favorite." He clears his throat nervously. "I'm rambling, sorry. My question is, do you know how to bake? Because they've asked me to either bake a couple cakes myself or find someone else and I'm afraid the only thing I know how to bake is the packaged cookie dough you buy at the store."

I chuckle. "Lucky for you, I happen to love baking. I can't promise it will be as magnificent as Mrs. Gardener's cakes." I remember how perfectly designed and delicious they were from the Halloween party last year. "Especially since I'll have to rush." Good thing it's early dismissal today with Halloween landing on a Friday. And the carnival doesn't start until six o'clock, so that gives me time to bake at least three cakes.

"You are a lifesaver. Literally. My cakes could have killed someone from salmonella or something."

I laugh. Ben has a sense of humor. "Happy to do it."

"Great. I guess I'll see you there," he says and walks out.

I'm surprised I was able to make it to the grocery store after school and bake three cakes all in time for the Halloween party. It would have been four cakes if the sugar butter cake with pumpkin frosting worked out, but that one was a fat fail. That's what I get for experimenting with a new recipe on the day of an event. I decided on a simple s'mores cake, another with key lime and cream cheese frosting, and a double chocolate with caramel drizzle. They don't look as pretty as Mrs. Gardener's, but I think they'll taste good. And to make it extra fun for the kids, I topped off each cake with a Halloween decoration.

After lots of excitement and laughter through each cake walk, the table is empty, so I begin cleaning up.

The kids are all hyped up on sugar and running around the gym with their prizes and games. It's been a successful night and I'm beat. Everyone seemed to love my cakes and I feel pleased. I can't wait to get this costume off and watch a scary movie in my pj's. Just as I'm cleaning up the last of the trash, Ben walks up to me with a slice of the key lime cake I had made.

"How did you manage to get a slice of that?" I ask him, remembering the redheaded fifth grader who won it. She had a hard time choosing which one.

"What can I say? I'm the students' favorite," he brags in the humblest way.

I arch my brow at him. "You're only the favorite because you don't hand out homework."

He laughs. "Touché. This cake is delicious."

"You like it?"

He takes another bite. "I was a little disappointed it wasn't red velvet. But I have to admit, this one is way better."

I smile, feeling even more pleased with myself. "I'm glad you like it, Ben."

His lips curl up into a smile. "Rumor has it that you're single, Scout."

He's flirting again.

"The rumor is true."

I've been hit on before, but it feels different being that Ben is a co-worker. Is this against the rules? I feel like it could be.

"I was wondering if maybe you'd like to go out with me sometime?" he asks.

Ben Dallis isn't bad to look at with his wavy dark hair, perfect jawline, and tall slender build. Honestly, if counseling doesn't work out, he should consider modeling. And he's really nice. I didn't even realize he was single. I'm surprised he is. But I'd be lying to myself if I said I was ready to start seeing anyone again anytime soon.

"Um…" I begin speaking when I'm startled by a girl screaming, "Stop!"

And then it hits so fast. Just in the blink of an eye, I'm having a flashback.

I can't breathe.

I drop the garbage bag I had been holding and trash spills all over the floor. *Breathe.* I'm trying so hard to steady my breath but it's so loud and crazy in here.

I turn and run out the front door before anyone else notices me. The cool air hits my lungs, and it helps a little.

A hand grabs my shoulder and I lose it. "Don't touch me!" I scream.

Ben immediately removes his hand from me, and I feel like a horrible person for yelling at him.

"Scout, are you alright?" Ben asks.

My heart is still racing, but I've got my breathing under control. "Why was that girl screaming?" I ask, remembering what triggered me.

"That girl who screamed 'stop?' Her dad was chasing her, pretending to take her candy. They were playing. Everything is okay."

I turn away from him so he can't see the tears rolling down my cheeks. "S-sorry. I've got to go. I'll see you Monday." I begin walking toward the parking lot to get to my car. I'm relieved when I realize I already have my car keys in my back pocket and that I can go home without having to go back inside.

"Wait, are you sure that you're okay?" Ben asks.

"I'm fine. Just exhausted, I guess. Have a good night." I wave to him as I continue walking away.

"Goodnight," he says.

He probably thinks I have some serious mental issues. I hope he doesn't mention this to Principal Charles. I can't be getting fired for being an unfit, psycho teacher. I'm so embarrassed. What is wrong with me? I'm really hoping that no one else saw my outburst in there.

Chapter Twenty-Two

Jameson

It's late and I'm on my way back home when I notice Scout running with her dog alongside her on the road. Even though this town is safe, she should know better than to be running this late at night, especially on Halloween. I quickly stop the car and jump out. She immediately notices me but continues running past me.

"Scout, what the hell are you doing?" I ask.

I chase after her. "Scout!"

She stops to face me. Her eyes are red and swollen like she's been crying. *Why is she crying?*

"Running," she says, seemingly annoyed that I stopped her.

"What are you thinking running this late at night?"

"I'm thinking running is literally the only time I have any fucking control over my life anymore," she says.

She's clearly upset. "What does that mean?"

"Forget it," she says through painful eyes. "I'm only a couple miles away from home." She begins running again.

I jump back in my truck and slowly follow behind her. She starts running even faster. She turns and gives me a few good glares, shaking her head after, but I don't give a shit. When she stops in front of a small house, I pull the truck into park and get out. Her place is nice and in a safe neighborhood.

She's panting hard as she hunches herself over, trying to catch her breath. When she notices me walking her way, she stands up straight with a questioning look. "You didn't have to follow me," she sasses.

"Are you going to tell me what's going on with you? Since when do you run in the dark?" I ask.

"There's nothing to tell, I just had a bad day."

"Dammit Scout, when are you going to stop with the lies?"

"Why do you care? You're not supposed to care about people you hate Jameson."

This fucking girl. "I don't. Harper is worried about you." That's not a lie. I remember what Harper told me about the other night at her and Will's new place, that Scout's been acting differently.

Her watery green eyes stare into mine and she looks like she is about to tell me something. But she doesn't.

"You can talk to me," I say, almost regretting how I'm inviting her in. But dammit, I have to know what the hell is going on with her. She's hiding something.

"I- I can't," she says with a shaky voice. It's almost as if she's scared. She's pushing me away. She's good at it. Always has been. Even though I wanted more than anything for her to let me in, I never pushed her.

"Dammit, Scout. Do you have any idea how much I loved you?" I choke.

Tears flood her eyes again, spilling over. I hate that I'm making her cry, but she needs to hear this.

"I loved you so much. And you never let me in. You've been through so much, Scout. Everyone can see that. You're bad at hiding it. But you're really fucking good at lying about being okay with it. You've always seemed to be so okay. I'm starting to wonder if that's not true at all. I dated you for four years. You were everything to me. I shared every part of me with you. Yet, I feel like I don't even know *you*," I admit.

She's crying hard now. Her chest is shaking with each uncontrollable breath. "I'm sorry," she says.

"I just need you to tell me why. Why did you ruin everything we had?"

She doesn't know what to say. She won't even look at me.

"Why?" I yell louder than I meant to. Sickem's ears stand up. Good dog. She's protective of Scout.

"James please."

I repeat, "Why?!" She left me like I never meant anything to her. Like she never meant anything to me. Like she wasn't my fucking world.

She stares back at me now and shakes her head. "I can't-do this."

I scoff. "Of course, you can't."

Her shaky hands wipe at her wet cheeks. I hate that I want to pull her into me and never let her go again.

"Can you at least tell me why you can't tell me?" I ask, feeling desperate. Desperate for any explanation at all. An explanation I know I'll never get.

I look at her lips that are soaked with salty tears and I want to kiss her pain away. But I know I can't do that.

"I loved you too," she says. I shouldn't believe her when she's so full of lies and secrets.

"I don't believe you." It doesn't make sense. You don't lie to someone you love. But I know Scout loved me. I felt it more than I'll ever let her know. That's what makes it all so confusing. I'll never understand, and she'll never let me.

She wipes her tears with the sleeve of her hoodie. I hate how badly I want to comfort her.

"You're right," she whispers, "not to believe anything I say. I don't tell you the truth. I *won't* tell you the truth. I care too much about you."

This girl is the most confusing person on the whole god-damn planet. She makes me feel like a crazy person. I step closer to her, and she sucks in a breath. Like she's afraid of me.

"What are you doing?" she asks.

I get as close to her lips with mine as possible without kissing her. She loved me. I believe that even though I said I don't. And by the looks she's been giving me, she misses me. She misses me just as much as I miss her. And I need it. I need her to miss me. I want her to miss me. Fuck, I want *her*.

"You drive me crazy," I whisper. She looks down at my mouth and gulps.

"I know," she whimpers. Her breath hits my mouth, and I can't move.

It would be so easy. She'll let me kiss her. She'd probably let me stay. It's all over her face how bad she wants me too. I'll kiss those tears off her pretty face until it's dry again, I'll put her heart back together piece by piece, and hold her until I'm enough for her.

She steps back and glances around frantically, like she's looking for someone. "You should go," she whispers.

She's doing what she does best, so I don't hesitate in doing what she asks of me. Without saying another word, I walk away. I glance back at her one last time as I'm getting into my truck, noticing her looking around again. *What the hell is she looking for?*

When I see that she gets into her house safely, I drive away.

Chapter Twenty-Three

Scout

I lean up against my door and cry. I'm crying about these new panic attacks I can't seem to get rid of, I'm crying for Jameson, I'm crying for my younger self and the person I am today, for everything that's happened. My favorite holiday really sucked this year. I slide down onto my butt as I stay pressed up against the door. Sickem tries to lick my face, forcing me to laugh through my tears. Rubbing behind her ears I say, "We'll be okay girl. Today was rough but tomorrow will be better."

I get up off the floor and spot the mess in my kitchen left behind after baking so many cakes. I didn't have time to clean up after myself. I don't want to wake up to this in the morning, so I better do it now. Instead of watching a scary movie like I planned on doing, I listen to a true crime podcast through my headphones as I scrub batter off dishes and wipe up the flour on the counter tops. I spot the cake I messed up on – it all came tumbling down in huge chunks when I was frosting it. Taking a fork from the silverware drawer, I have a taste of the messy butter cake with pumpkin frosting.

"Mmmm, oh my gosh. That's so good."

Sickem comes into the kitchen, her ears perked up, ready to devour the cake with me.

"This is not for you. It will make you sick." I reach up toward the top of the fridge and pull down her dog treats, her tail wagging with anticipation when I open the box. She catches the treat and I get back to cleaning.

After finishing up the kitchen, I take the whole pan of messy cake and a fork to the living room and plop down on the couch. The true crime podcast made me feel a little too unnerved and I realized I can't listen to this as often now that I live alone. A scary movie would only make that feeling worse. So instead, I flip through the channels and settle on an episode of *Friends*. Sickem lays by my feet, and I rub her back with my toes.

And I try to keep the image out of my mind of the way Jameson was looking at me tonight.

Chapter Twenty-Four

Scout

Most of my first paycheck goes toward rent and bills at the beginning of the month. But I like to splurge a little with my second paycheck. I shoot Rafe a text hoping he'll be up to shopping at the boutiques here in town. He immediately texts back that he'll pick me up in an hour. After letting Sickem outside, I get myself ready.

Feeling giddy that I finally get to get out of the house today and spend time with an adult, I practically skip toward the door. But this happy feeling doesn't last long because as soon as I open the door, Ethan is standing there. I try to slam it shut but he jams it back open with his foot.

"Hey sis, where ya headed?"

"That's none of your business. Get out of my way." I try to squeeze around him so that we can talk outside. I feel trapped being here with him and I don't like it. He practically knocks me down as he steps into the house, shutting the door behind him.

My heart drops. "Can't we talk outside?"

"No," he says. "Where are you going?"

"To the mall. With a friend."

"That friend have a badge?" It's his way of asking if I'm going to the mall with James.

"No. Will you just tell me what you came here to say so I can go? You already made James believe I cheated on him with you and he hates me. You got what you wanted so what now?"

The memory of breaking up with James flashes back to me.

I'm all smiles in the shower after the good morning I had with Jameson before he left for work. I hear something outside the bathroom and shut off the water. "James?" I call out.

He doesn't answer me, but I know I heard something. I wrap a towel around myself and walk out to the living room. I'm horrified when I see who's sitting on my couch. I dart toward the kitchen to grab a knife and aim it at him.

"What are you doing here Ethan?"

He laughs. "Your little steak knife has nothing on my twenty-two pistol. But I'm just here to talk."

"Talk about what? How did you even find me?"

"You think you can run away that easily? We've known for years that you've lived in Ohio. That you never went to California. That you ran on the track team at some college in Columbus. It was pretty easy to figure out. But dad decided to let it go since you were happy. JC too. Until he discovered you were dating a cop. We also heard about your boyfriend's little promotion. You know we can't let you date a U.S Marshal, Della."

"Scout. My name is Scout," I snap.

"Whatever. Somehow you haven't spilled your guts with him yet or he would have come after us already. But that's just a

matter of time since you're a rat. When JC found out you were dating a city cop a while back, we figured it was no big deal. We'd let it slide since we knew it wouldn't last anyway. It never does with you. But you're obviously getting serious about him, and we can't risk this. If you don't break up with the Marshal, we'll kill him. That simple. It's up to you. We have hit men lined up for these kinds of situations. But truthfully, I wouldn't mind killing a cop myself. I hate co-"

"No! I won't. I won't say a word to him. James doesn't even know where I come from. Please. Tell JC I won't say anything to him."

"JC knew you'd say that. He told me to tell you a U.S Marshal is bound to investigate your life. He'll figure it out even if you don't rat us out. You're lucky he's just letting you break up with the guy."

"Ethan please. I'll talk to JC myself. I can make it work."

"No, Della. You can't. You know JC. And I think his feelings are still hurt from you rejecting him, but he'd never say that. I promise this is the only way if you want the cop to live."

My whole world just turned upside down. They found me. Years ago. And now I have to lose the only real thing I've ever had. Jameson is my family. But I should have known this was how things would end. I hear a car pull up and my heart races. Please don't let it be Jameson.

I dart my eyes toward the window and my stomach drops when I see that's exactly who it is.

"Perfect timing. The boyfriend is home." Ethan rips his shirt off over his head and steps into me.

"Go along with this or I'll shoot your boy toy between the eyes. Got it?"

I nod as tears stream down my cheeks.

I'll never forget watching the color drain from Jameson's face when I told him it was true, that I had "cheated" on him.

Ethan interrupts my thoughts. "Just making sure you're staying away from the Marshal. Don't forget it's not smart for you either, considering you were involved with some of our shit. He smiles dangerously, causing my stomach to hurt. I wish JC wouldn't have sent him here to do this. He does whatever his leader says. I'll never forget how badly it hurt that Ethan just sat and watched JC assault me. I don't think he would have cared if JC killed me. Sickem starts scratching on the back patio door. I walk toward her when Ethan says, "Don't even think about letting that dog in."

I'm going to sleep a little better at night, knowing that Ethan is afraid of her.

"JC finds it odd," Ethan says.

"Finds what odd?"

"That you are renting your own place. A tiny little shit hole of a house, when you could be living at home in a house that's practically a mansion."

"I haven't lived there in five years and I'm not planning on going back."

"JC just wasn't expecting you to continue living here in the same town as the cop. By yourself. He thought you'd be back by now or at least found yourself a new man to take care of you."

This conversation is infuriating. They don't think I can handle being on my own. "I've never needed anyone to take care of me."

Ethan laughs. "Something tells me it won't last. You'll eventually find your way into someone else's bed. Or shit, maybe one day you'll cave and come home."

"I won't." My voice sounds pathetic. So weak. I hate it.

"You will sis."

I'm sick of Ethan's smile. The longer we talk, the smaller the room gets. I can hardly breathe as my brother acts as though he has control over me. I can't stand it any longer.

"I hate you." *Did I just say that out loud?*

"You what?" he snarls.

I'm sick of feeling afraid. I have to ramp up some kind of dominance, or I won't be able to sleep tonight thinking about how I let Ethan and his gang walk all over me. He is looking at me like he could kill me at any moment just at the pull of a trigger on his silenced gun. Would anyone look for me? Would they find me? I know who would. Our father.

"You heard me. I hate you." This time my voice sounds much stronger. Just as Ethan lunges toward me I say, "Careful Ethan, I'll tell dad the real reason I ran away. Wouldn't that be a bummer for you since you want his business so much."

His fist swings at me so fast, I'm not able to turn in time. He hits me on the cheek so hard that it knocks me down. Somehow, I catch my fall with the palm of my hand as I land on my side. I wish I wasn't crying. I wish I didn't feel so weak. So *afraid.*

Sickem is going crazy barking, whining, and scratching on the glass now as she watches everything that's happening.

Ethan kneels next to me as tears continue to roll down my face. I bury my face into my knees for protection and so that he can't see me cry.

"Tell me you haven't seen the cop and I'll know if you're lying," Ethan says.

"I only came back to Wood Lake to finish my contract with my job. I'll be leaving in less than a year. You don't need to worry about Jameson anyway. He hates me thanks to you."

He smiles. "Good." He touches my arm and I try to pull away, but this only makes him grab it tighter. "And don't even think about threatening me again. You have no idea just what I could do to you." He lets go of my arm and I fall back, my elbows hitting the ground to catch myself.

"Look at you. You're pathetic."

Suddenly, someone knocks on the door. It feels dangerous somehow even though I'm relieved at the same time. Ethan still looks like he wants to kill me.

Wondering who's there, I stand up. Instead of letting me answer the door, Ethan swings it open. "You must be the new one," Ethan spits out to Rafe as he storms past him.

Rafe watches as Ethan drives off with screeching tires. Then Rafe turns toward me and says, "Okay who's the sugar dad– Scout? Are you okay?" He rips off his sunglasses and touches the side of my cheek.

I hiss at the pain of his gentle touch. "My God, what happened?" he asks. "Did that guy hurt you? I'm calling the police." He pulls his phone out and begins dialing.

"Stop! Rafe no. It's not what it looks like. He's my brother."

He says, "Your brother hit you? What happened?"

I'm about to tell him I fell. Or come up with some other lame excuse to tell him. But honestly, I don't have it in me right now to lie. And Rafe isn't stupid. He just caught the villain dead in his tracks and Ethan didn't even seem to care. He knew I'd cover for him.

"You can't call the police," I tell him.

"Did he hurt you?"

I pause but finally nod. I feel safe again as Rafe wraps me in his arms.

"Oh, Scout. I'm here," Rafe whispers. I squeeze my friend even tighter as he holds me.

"My brother has a temper."

"He never should have laid a hand on you."

I stand back. "I know. I'm glad you showed up."

"Why was he here?" Rafe asks.

"To make sure I'm not snitching on him."

He gives me a questionable look.

"That's all I can tell you. I don't want you getting involved in any of this."

"Do you want to stay at my house for a while? Or even move in? I hate that these S.O.Bs know where you live."

"No. I'll be fine. And I don't live alone." Sickem has calmed down now but she's still eyeing me through the glass.

"I hate to break it to you but I'm not sure your dog would hurt a fly."

"Well, she made my brother feel intimidated. I'll be fine, I promise. He's going back to Washington."

"He lives in Washington?"

I sigh because I feel like a big fat liar. But it feels good to open up to someone a little.

"I lied to you when I first met you, Rafe. I'm from a nice neighborhood just outside of Seattle Washington. I'm not from Tennessee."

"What? Why would you lie about that?"

I stare at him, hoping he'll realize this is not something he wants involved in. I think he understands.

"I don't know what's going on but I'm here for you. You can talk to me about anything. And I won't go to the police but only because you said it will make things worse. If anything like this happens again, promise me you'll go to them yourself. What about Jameson?"

"What about Jameson?"

"Does he know any of this? Can he help you?" Rafe asks.

"Absolutely not. He can never know about any of this. And he can't help me. Please don't ever speak a word of this to anyone Rafe. Especially James."

He sighs but nods in understanding. "Let's get some ice on your cheek."

Chapter Twenty-Five

Scout

The next week drags by very slowly. It's the week before Thanksgiving and the students are extra excited and rowdy at the thought of their early dismissal next Wednesday after our class turkey party.

As I'm getting the students lined up for lunch, Ben smiles and waves as he moves toward me down the hall. We've seen each other a handful of times since Halloween and he told me if I ever needed to talk to him, he'd listen. He went all shrink on me instead of asking me out again, which I don't mind. I'd rather not go out with someone only to have it not pan out and show up to work feeling embarrassed to see him every day. That would just be awkward. Having a full-on mental breakdown in front of him and having to see him is embarrassing enough. I'm a little relieved he hasn't asked about a date again.

In front of the students he says, "Ms. Addison," but he steps closer to me and whispers, "Scout. How are you?"

"I'm fine, thanks. How are you?"

"Good. Have any Thanksgiving plans for next week?"

Harper and Will invited me over to their place. I don't want Jameson to feel like he can't go if I'm there, so honestly, I don't think I'll attend. I have nowhere to go for Thanksgiving this year, but I do have plans with my couch and some sushi. "Um... yeah of course I do." I'm not about to tell the man who thinks I have mental issues that I don't have Thanksgiving plans with family. Then he'd really sit me down in his office and make me spill my guts.

"Good. Look, I know I haven't brought it back up since Halloween. But I'd still like to take you out sometime. Maybe over the break?"

I did not see this coming. The lunch line begins moving as a student tugs on my hand. "I'll think about it," I tell him.

He pulls out his phone then instantly puts it back in his pocket. He's clearly nervous and I have to admit it's kind of charming. "I don't want to be pushy or make things weird by asking you for your phone number. How about you take my number and if you decide you want to go out for dinner or something over the long weekend you can reach out?"

I never take my cell phone to lunch. "That sounds great. If you want to leave your number on my desk, the door is unlocked. I don't have my phone on me."

"I'll do that. Have a great lunch."

"You too."

Ben walks off just as my student Dawson yells, "Ooooh, Miss Addison has a boyfriend!"

Ben hears and turns around and laughs. I know I'm probably beet red from embarrassment but I quiet Dawson down and tell him Mr. Dallis is just a friend. As if the eight-year-old needs an explanation from me.

When I get back to my classroom after lunch, I see Ben's number written down on a yellow sticky note. Underneath it says, **I hope I get to see you next weekend.** Wow, here I thought Ben Dallis had given up on me. I appreciate the fact that he gave me plenty of time to think about it. I honestly can't imagine going on a date with him. Ben is sweet. But he's also a co-worker. Not to mention the fact that I'm still trying not to get involved with someone else. I groan. I don't have to make this decision right now. I fold up the sticky note and place it in my purse pocket.

Chapter Twenty-Six

Scout

"How was the turkey party?" Harper asks as we plop down on my couch. I blow on my hot chocolate before taking a sip.

"It was fun. I'm ready for a much-needed break though, that's for sure."

"Dinner is at four tomorrow. Don't feel like you need to bring anything, my mom is planning a huge dinner."

She still thinks I'm coming tomorrow. "About that..."

"What do you mean? You're not coming? Why?" Then it clicks. "Jameson won't care. Will already told him you'd be there. We invited so many people, it will be like you don't even know that he's there."

"It's not that."

I don't mind being in the same room as Jameson. Although it does make it hard to try and get over him. "He's the one that has a problem with *me* being there. Don't you remember the last time we tried to have dinner? I don't want him to think he's getting pushed out so that I can be put in. He won't stay if I'm there. I know he won't. I don't want to ruin his Thanksgiving. I've already decided."

"But Scout. You can't be alone on Thanksgiving. Can't you at least come for a little while?"

"I'll think about it. But honestly, I'm looking forward to staying in my PJ's all day. I even picked up some of that delicious sushi from the market."

Harper lets out a breath. "Fine. Feel free to show up anytime if you change your mind. If you don't, I'm bringing pie over later."

"With your mom's homemade whipped cream?" My mouth waters just at the thought of the heavenly stuff.

Harper smiles. "Of course." She pauses for a moment then says, "Will is going to be so mad at James."

"Why?"

"He was really looking forward to you being on his team this year for the Turkey Bowl."

"Oh no, I totally forgot about the football tournament."

A smile tugs at my lips just thinking about all the fun the four of us have had together. We've even made traditions together like going to the Turkey Bowl to play flag football on Thanksgiving every year here in Wood Lake.

"Please don't ever feel like you're not welcome in my home," Harper says, "I never want you to feel like that. You're family."

"I know that. Things will get better between James and me. We just need time."

⁕⁕⁕

I'm trying to keep today casual and pretend it's not Thanksgiving. It's just a regular Thursday except my bar with the curly fries is closed. After my run, I shower and look into the mirror at the bruise on my face. I've been able to hide it with makeup for work and nobody has noticed it, thank goodness. But I do have a story lined up just in case. Rafe has been by to check on me almost every night. He's worried about me, but I still make him promise that he won't go to the police. He hates it but he does what I ask. I'm so glad I have a friend like him. Everyone needs a Rafe in their life. I'm sure the bruise will be completely gone after the break, so I won't have to cake so much concealer, foundation, and powder over it. I throw on some sweats and a t-shirt and just as I'm comfortable on the couch with my sushi and a romcom, somebody knocks.

A dreaded feeling overcomes me. What if it's Ethan?

My footsteps are soft as I very slowly and quietly tiptoe to the door. I'm shaking as I look through the peephole. But my fear quickly goes away and turns to confusion.

I don't hesitate before opening the door. "James?"

He freezes when he sees me. He looks like he's just seen a ghost when he was the one knocking on *my door.* But then he looks so angry I have to take a step back. He's studying me. *What did I do now?* His jaw twitches as he bites down on his teeth. His hand reaches up to the side of my face, touching my cheek.

"Who the fuck did this to you?"

Then I realize he sees the bruise Ethan left on my face. I'm not wearing makeup to cover it up. I quickly think of my story as I throw my hand up to cover my cheek.

"Sickem is a crazy dog when she gets hyper. I was playing with her when she knocked me dow–"

"Enough," he interrupts. "Stop lying."

"James," I stammer. I don't know what to say.

"Did you forget how to tell the truth with that lying mouth? The shape of the bruise on your face, that's from a fist. And by the size of it, it's from a man's fist. Now tell me who did it and I'll go find him right now."

It's not safe for him to know the truth.

"What happened?" he asks.

"I told you. It was just an accident," I say.

"You're really not going to tell me?"

When I don't answer he shakes his head in frustration and says, "Get dressed, you're going to Harper's for dinner."

"But– I've already decided to stay in today."

He puts his arm up on the door frame and I glance up at the definition of muscles I can see through his long sleeve shirt that squeezes onto his arms like a second skin. His tongue presses against his top teeth. It's something I recognize he does when he's frustrated. He has a lot to say but he's trying to hold his tongue. His big hand rubs the back of his head, his eyes stare into mine. "Harper told me what you said last night. About making me uncomfortable and that I would leave if you showed up to Thanksgiving dinner. I'm here to tell you that I won't leave. I'll stay there. You'll stay there. They're family to both of us."

James hates me for what I did but he's here. Ready for answers about who hurt me and to make sure I'm not alone on Thanksgiving. "You don't have to do this," I say, looking into those eyes I've hurt so much.

He ignores me. "Get ready. I'll wait."

By the piercing stare in Jameson's eyes, I can tell he's concerned for my well-being. He doesn't want to leave me alone. I know I can't argue with him right now so instead of pushing him, I quickly get dressed in black leggings and a sweater. I attempt to curl my hair after drying it and make sure to put on plenty of makeup to cover up my cheek. When I walk out into the living room, James is leaning up against the door, waiting for me.

His expression is loaded with anger and worry. I try not to let the fact that he still obviously cares about me tug at my heart.

"We better get going," I say.

James steps outside behind me and the tension I feel radiating off him is intense. I punch in the code to my garage and the doors take forever to open as I feel Jameson's stare from behind me. "I'll see you there," I tell him as I climb into my car. When I turn the key and the car doesn't start, I try again. And then again, but this time pushing on the gas pedal at the same time. Nothing works.

James knocks on the driver's side window. "Just get in my truck," he says, looking impatient.

I've needed a new car ever since the old bug decided that starting was an option, not a necessity, but I'm having a hard time letting it go. It's what brought me here after all. And I'm starting to get sick of change.

"You really need a new car," James grumbles when we move toward his truck.

He opens the passenger door for me out of habit.

"Thanks," I say before climbing in.

The drive over to Will and Harper's is super quiet as James keeps his eyes on the road, his fingers tightly gripping the steering wheel. He's clearly mad at me and I don't blame him. All I do is hide things from him, and I can tell that he despises me for it, which is good. I need him to stay mad at me.

Everyone is too busy getting dinner ready to notice Jameson and I walk into the house together. Harper's parents are here, Rafe and the date he brought with him, and a few other people I don't know. A tall man walks up to the two of us when he notices us. He whispers something in Jameson's ear, and I suddenly want to bail out when I hear him whisper, "What are you thinking bringing *her* here?"

But instead of running, I hold out my hand. "Don't worry, I come in peace. I'm Scout. But by the sounds of it, you already know that."

"Yeah, I know who you are," he says with a smirk. The man looks so skeptical. Like I'm some kind of wild animal about to attack at any moment. *Who is this guy?*

Jameson clears his throat. "This is Bond."

I can't help but smile at the name. "You're Jameson's partner?"

"Well, technically no but we work together a lot. How did you know that?" Bond asks.

"James Bond. I like it." I walk away from the 007 duo and make my way to the kitchen without offering an answer to his question.

I hear Bond hissing something at Jameson, clearly yelling at him some more for bringing me. But he seems like a good friend, and I love that someone is looking after James.

"You came!" Harper says as she continues stirring something over the stove.

James didn't give me a choice. "I did. I feel bad I didn't bring anything. Hi Mr. and Mrs. Pearson."

Harper's parents both say hello and her mom gives me a hug. "Scout, how are you?" She whispers, "You look stunning."

I smile. "Thank you."

Rafe smiles at me. He's probably surprised I left the house today. He also tried to convince me to come via text messaging last night. I turn around to see James, Bond, Will, and Rafe's date visiting in the dining room. James looks at me and I look away.

"How are you doing?" Rafe steps up next to me.

"Good. Who's the cutie you brought?" His date has perfected faded light brown hair with glasses on his handsome face.

"That's Trey. We've been seeing each other for a couple weeks. Are you sure that you're okay?"

If Jameson had any idea Rafe saw what happened a week and a half ago at my house, he'd most likely hold him by his collar, interrogate him and have him spilling his guts before dinner is even served.

I put my finger up to my lips to shush Rafe and he follows my eyes as they direct him to Jameson.

"He knows?" Rafe whispers.

"He saw my bruise. He's been asking questions, so if he asks you anything today, you know nothing. Right?"

"Right. But your brother hasn't been back?"

I shake my head no just as I notice Jameson walking past. He doesn't even look at us though so I'm pretty sure he didn't hear anything. I open my eyes wide to give Rafe a look that tells him to stop talking about it. "I'm going to help Harper in the kitchen."

Harper has been cooking all day and somehow didn't even break a sweat. Her hair and makeup are on point. Will sneaks up behind her, grabbing her sides and she laughs before leaning into him.

My eyes find Jameson looking in the refrigerator. I wonder why he didn't bring Ava. Maybe she's spending time with her own family. Or maybe... they're not together anymore.

Chapter Twenty-Seven

Jameson

I make sure to keep my distance even though my eyes catch Scout's every move. I'm relieved nobody else besides Bond realized I was the one who brought her here. They'd ask too many questions and ask if we're getting back together again. Which we definitely aren't. I just wasn't going to let her be alone. I'm not that big of a dick. Scout didn't have anywhere else to go today. We're the only family she has.

I leave the guys in the living room to sneak into the kitchen when I see Rafe and Scout having a serious conversation, but I can't make out their words.

I head to the fridge to grab a beer and pretend I wasn't just trying to eavesdrop.

A chocolate cake sits inside which is strange, because who eats cake on Thanksgiving when there's pie? But it reminds me of the time Scout first made me a cake when she threw me the first birthday party I've ever had. No one had ever made it such a big deal before. Hell, no one ever even got me a cake for my birthday since my mom died. Until Scout. That was the day I realized I was in love with her.

"Hands down, best sex I've ever had," Scout says as my heart races beside her in her bed. I look over at her as she tucks her arm under her head to prop herself up on her side, giving me a better view of the beautiful curvature of her body. Her confidence turns me on. She doesn't immediately hide her naked body under the covers, instead she wants me to see all of her and honestly if she'd let me, we'd be going again already.

"Oh yeah?" I ask.

"Definitely. I really mean that. It's never felt like... that before," she says.

Yeah, as soon as she's ready, we are going again. How am I ever going to get enough? I groan and pull her into me closer because I can't not touch her right now. "Like what? What did "that" feel like?" I ask, wanting her to say it.

I know without a doubt that I love her. But I kind of want to hear her say it first. Then Scout does the simplest act of telling me in her own way and she taps me three times on the chest, over my heart. She's too afraid to say the words out loud and I get it. I get her.

"I love you," too. I tell her not expecting her to say it back. She's not ready to say it but she feels it. That's all I need.

"Dude, it's time to eat. Why are you just standing in the fridge?" Will asks.

"Shit sorry, just grabbing a beer," I say, and Will shuts the refrigerator door.

"You have a lot on your mind?"

I clear my throat. "I'm good."

Scout is usually the life of the party but today, she's different. She's quiet and sad. Maybe even nervous. She fake smiles and laughs when someone talks to her, pretending she's perfectly fine, but I see straight through her. She's barely even touched her food. Everyone else is having a good time and doesn't seem to notice. When she's finished with an exhausting looking conversation with Harper's mom at the table, I watch her stand up and walk through the living room and down the hall. I need to find out what happened to her. I casually get up to follow her and no one seems to notice. I'm waiting outside the bathroom when she opens the door. She jumps a mile high.

"Geez, James, you scared me," she says.

I don't say anything but I step toward her, causing her to shuffle back into the bathroom. When we're both inside, I shut and lock the door behind us. Scout's breathing is rapid as we stand in here alone. The sadness in her eyes is ripping me apart.

"Tell me what's going on. I see the pain written all over your face today. Quite literally." My eyes drop below her left eye to her cheek bone, the one covered in makeup hiding the mark someone left. If I look close enough, I can almost see the darkened area, reminding me of a shadow. But the fact that it's a fucking bruise has the wind knocked out of me all over again. Just the way it felt when I first saw it today. "Tell me who hurt you."

She's doing that thing when she's nervous, chewing the inside of her cheek, causing the sexy puff of her lips to pout to the side. Her head is tipped down, her eyes on the floor and it's frustrating she won't look at me. Without thinking, my fingers roll through the back of her hair as I gently grab it. She lets out a soft breath as she tilts her head up, her eyes locked on mine.

"Talk to me," I say.

The feel of her silky hair through my fingers again has my stomach dropping but it's nothing compared to the way she's looking at me. She still looks sad, but I can tell she wants my hands on her. It's taking everything I have not to pull her into me and hold her the way I normally would when she's upset.

A single tear streams down her cheek. I want to catch it and examine it hard enough to figure out who caused it. Admittedly, I'm the one who has been making her cry since she's been home, I'm sure. I haven't been nice to her at all. I wanted her to feel like shit for what she did and have those eyes flooded with tears. But knowing that someone else made her cry that wasn't me has me wanting to murder the bastard that did it. With my right hand still in her hair, my left one catches her chin when she goes to put her head down again. My thumb pulls down her lip as it puckers out and trembles. The urge I have to bite on that bottom lip is so strong.

"James, what are you doing?" she whispers, as the rhythm of her breath speeds up.

I watch her chest rise and fall rapidly as she leans her head back against the wall. She's so ruffled up but in an absolutely perfect way. I let go of her and turn around because if I don't, I'm worried I'll kiss her.

"I'm trying to help you, Scout." She may look perfect but she's the most frustrating woman on the planet.

"Well, you can't James, okay? I need you to leave me alone. I need you to hate me. I need you to stop worrying about me before something terrible happens!"

I'm confused by her words. "What does that even mean?"

"No-nothing. I just want you to stay out of my life, okay? Where is Ava? You should find her."

My chest burns. Moments ago, I wanted to kiss her. Now it's taking everything in me to even stay in this very room. I'm fuming.

"That's exactly what I'm going to do," I growl.

The glare in her eyes lights something in me. I want to see this side of her. This anger. I'd much rather her be angry than sad. "Do you want to know what I'm going to do with her?"

She shakes her head no, but I tell her anyway.

"I'm going to kiss her exactly the way I used to kiss you."

Scout shakes her head like she doesn't want to hear it, but I'm not done.

"I'm going to strip her naked, layer by layer, just like I used to do with you."

"James, stop."

"Then I'm going to touch her, exactly the way I touched you."

Her eyes are flooded with rage. She's exactly where I want her as my words come at her like venom, poisoning her slowly.

"Then I'm going to fuck her, exactly the way I used to fuck you."

But there's a hurt in her eyes I've never seen before. She can't even say anything as she pushes me out of her way to throw the door open, leaving me in the bathroom alone.

As soon as I walk out, everyone is chatting away like they had no idea we were in the bathroom together. My eyes scan the room when I find Scout now sitting on the couch as if nothing happened. It's scary how good she is at hiding her emotions.

A hand grabs my shoulder and I turn to see Will wearing a football jersey with his flat brim hat on backwards. "You ready to get your ass kicked?"

I'm not really in the mood for flag football but it's a tradition that we do every year at Grant's Park.

Harper comes up next to me all decked out in her red football jersey and black stripes painted under her eyes. "No, James and I are ready to kick your ass," she tells her husband.

I force a smile toward my sister-in-law. "Let's do it."

Usually, we do couples on the same team but this year since Scout and I aren't together anymore, they decided to do things differently.

Chapter Twenty-Eight

Scout

Maybe Jameson is angry enough that he'll leave me alone about my bruise. The way he was looking at me, I had to remind him of Ava. If he would've kissed me today, I would've let him.

"Scout, you're on team yellow!" Will yells in my direction as he throws me a jersey at the park.

Last year James and I were on the blue team together. When we lost, I was such a sore loser, James felt the need to make it up to me on the drive home by pulling the truck over to kiss me until I felt better. Then things escalated and we got naked under the stars in the back of the tailgate of the truck.

After slipping on my jersey and putting my flags on, Will tells me we're playing the blue team first. Will, Bond, a co-worker of Will's, and his girlfriend are on a team as we line up to play the blue team. Rafe and his date, Trey, are on the blue team with three other guys.

We rotate positions and when I'm the receiver, I score a touchdown.

Will cups his hands and shouts excitedly. Then he says, "Damn! You're fast!"

I smile at the compliment before getting back into position.

After we beat the blue and green team, we line up to play the other winning team for the championship round, the red team. Harper, Jameson, and the others huddle up to plan their play and we do the same.

After that we line up on the field and I'm playing center this time with Bond as the quarterback behind me. Feeling competitive, I squat down in front of James.

"And here I thought you had plans with Ava. Looks like you decided to play with me instead."

"Oh. I have plans with her later. After I beat your ass at football."

The sting of his infuriating words from the bathroom earlier come back to me, making me angry all over again.

As I squat down with the football, scowling at the man in front of me, I realize that James is not looking at me but instead he's glaring at someone behind me.

"Eyes on the ball, Bond," Jameson grunts at his friend.

Before I can turn around to see if Bond is checking out my ass, Bond yells, "Hike!"

I throw the ball back between my legs and run into position. Will catches the ball just as Harper takes his flag.

Jameson intercepts the ball in the next play and ends up scoring a touchdown.

He gives me a cocky smirk as we line back up and I say, "You totally caught the ball out of bounds, but okay, I guess we'll let you have that one."

He scoffs. "Still a sore loser I see."

I let his words get to me, remembering exactly what we did last year when I was acting this way. The thoughts of Jameson and I in his truck cause me to lose a flag to one of the other guys on the red team.

But after the next three first downs, I finally score a touchdown. I make sure to give Jameson the side eye when I walk past him. But as soon as I start walking by, he pulls his shirt up over his head, revealing the torso of his beautiful body. I hate that I turn around just to look at him and the sweat running down his abs. The definition of his body has me in a trance.

"Scout! Why aren't you running the play?" Will asks.

I look around, realizing that I'm a complete idiot since I was distracted. I didn't even hear them run the play. I'm going to lose us the game if I don't get out of my freaking head.

I get into position and say, "Sorry. Run it again, I'm ready."

I glance up at Jameson to see him smirking at me like he knew exactly what was going to happen. *He did it on purpose.* I feel like there must be flames coming out my ears because I'm so mad. Making sure to keep my eyes glued to the ball instead of my ex, I end up scoring another touchdown, winning us the game.

Chapter Twenty-Nine

Jameson

If Scout would have lost the flag football tournament today, she probably would have pouted the whole way back to her house. I would have loved every minute of it. But instead, I'm the one pouting on the drive home as she turns to look at me with an overconfident smile. No wonder she was so good at track, she loves to win. And she definitely hates to lose. As much as I don't want to admit it, it's nice seeing her smile today, especially after everything that's happened. We don't dare say a word to each other because if we do, it most likely won't be pretty. I never in a million years expected this is where we would end up.

When we pull into her driveway it's almost dark.

Just as I'm about to apologize for being such a dick earlier, Scout decides to open her sassy mouth again. "Have fun with Ava."

She opens the passenger door, slides out and slams it shut. Not even a thank you for picking her up for Thanksgiving dinner or letting her win flag football. Okay, I didn't let her win, but still. Not even a thank you for bringing her home.

Then she quickly walks to her front door as she pulls out her key, unlocks it, and slams it shut behind her.

It reminds me of the day we broke up. When she slammed the door after walking out on us.

Six months earlier...

Scout's alarm went off for the fourth time. She finally sat up to get out of bed with a groan and I'm tempted to pull her back under the blanket with me, but I know better. She may hate waking up in the morning, but she hates skipping a run much more. Honestly, she's a little crabby when she doesn't run. So instead of pulling her back down, I pat her on the ass as she stands up to get her running gear on. A small gesture to let her know I'm rooting her on to get up and go. We never really talk at this hour since we're both still half asleep but Scout looks at me and yawns before leaning over to kiss me like she does every morning. She slips out of my t-shirt, the one that she slept in last night. My clothes look so much better on her. When she's finished getting dressed, she shuts our bedroom door behind her, and I lay in bed for a few more minutes before getting ready for work.

I push the button on the blender and smile knowing Scout will be home from her run any minute to try the perfect smoothie. Yesterday, I made sure to study each portion of fruit, vegetable, protein powder and chia seeds she put into it. I'm pouring the fruity green smoothie in two tall glasses just as she walks in the door. Scout's smoothies have grown on me. They taste pretty good and drinking one each morning makes me feel healthy knowing that I at least got a serving of fruits and vegetables for the day. She kicks off her shoes and takes out her ponytail. She still has her headphones in as she's breathing heavily. Mouthing the words to whatever rap song she's listening to, she pulls off her sweaty tank top. Leaving her only in her shorts and sports bra. Sweat drips down her tiny waist as she takes out her earbuds and smiles. Her smile is the most beautiful thing I'll ever get to see. This is why I'll never complain about her alarm going off three or four times a week at the crack of dawn before she leaves me in bed alone to go do what she loves.

"Were you just checking me out Marshal Karter?" she asks before taking a drink from her water bottle.

"Always. And you can't call me that yet."

She rolls her eyes. "Tomorrow it's official."

She walks around the kitchen island and wraps her arms around me from behind. "I'm so proud of you for working so hard to get what you want."

God, I love this girl.

"I'm proud of you Miss Addison." I've never seen a sexier teacher...

"You can't call me that either. The school year just ended and I'm not a teacher again for another three and a half months."

"Just because it's summer, doesn't mean you're not a teacher."

She sighs. "Is it weird that I miss it already and it's only been three days?"

"No, it's great that you love your job so much." I hand her the smoothie I made, and she smiles before taking a drink.

"Mmmm," she says, licking her lips. The sexy sound that just escaped her mouth instantly turns me on.

"Say that again."

Scout laughs as she takes another sip. "You made it just right this time."

I pull her into me and kiss her neck.

She giggles. "James! I'm all sweaty and gross."

"You couldn't be gross even if you tried," I say before kissing her fruity mouth.

"I'm going to go get in the shower if you want to join."

I look at the clock. Shit.

She giggles. "I know you don't have time. Don't worry, I'll sneak into your shower tonight when you get home."

I look down at her flushed face and the urge to take her right here is almost unbearable, but I'll have to wait. My fingers slide into her hair before I kiss her on the head. "Can't wait."

She melts into me as she taps her finger three times over my heart, reminding me of the first time she did it. I love how we secretly pretend it's nothing but we both know it's her way of saying she loves me.

"I love you baby," I whisper.

She tips her head back and looks up at me with a slight smile. Her green eyes are glossy like they always are after she runs. "I love you too," she says even though she already told me.

***

As soon as I stepped foot inside my office this morning, I realized I had forgotten the paperwork Captain Berkley needs for my release. I left the folder right next to the smoothie maker. I'm ready to take on a new unique role of finding criminals and taking on actual bad guys. Working for the Wood Lake sheriff's department was an experience, but I'm ready for something a little more exciting. Not that giving out parking tickets and arresting some of my father's old buddies wasn't fun. But I'm ready to take on the job as a U.S Marshal. When I pull up to the house just thirty minutes after leaving it, I see a black Ferrari parked in the driveway. Who could that be?

I walk in the front door to see a shirtless man standing too close to Scout, who is wearing only a towel. Why the hell is she only in a towel? She looks shocked and I'm taken back at what I'm seeing. She wouldn't do this. It's not what it looks like.

"What's going on?" I ask.

The bastard next to her speaks first. "Are you going to tell him that I'm fucking you? Or should I?"

My heart stops. "Scout what's going on? Who is this guy?"

She's crying. No. She wouldn't do this.

"It- it's true," is all she manages to say through her sobs.

Then the guy next to her pulls her into him and I come apart. "Get your fucking hands off her!" Before I realize what I'm doing, I thrash his head with my fist and the guy lands on the ground. "Get out of my house before I bash your fucking skull in."

How I haven't already killed this guy is beyond me. He gets up and smiles. Why is he so goddamn happy? If he isn't gone in two seconds, he's dead. "Get. Out."

"Just go Ethan," Scout tells him.

When he shuts the door behind him, I can't even look at her. I hear her crying when I close my eyes. "How long?" My voice cracks.

She doesn't answer me.

"How long?!" I yell, looking down at her now.

"This was the only time," her voice shakes. "But it will probably happen again. You deserve better Jameson. I'll be gone when you get back."

"The hell you will. Tell me what's really going on," I beg. "Tell me you wouldn't do this. Not to me. Not to us."

"James. I'm going to be honest with you. I've lied to you, a lot. And I'm going to continue to lie to you. You have to let me leave. You deserve someone honest. Someone who wouldn't..." she pauses as I try and find some sliver of hope left for us. "Who wouldn't cheat on you."

"You're telling me you slept with that guy? After four years of commitment to me? After everything?"

She turns away from me and says, "Yeah." Her voice is different. She's acting different and I don't understand.

I come up around her and stand in front of her. "Scout, why are you doing this?" I ask, feeling myself break. I've never felt this kind of pain before. Scout is slipping away from me, taking my heart and soul with her.

"I have to go. We're done Jameson. I- I'm sorry." She tries to walk away but I follow her to our bedroom.

"You're sorry? Are you fucking kidding me? We talked about getting married last night and you seemed more than ready. Is that what this is about? Because we don't have to get married. We can keep doing what we're doing. I can't- fuck- I can't lose you Scout. Please. We have to make this work. But God dammit why? Aren't you happy?"

"No, Jameson. I'm not happy. You have to let me go. I can't love you anymore."

My whole world comes crashing down on me as Scout's words destroy every last hope that's left of me. The love of my life, my everything, gone. Just like that.

I try and swallow my anger, but it doesn't work. "Don't ever come back and ask me to love you again. Because I won't be able to."

She falls on the floor and breaks into uncontrollable sobs as she throws her clothes out of the dresser and into a suitcase. I'll never understand why she's breaking down if this is what she wants. But she doesn't let me stay to pick up the pieces.

"Go!" she screams.

I step out of the bedroom and just when I think she's following me, she slams the door shut behind me.

The day I let Scout go will always be the worst day of my life. My heaviest heartbreak. Because she was it for me. The day I lost Scout, I lost everything.

Chapter Thirty

Scout

All that wine I had last night when I got home from Thanksgiving was a bad idea. I groan as my alarm goes off for the third time. I'm not about to let a hangover stop me from running. My head doesn't hurt too badly, I'm just tired. As I turn off my alarm, I remember that I ended up texting Ben Dallis and he's picking me up for dinner tonight. I groan again. Drunken me figured if James could move on, maybe I should at least be trying to move on too. I absolutely don't think I'm ready for this but I'm not going to cancel on him. Maybe it will be good for me. Maybe I can forget about Jameson Karter for one night. Who am I kidding? I could be on a date with my celebrity crush, Ian Somerhalder, and even he couldn't help get James out of my head. It's six am when I step outside into the brisk fall morning. It's getting colder and darker at this time of day, but my legs are feeling antsy. After stretching a little, my feet begin pacing down the paved road. As my heart rate speeds up, my stress level slows down. I come to a complete stop when I notice Jameson's truck parked on my street just down the road from my house. Moving slowly, I can see that he's inside.

Was he parked here all night?

Emotions I don't want course through me while I look at the man sleeping inside his truck. I could tell he was worried yesterday when he saw the bruise on my cheek, but I didn't expect him to stay outside my house to keep watch. He's looking out for me. He still cares about me, enough to protect me, and that has my stomach twisting in knots. Not only because it makes me fall in love with him all over again but because of how dangerous it is for him to be near me. My eyes feel heavy at the sight of him finally getting some rest after a long night of keeping watch.

I take off again, my pace speeding up. Running tricks my brain into believing I'm leaving everything behind. And it feels good to run away from it all, even if it is only for an hour.

When I get back home, Jameson's truck is gone.

***

Police cars were literally driving by my house all day. I know Jameson sent them to check up on me. After putting on my red dress and clear strappy heels I'm anxiously waiting for Ben to pull up any minute now. It's been a while since I've been on a date. I used to love the thrill of going out with someone new. Now I'm unable to stop myself from feeling like I wish I were going out with James. But that's not fair, so I quickly brush that thought out of my mind.

I watch Ben's blue car pull into the driveway and I head out the door. The cool, fall breeze hits my bare legs and I'm immediately pleased with myself for wearing a leather jacket over my dress. He steps out of his vehicle and smiles. He's dressed in a button up shirt and khaki pants.

"Hey there. You look amazing," he says, rushing to the passenger door to open it for me.

A hint of fresh cologne wafts off him as I get closer. His hair almost has a little curl to it with a shiny looking gel he must have put on it, giving it a wet look. "You clean up well too, Mr. Dallas." I wink before sliding into the seat of his car.

"I feel terrible," Ben says, getting in the driver's seat.

I look at him, wondering why he feels so bad.

"I know you wanted to go on a date in the city but when I tried making reservations, everything was completely booked. That's what I get for calling last minute, I guess. Anyway, how do you feel about Allessio's here in town? It's the only nice restaurant available for tonight."

I told Ben I wanted to go on a date in the city only because I didn't want to risk running into James. But James could also be out of town tonight. He did have other police officers driving by instead of him earlier, so there was the possibility that he's not around. But even if he's not around, he's an adult. An adult who also goes on dates. With Ava. "I love Allessio's," I answer.

Ben grins. "Good."

✼✼✼✼✼ ✼✼✼✼✼

Ben really is a nice guy. He's polite, he makes me laugh, he's not bad to look at. After dinner, Ben and I walk down the quiet street. I hear music playing from one of the bars in town. A bar James and I used to go to. I try to push those memories out of my mind while I walk with my date. Ben brushes his fingers up against mine before holding my hand. I've already discovered he grew up in Michigan and moved here for a fresh start after college, he's three years older than me, and he has a cat named Nancy. I've talked mainly about my college years in Columbus.

"You're great with your students. Do you want children of your own someday?"

I want children but I can't imagine ever having them with anyone else besides James. My heart is still wounded. I wasn't ready for this. I let go of Ben's hand. "I'm feeling really tired. Can you take me home?"

I don't look at Ben when he says, "Are you sure?"

I nod before we get into his car and drive back to my house.

I'm anxious when we pull into my driveway, and I see Jameson's truck parked down the street. But I try to ignore that as Ben walks me to the door and I thank him for the date before saying goodnight.

"Are you the piece of shit that hurt her?"

I immediately whip around to see Jameson all up in Ben's face, backing him up against my house.

"James!" I yell.

"Who the hell are you?" Ben asks Jameson.

"Did you *hurt* her?" James pronounces his words slowly this time. He won't let go of Ben until he has an answer.

Ben shoots me a concerned glance before he glares at James. "I would never hurt her, no," he answers.

James isn't budging. He keeps Ben pinned up against the wall.

"James, he didn't hurt me." I step closer.

"How am I supposed to believe you?" James asks, still studying Ben.

"What's going on Scout? How do you know this guy?" Ben asks.

"He's my ex-boyfriend. I'm sorry about him."

James lets go of Ben, almost looking disappointed that he's not the one who hurt me. Then his eyes find mine and there is so much pain in them that I want to look away.

Ben clears his throat and adjusts his collar. "It's fine. Are you going to be okay?" he asks me.

"I'll be fine. Thanks for the date."

Ben nods at me before walking away. James follows and stops him from getting in his car and says something I can't hear. Probably threatening him some more.

When James walks back I say, "What were you thinking?"

His hands are in his front pockets. "I was thinking I needed to make sure you're okay and that this wasn't the guy that hit you."

"By threatening him?" I snap.

"Who said I was threatening him?"

Feeling frustrated, I close my eyes slowly. He has to stay away. "I saw you this morning, parked by my house. You don't have to do that."

By the look on Jameson's face, he's not budging. He'll be here tonight because he's too good not to stay. Feeling myself about ready to fall into another panic attack, the words come out faster than I can think. "Ben is staying over tonight. I'm going to ask him to come back."

Jameson's jaw twitches as he clenches his teeth. The heated glare he gives me, sends shivers down my spine. "What?"

"Ben will stay with me. You don't have to be here."

"You're telling me that guy is sleeping in your bed with you tonight?" he asks with fire in his eyes.

"Yes," I choke, hoping he believes the next lie.

When I see the pain on his face, I want to tell him the truth, but I can't.

"No," he growls.

Jameson

I hate the way I'm reacting to the fact that Scout has a man sleeping with her tonight. But I feel like I could explode at any moment.

"No?" she asks. "You can't tell me what to do James."

If she wants me to hate her then it's working. But I need her to hate me back. I can't be the only one feeling this way. Even though I don't believe it one bit, I'm going to take the ammo while I can.

"Does he know the only person you'll ever love is yourself?" The words roll off my tongue, knowing I won't be able to take them back.

"That's not true," she says.

"It is true. You don't care about anyone but yourself. I feel bad for the guy. You're only going to get close to him so you can watch him hurt when you break him. Then you'll move on to the next man, eager to destroy him too, doing all of it so you can feel powerful or some shit. You're like this pretty, tempting little flower that every man wants. But when they get to know you they'll see how ugly you really are inside."

All the color drains from her face as she looks at me in disbelief. If an already broken heart can shatter all over again then mine just did as I watch how badly I just hurt her. The silence pierces my ears as her tears splatter at my feet. I wish she'd drown me in them. I deserve it.

She steps toward me. "Is that what you think of me?"

"I don't know what I think anymore Scout."

I needed her to look at me like this because it's been taking everything in me not to take her lying mouth to mine. If she didn't hate me before, I think she does now.

"Leave me alone," she says, her voice breaks.

I do exactly what she says because I can't stay and watch another man be with her. He'll sleep next to her, and he'll get to wake up to those green eyes. He'll fall in love with her. Because how could he not? And she'll still hate me.

When I get to my truck, I punch the steering wheel over and over again. I hate myself more than I hate her. Because I still fucking love her.

When I pull my shit together, I call Tyson. "Hey. I need you to take watch at the same address you were scouting earlier. On Nestlington."

"You got it."

Tyson is good at his job. He's a police officer I trust to keep her safe. He has a damn good eye. Even at night. Scout may have a man sleeping with her tonight, but I don't trust him. Not one bit.

Scout

I slam the door and lock it behind me. Painful words hurt a lot worse when they come from someone you love. It's just words. Why does it hurt so much?

Does he know the only person you'll ever love is yourself? I scream out of anger as I kick the side table in the entryway, knocking the lamp over. Pain shoots up my leg causing me to drop down on the floor. I hiss as I take off my heel. My foot is already starting to bruise, and it makes the runner in me so mad that I chuck my shoe hard across the room. That's when I hear glass shatter. *Shit.* As I hobble over to the damaged sliding glass door, Sickem is waiting outside, tilting her head at the mess.

"Sorry girl." I carefully slide the door open, even though it shattered completely.

Hoping Sickem doesn't get glass in her paws I call her inside as I hop on one foot. She follows me to the door in the kitchen that leads us directly into the garage. A tarp will have to do for now. It's difficult cleaning up the glass and putting the tarp up with my injured foot but I do the best I can.

Chapter Thirty-One

Jameson

I'm headed to the city to do research at the office this morning when Tyson calls me.

I answer over Bluetooth. "Yeah?"

"Hey, just thought I'd let you know I just left Nestlington Street. Nobody has come in or out of her house in the past ten hours."

She was lying about Ben staying over. I should have known. Wait, nobody came in or *out*?

"You saw her leave for her run, right?" I ask, on the edge of my seat.

"No. Must have skipped it this morning. I gotta go. Boss is calling."

"Wait, Tyson." But he's already gone as he switched to the other line.

Today is not Sunday. Scout *never* skips a run. "Shit!" I flip a U-turn and head back into Wood Lake.

Maybe Tyson didn't see her leave or maybe she left after Tyson did. But I don't spot her running as I speed to her house. I pull into her driveway and jump out before I pound on the door. She doesn't answer. *Goddammit.*

"Scout. Open up!"

When she still doesn't answer, I peek through the window. My blood turns to ice when I spot a knocked over lamp. I run to the back of the house after hopping over the fence. I'm flooded with fear when I see the back glass door is broken. The door is locked so I shove my arm through the tarp to unlock it. I step inside the house to see Scout baking in the kitchen.

"Why the hell didn't you answer the door?" I ask, my heart still racing as I try and catch my breath.

She's ignoring me. Sickem gets excited to see me and comes running up to me to lick my hand.

"Scout. What happened to your glass door?" I ask, stepping around the kitchen island. That's when I get the full view of her. She's wearing her Captain America tank top and no pants. She's just in her panties. Not only panties, but a thong. Her headphones are in so that explains why she didn't hear me. She hobbles over to the pantry on one foot as I watch her ass jiggle from behind. *Holy fuck.*

When she turns around and notices me, she squeals before she chucks the bag of flour at me. The bag of flour breaks in front of me, covering my pants in white dust.

She rips her headphones out and gives me a death glare. "You scared me! What are you doing in here?"

She scared me first. "What the hell happened to your door? And what's wrong with your leg? You're limping."

Scout hands me a towel to wipe the flour off my pants. "I hurt it last night. About right after you called me ugly inside," she says angrily.

"That doesn't explain what happened to your door."

She sighs, looking at the broken glass door. "I threw my shoe after I hurt my foot and it hit the glass."

A pang of guilt hits me looking at the damage. Scout was upset after what I said last night. I'm the one that caused this. *I'm an ass.*

I link my hands together behind my neck, feeling frustrated at both Scout and me.

Scout stands directly in front of me, taking a deep breath and my eyes immediately land on her chest. She's not wearing a bra and it's visibly noticeable. She's making me insane, so with my hands still locked behind my neck, I turn around.

"Look who's breaking and entering now," she sasses.

I could spank her for talking to me like that.

"I was worried when Tyson told me you didn't go for your run."

"Tyson?" she asks.

"The police officer that was parked out front all night," I explain.

"Oh. Why was someone there when I asked you not to do that?"

I huff. "You told *me* not to be here. You didn't say anything about anyone else."

"But why should anyone keep watch?" By the sound of her raspy, whiny voice behind me, she's clearly frustrated.

"Scout, you know why."

She groans. "I don't know why you worry about me when you've made it very clear how bad you hate me."

"I'm only doing my job as a police officer," I say, knowing damn well I'm obviously going above and beyond for her. But I'm not going to admit that.

"Why can't you face me, James?" she asks, clearly unnerved that my back is turned. "Wait, you're bleeding."

I look at my forearm and see the gash I must have gotten from the broken glass door.

"Sit down. I'll get the first aid kit," she says.

Now I feel like a jerk that she wants to help me when she can hardly walk. "You don't have to do that."

Scout ignores me and comes back with a first aid kit and still no fucking pants. *Jesus Christ.* She pulls up a kitchen table chair for me to sit down on. I close my eyes as I feel the heat of her body in front of me.

While she cleans up my cut, she says, "Why are your eyes closed? I didn't know blood made you queasy."

"It's not the blood I can't look at. It's you."

"Why?"

"Have you seen what you're wearing?"

She stops what she's doing for a moment and whispers, "Oh."

Then I hear her opening wrappers and she has my arm bandaged up in minutes.

"You should probably have it looked at. You might need stitches."

"Thanks," I say, my eyes still tightly closed even though the image of her is permanently on my mind. It probably will be all day. "You should probably get your foot looked at too."

"Planning on it," she says as I hear her walk off. I slowly peel my eyes open.

When she comes back in, I appreciate the fact that she put on some sweatpants. "You can leave now," says the girl who was sweetly taking care of me just moments ago.

I don't think Scout notices me measuring the size of the glass door after I get the measuring tape out of my truck, or she'd be yelling at me to leave. But I'm not letting her deal with the broken door alone when I know damn well that I'm the one that caused it.

❧ ❧

When I get back to her house after going to the hardware store thirty minutes later, I'm surprised Scout hasn't chewed my ass to leave. But I think she must have figured out that I'm just here replacing her glass door. I'll take what's left of her old one to replace a new one that has a doggie door connected. That way Sickem can come in and out when she wants and needs to, but more importantly, if Scout needs her.

"James," I hear Scout say almost in a whisper.

I slide the door open and take down the tarp. That's when I see Scout on the couch. *Touching herself. She's just as pretty and pink as I remember.* Her eyes are closed, and she has her earphones in.

As soon as she sees me, she quickly pulls her panties up. Her cheeks are flushed pink, her hair a mess as she chews nervously on her bottom lip.

Scout

Jameson's eyes are so dark as he watches me from across the room. "How long have you been here?" I ask, feeling humiliated but completely turned on by the way he's looking at me.

"You were thinking about me while touching yourself," his voice deep, his eyes fierce.

"N-no. I wasn't," I lie.

"Don't lie. Not about this. I heard you say my name. Tell me exactly what you were just thinking."

After James left, I was sexually frustrated. I hate how my body reacted to the reason Jameson's eyes were closed when I was bandaging his arm. I wanted him to open his eyes and see me. Because I wanted to find out what would happen if he did. Thoughts of how he would have taken me racked my mind. The feel of his hard bicep and how tense he felt as I bandaged him up made me want to straddle him to feel other places I know were hard. Because I could see him growing through his pants. His eyes were closed, but clearly he was aware that I was half naked and that was enough for him to want me.

I tried like hell to forget the tall, blonde Marshal who drives me wild. But I couldn't. I laid down on the couch after putting my headphones back in. I had no idea he'd be coming back.

"James," I whimper.

"Tell me every detail Scout."

The way he's looking at me makes me weak in the knees. "I-I was imagining things were different this morning when you had your eyes closed. Instead, they were open. Watching me." I sit here on the couch as I confess what I was just thinking.

"And?" he asks, keeping his distance.

"And you ended up bending me over your knee to spank me for not wearing pants," I say, feeling nervous about how he'll react. *Why did he come back?*

James inhales my words, looking angry as ever. "You deserve to be spanked. Then what?" He steps closer, desperate for answers and my breath catches.

"Then you made me take off my panties."

"Why?"

"Because you wanted me."

James tilts his head back and I watch his thick neck as he swallows, his eyes still on me. "Keep touching yourself."

"What?"

"Don't let me stop you. I want you to keep that imagination going while you touch yourself." His eyes roam over me as he walks toward me slowly. "And I want to watch."

The throb between my legs is so intense, it's almost painful. I know I'm not thinking rationally when I say, "Okay."

When he gets to the back of the couch, he stands over me, his tongue glides across his bottom lip, ready to watch. He watches me closely as I slide out of my panties, leaving me only wearing my tank top when I lay back down.

"Close your eyes."

I do as I'm told. I keep my eyes closed but I can feel Jameson *watching* as my fingers slide against my soft, slick lips. "What did I do to you in the kitchen Scout? Keep going while you tell me."

Feeling the heat in my core, I do circles over the sensitive nub. I moan softly before I say, "You took me on the floor."

"Yeah? I was fucking you on the floor and that's why you were moaning my name?"

"Yes," I breathe.

"How did it feel?" he asks.

"So good," I moan, moving my hand faster.

Just as I'm on edge, James says, "Open your eyes." He can't help himself. This is his favorite part. It always has been. When I look up at him, he's hunched over the back of the couch, his eyes dark and thirsty as he watches my every move.

He says, "That's it. Keep going. I want to watch you come while you imagine what you can't have anymore." My body reacts to his eyes on mine and before I'm able to fully comprehend what he just said, my mouth opens, and I fall apart.

I'm out of breath after I finish and slightly embarrassed about what just happened. I was so in the moment I wasn't thinking of how I'd feel afterward. Especially when I realize what James just said. I sit up and slide back into my underwear. I feel so stupid. "Sorry, it's been a while," I confess. I wonder if James enjoyed watching me or if he just liked seeing that I'm not over him.

"How long?" he asks, backing away from the couch.

"What?"

"You said it's been a while. How long?"

I haven't slept with anyone since him, but he can't know that.

"I can't remember," I lie.

His eyes glare straight through me, like he knows I'm lying. The way he looks at me, forces me to look away.

Then my whole body tenses up when I hear a knock on the door. I drop down to the floor to grab my sweats and slip them on fast. "You have to go. Now."

"What's wrong?" he asks. "Worried your boyfriend will have his feelings hurt?"

James doesn't move a muscle and all I can think of is how scared I am to open the door. "James, please."

He glares daggers but walks toward the back door. If it's Ethan, I'll just have to lie and say he's here to help me with something. He'll believe me. Right? No. I won't be able to answer it if it's Ethan. *Please don't be Ethan.*

My steps feel heavy as I walk toward the front door, taking my time. I look through the peephole to see Ben holding flowers and I don't think I've ever felt so relieved that it's not my brother.

"Hi Ben," I say as I answer the door.

"Hey, I just wanted to say thanks for last night. I had a good time. I felt terrible that I didn't get you flowers before our date so that's what these are making up for." He hands me the bouquet of red roses.

I smile. "Thank you."

"She likes pink dahlias," James says behind me.

Ben's face looks completely shocked and a little hurt. Then I realize it's because my ex is standing behind me.

"James was just checking in on me," I quickly say before he gets the wrong idea. Even though we just had a very intimate moment in my living room. If you can call it that.

Jameson scoffs behind me and I feel like I could gut punch him.

Ben half laughs nervously. This is awkward and I hate how uncomfortable Ben probably feels.

"I love the flowers," I tell Ben. "And I had a good time last night too." I can feel James burning us with glares from behind.

"You bet. See you tomorrow," he says before walking away.

I shut the door and turn to face James.

"Looks like he didn't end up coming over last night after all," James says.

"You didn't have to be rude. He's a nice guy."

"Clearly, you're not into him. So why are you seeing him again tomorrow?"

I feel my eyes roll. He's getting too involved right now. I don't even want to explain that I'll only see him tomorrow because we work together. "That's so unfair of you to ask. Especially since you moved on with Ava about five minutes after I left."

"That's unfair for you to say when I'm the one that caught you cheating."

The fire in his eyes causes me to look down. All I do is lie to him.

"Please. Just go," I whisper.

I leave him standing in the entryway and go to my room and shut the door behind me.

I can't stop the tears from coming as I lay on my bed and fall asleep.

After my nap, I go to let Sickem out, but can see that she's already out. James built a dog door! Sickem sees me through the glass and comes flying through the small flappy entrance. "You like it girl?"

She runs back out like a mad woman, and I can't help but smile that he did this. I thought I would have to pay a fortune to fix that door. As I stare at the fixed problem that now has a way for Sickem to get in and out of the house, I think about how hard James makes it to stop loving him.

Chapter Thirty-Two

Scout

Another teacher, Mrs. Freemond and I, thought it would be a good idea to plan a field trip right after Thanksgiving break so that the students would be happy to be back in school. The principal agreed when we explained the educational benefit they'd get out of it. Usually, the students would be dragging their feet being back in school, but they're excited to be here, and I smile at that. They all scramble toward the buses full of anticipation and excitement for our field trip to the nature museum. I follow my class and sit in the front seat of the bus after counting down each student.

"How are you doing, dear?" Mrs. Freemond asks. She's seated across the bus aisle from me. She's the only other first grade teacher and I usually go to her when I need advice since she's been in the profession for so long.

"I'm great. How are you doing?" I ask.

"Surviving. I would be lying if I said I'm not a little sad this is my last year though."

"You're retiring?"

"I am. It's time. Hank really wants to start traveling next year." I remember her telling me her husband retired a couple of years ago and has been patiently waiting for her to start their adventures together.

"That will be fun. I love traveling."

"Well, you're single, aren't you?" she asks. "Next year maybe teach in a different place. Then a different one the year after that. Nothing is holding you here. If only I was smart enough to do something like that when I was younger. Take my advice honey, see the world while you're young. Thinking about doing it now is already making me tired."

I laugh. "Maybe I will." It's not a bad idea. It's honestly probably the best thing I could do, for not only myself but for James. That was always the plan anyway. To leave when my contract ended.

Ben walks onto the bus and gives me a small nod. He must have volunteered to help chaperone. I need to talk to him, but he won't even look my way. I don't blame him really.

The bus is loud the whole way to the museum, but I don't mind it. Listening to children get excited about something so simple makes me happy. If only we could stay that way as adults. As we grow up and adapt to the world, it's as though things aren't as spectacular as when we were kids. I miss the feeling of having no worries, being carefree and naive to the responsibilities of being an adult. Unfortunately, my childhood was cut short when I started figuring my family out. Especially my mom.

After unloading the buses and making sure to keep my students in groups of five with a parental chaperone, we embark on our adventure.

We start off with the fossils and minerals. The students are fascinated at what they uncover while digging through the sand and explore the different types of rocks.

I spot Ben on the other side of the sand and move toward him. When I stand next to him, the uncomfortable shift of his body language tells me that he doesn't want to talk to me.

"The kids are loving this," I say.

"They are. I'm glad you and Mrs. Freemond made it happen."

I smile. "Me too." I wipe my hands on my jeans. "I wanted to apologize for the other day. When you came over and Jameson was there. He was rude and I felt like it was probably a slap in the face to you, seeing me with him right after our date. I want you to know that he and I aren't together. And although we're through, I think you should also know that my life is just too complicated at the moment for me to start dating again. I thought maybe I was ready, but I'm not. I really did enjoy our date the other night though."

Ben nods. "Listen, I get it. You don't even need to apologize for any of it. I understand things are complicated between you and your ex."

"It's not that. It doesn't have anything to do with James." I *just realized how stupid that sounded.* I shake my head. "No, sorry. You're right. It has everything to do with James and you don't deserve that."

He scratches the back of his head. "I appreciate your honesty, Scout."

"Thanks for understanding," I say. "And I really did appreciate the date and flowers."

"My pleasure. If you ever need to talk, my door is always open to you," he mentions.

"Thanks."

"Look what I found Ms. Addison!" my student Cashton yells. After he shows me all the cool rocks he's found, I round up my students and we move on to the next stage of the museum.

All the beautiful flowers and plants in the greenhouse take my breath away. I'm excited for spring to come just so I can plant my own flowers in the front yard. The tour guide shows us around and tells us about the different types of plants and butterflies. The kids are most fascinated by the butterflies hovering all around us. They are landing on the flowers and lily pads in a tiny pond with a waterfall.

I hear a giggle and turn to see one of my students with a butterfly that landed on her shirt.

"Wow, look at that. It likes you," I tell her.

All the students gather around to see the butterfly and I love how much they're enjoying this. Then I notice a butterfly that looks all too familiar. Its black and white wings are tattered and broken. I flashback to the memory of the butterfly I found on a hike with Bailey. In my eyes then, I saw it as a broken, sad little thing. I felt bad for how hideous it looked compared to the rest of nature's beauty. I kneel to the butterfly and pick it up with two fingers.

"You got one too!" the students shout.

"That one's... kind of broken. Look at its wings," Dawson says.

"That's sad," another student says.

"Kind of," I say to the students that gathered near me and the butterfly. "This butterfly may be broken but that doesn't make it any less beautiful. It's been through a lot. It may look weak but it's probably the strongest butterfly here." It flies off my finger. "See? It's a survivor."

Chapter Thirty-Three

Scout

I t's been cloudy all day today and I think it's going to snow soon. It's been a couple weeks and I still feel embarrassed as I think about how I selfishly let James watch me on the couch a couple weeks ago. And I wish I could stop thinking about it. Sickem barks by the front door. She does that when she wants to go for a run. I haven't been able to run all week because of my bad ankle and that's been driving me crazy. Sickem too, apparently. We both miss it. I don't think it will hurt to walk her to the bridge only a half mile away and back. Sickem's tail wags as I put the leash on her collar.

"Come on girl, let's go out."

I open the front door and step out into the cold, and the chilly air hits my face. I walk through my quiet neighborhood and when we get to the bridge we turn right back around. I spot a couple runners in the distance and instantly feel envious. I know I should probably do something besides mope around today. I might go crazy. As if Harper can sense my misery, she sends me a text.

Going on a Target run in the city. Want to come?
Absolutely.

"Would you tell me if someone hurt you?" Harper asks as we walk through Target with our iced coffees in hand. "Physically I mean?"

I sigh. James obviously talked to her. "I already told James it was an accident. I don't want to talk about it."

I wish I didn't have to lie to her too, but I want to keep the people I love safe.

Harper watches me skeptically as I look at some hoop earrings. They seem to be my favorite to wear lately. "Okay. Just know I'm always here for you," she says.

"Of course." Harper has never asked me too many questions. She knows how to be here for me without prying. I love her for that. And I really don't want to talk about my brother hitting me. Last night I had a nightmare that he came back to my house after he found out Jameson had been around me. I don't even want to think about the rest.

Letting him inside my house was a huge mistake. One that I can never do again. Coming back was a mistake. I should have listened to my gut screaming at me not to. Instead, I let my heart get the better of me. Well, that and my contract with the school.

"When my contract ends with Blue Hill Elementary, I'm moving," I tell Harper. I don't know why the hell I felt the need to say that out loud because my friend now looks sad, and I feel bad.

She immediately frowns. "You're going to move? Why?"

I pick up a gold set of hoop earrings I like and hold them up to my ears. "Do you like these?"

She nods. "Scout, talk to me. Why are you thinking about moving? You just came back."

"It was always part of the plan. And you know why," I say, throwing the earrings inside my basket as we move on to the handbags.

"Because of James?" she asks.

Harper still hasn't even looked at anything when it was her idea to come shopping. This was obviously just her way of getting me to talk. Sneaky woman.

"It's just too hard being around him. And I always knew in the back of my mind that I wouldn't be able to live here forever." I admit with a shrug. But it's so much more than that. I just can't tell her, or anyone.

"Do you ever just think about trying to make things work with James? You both clearly love each other. He even ended things with Ava."

"Harper, stop."

I touch my best friend's arm. "James and I can't work. We just can't and I'm done talking about it."

I feel like I could burst into tears at any moment. I feel so angry at myself for always hurting the people I love.

Harper looks concerned. "Are you okay?"

I nod even though I'm clearly not okay. "I just wish things were different."

"Different how?" she asks.

I shrug as I hold in my feelings. Harper lets me but I know she is wishing I would open up. "Honestly, I've kind of had a rough week. I'm moody." Most likely from what I did with James and for not being able to run.

Harper smiles with sincerity in her eyes. "Really? I haven't noticed," she says sarcastically.

It feels good to laugh. "Thanks for today. It really has been nice even though I've been a bitch."

"It's okay. I shouldn't pry." She sighs. "I just want you to be happy, that's all."

"I know."

"How about we drive back home, and you come to my place?" Harper offers. "Mint chocolate chip ice cream is waiting for us in the freezer."

She gives me those puppy dog eyes knowing that I can't say no to ice cream.

⁘ ⁘

I slip off my coat at Harper's house and pull my hair back into the clip from my purse. I look in the entryway mirror at my new hoop earrings and smile. It's the little things in life that make a woman happy.

Harper brings out the tub of ice cream and two spoons.

"Sugar therapy is a real thing. I could use it right now," I admit.

"I figured." Harper smiles as we both drop down on the couch and rip open the lid. "Have you ever thought about actual therapy?" she asks.

I take a spoonful of ice cream and shovel it in my mouth. "Yeah, but I'm just not great at talking about myself. Do you feel like therapy has helped you?" Harper has been going to a therapist ever since the shocking events that happened four years ago with her stalker ex-boyfriend.

"Absolutely. Will can tell if I miss a session with her. I get more anxious and moodier. She's really helped me understand and cope with my emotions. I can give you her number if you want," she offers.

"I'll think about it."

Someone walks through the back door, and we turn around to see Will standing there with *Jameson*. Dammit. It feels extremely awkward between us after what happened last week, and we still haven't said a word to each other since. I've seen him drive by my house to check on me and that's it. But usually, he sends another police officer. He's avoiding me and I don't mind at all. Harper gets up to greet them and as much as I don't want to, I follow. I can tell Jameson just got done working out because his blonde hair is damp from the shower. He's wearing gray sweats, and he smells amazing. He and Will look so much alike since they're so close in age. They've even been asked if they're twins before. But Jameson will always be the more attractive one to me. His blue eyes find mine, but he quickly looks away, obviously feeling just as awkward as I do.

"Hey guys, how was the gym?" Harper asks them.

I drop my spoon in the sink as Harper puts the ice cream back in the freezer.

"It was good," Will says and James nods in agreement. "Oh no. The ice cream is out. Is everybody okay?" Will jokes.

Harper shoots him a look and I feel so hot in the face, I can't look Jameson's way. He probably thinks I told Harper about what happened. What if he told Will? He said he wouldn't but they're so close I wouldn't be surprised if he slipped up. I used to trust this man with everything I have but now that we're not together and he doesn't like me much, I'm not so sure he'd care.

When Will gives Harper a questioning look, I quickly change the subject. "I was just telling Harper I was thinking about moving next year. When my contract ends with the school."

My eyes immediately fall on James and the stoic expression he has on his face catches my breath. He really doesn't care -- or he's good at acting like he doesn't.

"Why?" Will asks as he pulls out a large container of protein powder from the pantry.

Suddenly Jameson walks away, and it's obvious that he doesn't care to be part of the conversation.

"I'm just thinking about trying something different. Going somewhere new. Traveling." The front door shuts, causing me to wince. "But I haven't decided yet. I'm still trying to figure it out."

Will looks at Harper who now looks sad again. Ugh why can't I keep my big mouth shut?

"Oh," Will says, "Well, that's cool I guess."

Harper smiles at me even though she's not at all happy about it. I'm relieved when she and Will start talking about going to get a Christmas tree.

"Do you want to come with us to get a tree next week over Christmas break?" she asks.

"Yeah, that sounds great."

"I'm going to go see if Jameson left," Will says and I stop him.

"No, I'll go. I want to talk to him."

I don't stay in the kitchen to see if Harper and Will are looking at me as I go find him.

Jameson is outside leaning up against his truck as he watches me walk out. I don't know if the chill coursing through me is from the cold or the glare he has in his eyes.

"Hey. I wanted to tell you thanks for fixing my door. Sickem loves it."

He just nods. In fact, he hasn't said one word.

"Are you okay?" I ask as I stand in front of him, my arms wrapping around myself for some kind of extra warmth.

"Why wouldn't I be?" he asks.

"I- I don't know. You came out here when I said–"

"That you're leaving. Again," he says like he couldn't give a crap. But I'm starting to wonder if he does.

Sadness overtakes me when I think about not being able to see him anymore. And how hard it was when I was in Hawaii.

"James."

"It's for the best," he says, his jaw clenches.

It would be so simple to tell Jameson everything right now. If I did, he would understand. He would wrap me in his arms and tell me everything would be okay and for once maybe I'd feel safe. Protected. But then that means he wouldn't be. And although I'm a selfish girl, I could never do that to James.

I bite my cheek just when Jameson looks down at my lips with a sharp expression. He wants to kiss me.

"Don't look at me like that," I whisper, realizing the words literally just came flying out of my mouth.

"Like what?" he breathes. His eyebrows pulled down with a pained expression.

"Like you want to kiss me." My head tips down toward the ground. I don't dare look at him when I say this, but my eyes are forced back to him as he steps forward.

"Don't look at me like *that* then," he says.

"Like what?"

"Like you still love me."

My eyes are on the ground, but my mind is somewhere else completely. Somewhere that I can love James again. I want to be there so bad it hurts.

I feel him approaching me closer, like he wants to be there too.

Will walks out and James immediately moves away from me so quickly, Will now looks suspicious.

"We're ordering pizza if you guys want some," Will says, throwing a bag of trash into the dumpster.

"I was just leaving," I answer.

"In that case, I'm up for some pizza," Jameson says rudely. Like he didn't just look at me the way he did seconds ago.

I glare at him before looking at Will who is also looking at his brother like he could smack him.

"I'm going to go tell Harper bye."

When I slip inside, Harper gives me a suspicious look. "What?" I ask.

"Nothing," she says. "Everything okay?"

"Fine. I'm going to go. Thanks for the ice cream."

"Of course," Harper says from the couch. "We'll see you next week?"

I'm confused so Harper reminds me, "To get a Christmas tree."

"Right."

I wish she'd stop giving me such a suspicious look. I ignore it. "Let me know what day and I'll see you then."

"See ya," she says when I step outside back out into the cold. James and Will are both walking back in, so I leave the door open for them.

"Bye, Will," I say, making sure to leave out the name James.

Chapter Thirty-Four

Jameson

We only rented out two snowmobiles since everyone failed to mention Scout was coming. Another holiday tradition the four of us used to do together was to go get Christmas trees. Of course, they were going to invite her. We did this every year. I remember the first time we did it and Scout came out to my truck with her purse, the only warm clothing she had on was a coat and scarf.

As soon as she hopped inside the truck I said, "You're not dressed warm enough. We're going Christmas tree hunting, remember?"

"It's not that cold out. I know the perfect place downtown on Main for tree shopping. I've heard the trees there are beautiful. And they even serve hot chocolate." She smiled and if she wasn't so damn cute, I'd be ripping my hair out.

"We're not going tree shopping. We're going Christmas tree hunting," I correct her.

She frowns. "There's a difference?"

"Yeah, we're going to go find one in the canyon and cut it down ourselves. I picked up the permit today. We'll be riding on snowmobiles so you're going to want some warmer clothes."

Her eyes were wide, but her smile convinced me that she was excited to try something new. "Wait seriously? Like an actual snowmobile? I've never even been on one! I can't wait. Your plan is way better."

While she went back inside and changed into warmer clothes, I made us hot chocolate to take with us. She was so happy, and I knew when I saw the look on her face that I would never let her down and forget the hot chocolate.

Scout took forever but she eventually picked out a tree that day. Although it wasn't as full as she would have liked she said she'd never want to get a Christmas tree any other way. The experience was worth more to her.

So here she is. Looking just as surprised to see me sit here on the snowmobile. Harper and Will are staring at us from theirs as if they didn't know what they were doing.

"I can ride with Scout," Harper mentions as she stands.

"No, it's fine," I say, "Scout, sit down."

"Behind you?" she asks, holding her helmet.

"Don't you want a Christmas tree?" I ask.

"Well, yeah," she says, looking back at Harper and Will, who are waiting.

She slowly walks up to the vehicle and steps up before throwing her leg around the seat to sit down behind me. She puts her helmet on as I stand up to pull-start the machine. I sit back down to get ready to drive, but when Scout doesn't hold on to me, I look back to see her holding on to the seat. That's not safe. She can't hear me over the engine, so with my left hand, I reach back to grab her arm and make her hold onto me. Keeping her hand on my waist, she brings her other one around and holds on tight. Will and Harper drive off, so I follow behind, trying hard not to focus on the hands I feel sliding up my chest.

The drive up the canyon is beautiful since the snowfall last night has dusted the trees with white powder. I don't know if I believe in God, but it's moments like these that make me wonder if he's real. Someone or something had to create this, right? I know I'm the one who put Scout's hands on me but the feel of her holding me is doing stuff to me I don't want it to be doing. Her glove slides across my coat and over my fast-beating heart. Is she trying to feel what she's doing to me? Then she does something that causes me to tremble. Maybe she doesn't think I can feel it, but the three small taps I feel through both my coat and her glove over my chest are obvious. The power it holds over me is clearly distracting because I don't see the snowplow that's coming at us head on. When I swerve to miss it, we go rolling off trail and down the hill. The first thing I notice when we crash is Scout's hands leaving my sides. Then the sudden shock of whiplash hurts my neck when I crank it back to see if she's okay. I don't have time to see her when my body rolls against the crunchy snow. I stop myself from rolling and slide to a standing position. My eyes immediately land on Scout laying in the snow. An unknown feeling of panic floods through me when she's not moving. A feeling I've never felt before.

"Scout!" I yell as I sprint the twenty yards down to her.

She turns her head toward me and I've never been so relieved in my life to see a person move. I try to hold myself together so that she doesn't realize how fucking worried I was two seconds ago. When I get to her, I search her face and body to find any possible form of injury. Then she does something only Scout would do -- she smiles. Then she laughs as she stays in the snow. I hate that the most beautiful creature ever created had to be Scout. I look down at her, my shadow covering her face as she looks up at me through her helmet with snow in her eyelashes.

"Are you hurt?" I ask.

"No. That was actually a lot of fun, if I'm being honest," she says as she stands herself back up.

"Fun? You could have gotten yourself killed," I grunt.

She tilts her head while she dusts herself off. "The last I checked, you were the one driving."

"You were the one distracting me though." I begin walking down the hill to retrieve the snowmobile and she follows behind me all huffy and puffy.

"Distracting you how exactly?" she asks.

I turn to look at her. "The way you were touching me. The way you just told me you– forget it."

She closes her eyes at my words, and I know for a fact that I'm right. *She* knows that I'm right.

"What James?" she asks, playing stupid. "I was just holding on like you made me do."

If I didn't know she was such a damned good liar, I'd almost believe her. "If you want to pretend that you're not messing with my heart again, then fine. Right now, I need you to walk back up the hill so it's easier to drive the snowmobile. It will be too hard to drive up the steep hill with you on the back."

"Fine then," she says and does what she's told, turning around to walk back up to the trail.

Feeling frustrated, I finally get the snowmobile rolled back over and started when Will and Harper pull up at the top of the hill. When I speed up to the trail, Scout is standing next to them.

"You okay man?" Will asks after I turn off the key. "Scout told us you rolled the machine."

Yeah, because of her. "I'm fine."

"Good. We found some nice-looking trees up here. Want to go check them out?"

"Yeah, let's do it!" Scout says, sitting behind me again.

We follow Will and Harper as they show us the way and I'm thankful Scout keeps her hands lower this time. Off my chest.

As soon as we stop the machines, Scout gets off and starts looking for a tree herself. She always takes everything so seriously. It's one of those things that drive me absolutely crazy about her but also makes me love her that much more. But I immediately shake it off and try my best to ignore her, searching for a tree in the opposite direction.

I find myself a Charlie Browner because honestly, I don't care what my tree looks like. The tree will be lucky if it even gets decorated. Then I find a small, full tree and cut it down too.

"You're getting two Christmas trees?" Will shouts while he cuts Scout's tree for her after cutting down his and Harper's.

"Yep," I say.

Scout's excited energy radiates off her as we tie the Christmas trees behind us on ropes.

Then she suddenly says, "Oh no! We forgot the hot chocolate."

"No, we didn't," Harper says, "Jameson brought the thermos and reminded us to get the cups." She walks toward my snowmobile where I left the hot chocolate in the compartment underneath the backseat.

Scout turns my way, but I can't watch her when she gives me that look. She knows damn well the hot chocolate was always most important to her, which, in turn made it important to me.

I pour the hot chocolate into cups and Scout drinks hers while sitting on the snowmobile. Then leaning up against a tree to talk to Will, I try like hell to keep myself from stealing too many glances at Scout and how happy she looks.

"You coming to the game tomorrow?" Will knocks me out of my trance.

"Yeah. I'll be there. What time?"

"Seven," Will answers.

Guys night is the only night I don't have to worry about running into Scout. I hate to admit it's now turning into my least favorite day of the week. As much as I've said how much I hate the fact that Scout came back, being near her is better than not at all. That's why I don't want her to move. Just the thought of never being able to see her hurts my chest. I have to know if what she did by tapping on my chest three times is true. I flashback to when she told me she doesn't love me and realize she didn't say that at all. Her exact words were "I *can't* love you anymore." She never said she doesn't love me anymore. They sound the same but are completely different. How did I not figure that out before?

As we drive back down the mountain, I can't help but hope that those three taps didn't mean what I think they mean. If so, Scout has more power over me than I ever even imagined could be possible. Because although I'm hoping the three taps on my heart didn't mean *I love you*, I'm also hoping more than anything that they did.

Chapter Thirty-Five

Jameson

I've found out a whole lot of nothing and it's almost been a month. I know by the mark that was on Scout's cheek that someone hit her. I'm not wrong. But I've talked to everyone, and nobody has seen her with anyone else. She's never going to tell me the truth either, and the frustration is not going away.

After the long day I had driving back and forth for work, I'm exhausted. I pull up to my house at six o'clock and my neighbor Lottie is outside her door. She's an older woman that lives alone after her husband died last year. She likes to use me as a handyman, but I don't mind. She's constantly baking things for me and lecturing me. But I've grown to really like Lottie. And for some reason she's really grown to like me.

I wave. "Hi Lottie."

"You could be coming home to a nice young woman you know? If you wouldn't have let her go," she says, sitting on her front porch.

She could be referring to Ava, but I know she's talking about Scout.

"Women are complicated," I say, pulling out my keys to unlock my front door.

"A good, complicated woman is worth fighting for. I saw the way you were around Scout. I know what a man looks like when he's in love. I expected the two of you to get married. You're too handsome and kind to be alone, that's all I'm saying."

Lottie is so blunt. This isn't the first time she's brought up Scout but she's the last thing I want to talk about right now. It was a long ass day thinking about her. I wish I had a little more self-control around her. I shouldn't be alone with her again, that's for damn sure.

"What are you doing sitting in the cold?" I ask Lottie, changing the subject.

"Waiting for you. I wanted to say thanks for my Christmas tree."

"How'd you know it was me?" I ask.

"Because you're the only gentleman in my life now. I still can't believe you're Frank Karter's boy. Now come inside and warm up. I baked you some chocolate chip cookies."

I chuckle. "Okay, Lottie."

After eating a cookie with Lottie and shoveling her front sidewalk, I head to Red's bar for guy's night. It has numerous large screens with all different sports playing and the best tap beer in Wood Lake.

Will, Rafe, and Bond are seated at the bar with their eyes glued to the game. Rafe is the only one that has to drive from the city, but he doesn't mind. He loves football just as much as my brother and I do. Or maybe it's the beer he loves, but whatever it is he never lets the hour drive stop him from joining us on guy's night. My day gets a little better when I see the score and that the Bengals are winning. It's a close game.

After sitting down, the bartender hands me my regular drink and I tell her thanks before taking a swig of the cold beer that covers my tongue like a smooth blanket.

"Long day?" Will asks.

"Long *month*," I answer.

"Did you ever find out what happened to Scout?" he asks. I even grilled my own brother and his wife about who hurt her. They don't know a thing.

"Not a clue."

As soon as Rafe clears his throat, my eyes are on him. "What do you know?" I ask.

He takes a drink before answering me. I know a hell of a lot about body language and the way he's glancing his eyes around while he procrastinates makes him look suspicious as fuck.

He doesn't look at me when he says, "I already told you when you questioned me at my apartment days ago that I don't know anything. I want to find the bastard just as much as you do. Trust me."

I want to believe him, but I don't think I do. "You sure about that?"

Bond gets up and stands next to me before patting me on the shoulder. "Re-the-hell-lax. It's guy's night. We're off the clock."

I look back at Rafe knowing damn well I'm not done with him, but I don't want to be the asshole that ruins a guy's night. "Sorry man. Like I said, it's been a long week." Then I order him another drink.

And then another.

⚜

I offered Rafe a ride home since he's clearly had too much to drink -- thanks to me. I decided maybe a little alcohol will get him to open up about what he knows. From what I remember, he's always been an honest drunk.

After bullshitting on the drive to the city in my truck, we're almost there when I finally ask, "So, you're worried about Scout too, huh?"

It might as well be daylight from the city lights shining on him through the window. I'm able to really see him which is good, so I can read him and know if he's lying. He leans his head back against the seat and looks over at me. "Yeah, but I'm not supposed to be talking to you about it. Like at all."

I should have known. "Yeah, I get it. But don't worry, I already figured out who hit her," I lie.

As if he forgot about our conversation at the bar, relief crosses his face as he sits straight up in his seat. "What kind of brother does that to his own sister?"

Her *brother.* Scout hates her brother, and I never pressed her enough to find out why. Every time I brought him up, something in her shut off completely. I loosen my grip on the steering wheel and take a breath before I crash from the anger radiating through me.

Rafe goes on saying, "I could punch the guy if I see him again. Scout's terrified of him. They have some serious family issues, and she won't go into any detail about it."

All I can think about is that it was her brother that hit her and how badly I want to kill him.

"So, are you going to go to Seattle to beat his ass or what?" Rafe asks.

Seattle?

"What's her brother's name?" I ask.

Rafe squints his eyes as he tries to think. "I don't know. She never said his name."

I park the truck when we get to Rafe's apartment. "Is there anything else you know that I should?" I ask.

"He drives a black Ferrari," he says, and the familiar car instantly comes to mind. The one I saw parked outside my house the day I caught Scout with another man. *Holy shit.* As Rafe climbs out of my truck I say, "Alright, thanks man. I'll see you next week."

"See ya," he says before stumbling up his steps to his apartment.

After making sure he gets inside safely, I drive away knowing damn well I'm not getting any sleep tonight.

I've been doing my research wrong all along, digging into the people Scout knows and loves when I realize that the person I really should be digging into is *her.*

Chapter Thirty-Six

Scout

Even though I'm not feeling in the Christmas spirit tonight, I put on my long-sleeved black dress with a square neckline. The long, form fitting garment hugs my body. Harper's parents are throwing a party like they do every year on Christmas Eve. And there was no getting out of it. In the hallway mirror, I apply a little more lipstick before sticking the tube in my purse.

The doorbell rings. Fear shouldn't keep me from answering the damn door. I'm a grown woman for crying out loud. But my high heels stay glued to the floor as I stare at the closed door. The bell rings again followed by a knock. I guess I'm not going to be able to ignore it. When I look through the peephole, I see James standing in the doorway with his hands in his pockets.

I take a deep breath before answering.

"James you shouldn't be here," I say, taking in the familiar, natural scent of him as the door opens. It makes my head spin a little, but I close my eyes to compose myself and try to stop myself from missing even the smell of him.

"Which one of us said 'I love you' first?" he asks.

I think back to the night of his birthday party, when he told me he loved me for the first time after making love to me.

"You did," I say, feeling like there's something lodged in the back of my throat.

"No. It wasn't."

What is he doing?

"James, you're making this so much harder on the both of us. You can't be here saying these kinds of things."

"You said it first," he says fiercely. His hand grips the door frame above his head.

"Why are you doing this?"

He ignores my question. "We were laying in your bed on my birthday and even though I was ready to tell you, I was waiting for you to say it first. But you weren't mentally ready to say it out loud so instead you tapped your hand over my heart three times. I knew exactly what it meant then, when you randomly did it while we were together, and what it meant the other day on the snowmobile. What it means *now*."

I never once told James that's what I was doing. But the fact that he could feel that I loved him sends shivers down my spine. He's right. I loved him and I was way too scared to tell him that night. Then guilt bites at me when I realize what that must have done to him the other day. I don't know what I was thinking. It was more instinct than anything. Being around Jameson makes it absolutely impossible not to love him.

"Admit it," he says. "I need to hear you say it."

"Fine. I love you!" I yell. "I've never stopped loving you James, is that what you want to hear?"

"Yes," he says, his voice calmer now.

My heart dances and I can't make it stop. "What are you doing here?"

"I know who you are," he says so fiercely that I feel my stomach drop.

"Of course you know who I am." I'm trying my best to play it cool. But I'm so worried he actually knows something that I'm starting to shake. I'm scared. "I'm going to be late for the party. I have to get going."

I walk around him and out the front door when he says, "Della Whitlock."

I freeze in my tracks at the sound of that name rolling off Jameson's tongue. The name that's been long forgotten. The girl I never want to be again. I want to lie. I need to lie. But Jameson clearly has figured out who I am. I'm caught. I don't know whether to feel relieved or terrified. I guess I feel both. I close my eyes, not knowing what to say. Instead of having this conversation, I begin storming off toward my car in the driveway, get in and turn on the engine. I back out of the driveway, knowing Jameson is watching me leave. But I don't look his way as I drive off.

I'm still shaking when Harper pulls me in for a hug at the Christmas party. "You made it," she says.

I nod and Harper studies me. "Are you okay?"

I smile. "I'm good. Thanks for inviting me."

The house is warm and Christmas music plays quietly as dozens of people from Wood Lake stand around talking among themselves.

"Scout! We're so happy you're here. You could have brought a date," Harper's mom says, holding out a tray of fudge.

"I wouldn't miss it," I tell her. The milk chocolate fudge melts in my mouth when I take a bite. "This is delicious."

Harper takes me by the arm and drags me off to meet some of her co-workers. I'm trying to be friendly but I know that I'm more quiet tonight than usual. All I can think about is James abruptly showing up to my house, and the way he called me *Della Whitlock*.

I wonder what he knows. I'm sure he's furious with me for lying, again. I can't imagine how he must feel. My stomach is in knots.

"I need a drink," I tell Harper.

"Good idea," she says. "The bar is this way."

I follow Harper toward the kitchen where they have a beverage menu and bartender. *Thank God.* But when I see Jameson standing next to Will with their backs turned from us, I stop walking.

Harper looks back at me. "Don't you want a drink?" she asks.

That's when Jameson turns around to look at me. When my eyes meet his, they're lit up with a warm understanding. I expected him to be angry. I look away, confusion racking my mind when I ask for a sour amaretto. Harper says something to me, and I feel so distraught that I can't even make out her words. All I'm focused on is James as he starts to walk away. I try not to make it too obvious that I'm watching him go out the back door. I sit down on a bar stool next to Harper and cross my legs, my conscious telling me I shouldn't follow him. I definitely shouldn't follow him. My foot twitches as I keep glancing at the backdoor, waiting for James to come back in. My eyes wander the room. Everyone is distracted eating, drinking, or playing games. Including Harper, who is now in deep conversation with Will. It's risky but after gulping down my drink, I realize my mind is made up, and I'm headed to the back door.

It's dark when I step outside and look around to find James. I hear the horses neighing and follow the sound, hoping James is there. Surprisingly, today was a warmer than usual winter day so most of the snow has melted. And it's raining. The warm winter night will probably bring a snowy blizzard tomorrow. I'm just glad I don't have to walk through deep snow in my heels and dress, because if it's to get to James, I would.

"James?" I say quietly.

I'm walking past the barn when I see him leaning up against the red doors.

He examines me and I can read the expression on his face. He *knows*.

"How did you–"

"It didn't take much to figure out you changed your name. Why I never thought of it before until now, I don't know. But I know who you are. I know Ethan Whitlock is your brother and that's who I saw you with that day in our house, the day you left. You never cheated on me. I also know he's the one who hurt you. I know about your family's company. And that your brother is part owner of a strip club that makes way more money than any other strip club in Seattle. So much money that I did some digging. I'm confident that he's involved in money laundering, and most likely, drugs. And I know how much power they clearly have -- even over you."

My voice shakes as the words try to come out. "Th-they will come after you."

He laughs at my concern, "They're the ones that should be worried. They laid their hands on you."

I stare at him. "No James. Promise me you won't do anything. They're bad men. I need to leave. I should've never come back and put you in danger."

"Scout, you're not going anywhere," he says.

"I got involved with them and this is now what I must do to pay for it. I never wanted to lose you. But I had to. And I thought somehow coming back to Wood Lake, just even having a sliver of you would be enough. I know I said the reason for coming back was for my contract, but I probably could have gotten out of it. I realize now what I really wanted was to be near you, even if you hated me. Even if that meant only looking at you from a distance. I tried to stay away. But gravity somehow pulled me back to you and now you have it all figured out. James, don't you understand how bad this is? I have to leave. Tonight."

I turn to walk away and James pushes me up against the barn doors and covers my mouth with his hand. "Shhh," he whispers.

Then he slides his finger down my mouth, pulling my lip with it as he stares at me. Without thinking about it, I let Jameson kiss me. As soon as our lips touch, our love takes control as we forget every last obstruction between us that ever existed. I hum at the feel of his lips, the familiar way he brushes his tongue up against mine and the way he takes me in like he never thought he would again. He pulls apart, looking down at me. His blue eyes darken as they look at me full of much more than want. "I need you," he says.

I grab him by the shirt, pulling his mouth back to mine. He doesn't stop me as I frantically kiss him. Jameson reaches behind me and pushes the barn doors open and we slip inside, our lips never coming apart. The barn is empty except for the stall with Taffy in it. The rain is pouring down harder now, making a lot of noise on the tin roof. It's dirty in here yet this moment feels incredibly romantic.

"What if we get caught?" I ask.

"We won't." He says while kissing my neck.

Chills rack my body. "But what if we do, what will we say?"

He looks me dead in the eyes and cups the side of my face. "Scout, if we get caught, I'll say whatever you need me to say. I'll lie. I'll protect you baby. But right now, I really need to make love to you in this barn."

He looks at me like he's waiting on me for the signal to keep going. The need for him is much stronger than the will to stop but I really love seeing him like this. Like he's a starving predator and I'm his prey. Chewing on my bottom lip, he backs me up until I'm leaning up against the pile of hay. I let out a breath as he blocks me in with his arms, his hands on each side of me.

He says, "If you want me to stop, I'll stop. But please, for the love of God, don't ask me to."

"But–" I begin to say.

"But nothing," he says, "I love you."

I never thought I'd hear him say those words again. I want to hold onto them forever. "I lied to you. I hurt you. I destroyed us."

He's looking at me like he truly sees me now. "I know. But now I know you did all of it out of love."

I take in a breath. My head leans back against the straw when Jameson's mouth meets mine full of hunger. I gasp as he yanks my dress up over my hips. His eyes flare with desire before he kisses me over and over again. His fingers graze the outside of my panties before he tugs them down. He kneels in front of me, slipping my panties off my ankles but making sure to keep my heels on. When he stands back up, I unbutton his dress pants wildly and he picks me up and pushes against my entrance with his hard cock. My mouth gapes open with a moan as he gently slides himself inside of me. When I'm completely full of him, the shock of how good he feels causes me to cry out, "James!"

James groans. "You're so tight, Scout."

It's too difficult to stay quiet as James begins pumping himself in and out of me. My moans get louder as I feel myself letting go quickly.

"James!" I cry before he stifles my screams by covering my mouth with his hand. He buries his face into my chest and my hands run through his hair. My eyes shut as I throw my head back, moaning hard against the palm of his hand. Before I'm about to come, James says, "Open your eyes." When my eyes open James is looking so deeply at me and it's so beautifully raw and true. There are no more lies between us. As soon as

I start to come apart against the haystack, his eyes stay on mine as we finish together.

James sets me down, kissing me softly. Then being the gentleman he is, James finds my panties and helps me step back into them before pulling my dress back down.

Panic starts to set in when I realize how dangerous this is, Jameson knowing all of this and what could happen.

I don't know how he knows but he instantly responds to how I'm feeling and pulls me into him, stopping the panic attack. "Everything will be okay."

Even though I still feel unsure of all of this, I trust James.

"Nobody can know about this. Not even Will and Harper. We have to keep us a secret. And whenever you come over, you have to go through the garage. The code is your birthday."

James nods with a grin. "Anything else?"

"Promise me you won't do anything to fix this without talking to me first.

"Okay. I promise."

"We better get back inside before anyone suspects any-thing," I tell him.

He says, "You go back in first. I'll wait a few minutes," he says before pressing his lips to mine one more time.

I stop and pet Harper's horse, Taffy on the way out. When I get back inside the house, I casually get myself a drink from the kitchen and I'm relieved when everyone seems to be too busy with festivities to even know I was gone. After loading my plate up with appetizers and all kinds of finger foods, I join Harper on the couch.

"Hey," Harper says as I plop down next to her. "Oh, good. You got some food."

Will comes up behind us and rests his forearms on the back of the couch. "Have you guys seen Jameson? I think he might have left already."

Being the experienced liar I am, I say no and so does Harper.

"Is that straw in your hair?" Will asks and I immediately grab the back of my head to feel what he's talking about.

"Probably," I say. "I went out to say hi to Taffy."

"Of course, you did." Harper smiles at me before looking at her husband. "Are you about ready to go? I'm exhausted."

"Whenever you are," Will says.

When I dump my plate in the trash, I spot James. He's eating fudge as he talks with Harper's dad in the kitchen.

We say our goodbyes and I thank Harper's parents for inviting me. It looks like Jameson is leaving too. He glances at me, and I wink at him before getting into my car. All I can think about right now is how good it feels to be loved by Jameson Karter again. And how I'm going to love him with everything I have.

Chapter Thirty-Seven

Scout

After changing out of my black dress and into fleece pajama bottoms and a t-shirt, I turn on "The Grinch" before making hot chocolate and popcorn. I heard Will and Harper invite James over, so I assume he's over there to spend Christmas with them. After taking my buttery popcorn bag out of the microwave, I check my phone just as I hear a knock on the garage door. I smile because the only person knocking on the garage door would be James since I gave him the code earlier. When I swing it open, he stands with a crooked smile, his hands in his pockets.

"You're here," I say excitedly. "I wasn't expecting you tonight."

He pulls me into his strong arms. His corduroy coat smells like his cologne, and I bury my nose in his chest. "You smell so good."

He chuckles. "What do I smell like?"

I smile, "Like you. I just can't believe you're here."

"Nowhere else I'd rather be," he says. "I smell popcorn and hear "The Grinch" so let's get this party started."

We hardly watch the movie while it plays since we have a lot to catch up on.

I tell him all about Hawaii and he tells me how much he loves being a U.S Marshal. Then we begin to reminisce. "Remember that time when Will and you made that bet about who could drink a whole carton of eggnog first?"

James laughs. "I remember kicking his ass."

"I felt so bad when he almost threw up." I giggle.

"The loser had to wear their girlfriends' pajamas the whole Christmas day. I'll never forget the look on Harper's dad's face when he came in for Christmas brunch to see Will wearing his daughter's pink tank top and matching shorts."

Still laughing, I stand up to get myself some water when I wince at the pain in my ankle. It was almost healed and now it's sore again.

"Are you okay?" James asks.

"Yeah, it's just my ankle. Maybe wearing high heels tonight was a bad idea," I tell him.

James gets up and says, "I have an idea, I'll be right back."

I can't help but smile at him and how sweet he is when I hear what he's doing for me. He comes back out and I squeal as he scoops me off the couch to carry me to the bathroom where he's running a bath.

He sets me down. "This is perfect," I say.

"A bath might help," he says. I'm going to let you get in and I'll get you a drink."

After he walks out, I quickly undress and step into the warm and bubbly bath water. I let my body relax and James walks back in the bathroom with a glass of wine.

I smile. "Thanks, this feels amazing."

I turn off the faucet when the tub is completely full. I feel James watching me as I lean back to wet my hair. I lather it with shampoo and rinse it out. Then I glance up at James who looks way too good with his white button up shirt rolled up his forearms and his back against the wall.

"What's on your mind?" I ask.

He rubs his scruffy chin as he thinks. "I'm thinking about how hard your life must have been if you had to run away and change your name at such a young age."

I think about how good it feels that he knows the truth. And I'm relieved that I can finally talk to him about it. "Scout was my middle name. I just took Della out."

"Did you do it because you were hiding from someone? Or because you didn't want to be Della anymore?" he asks.

"Both I guess." James listens carefully as I speak.

"And the last name Addison?" he asks.

"It's my mother's maiden name," I explain. "There were so many times that I wanted to open up to you about things, but I just didn't know how. I was literally running from my past, afraid more than anything that it would come back. And everything was perfect the whole time I was loving you. Until JC found out I was dating a police officer who was being promoted to a U.S Marshal."

"JC?" James asks.

I nod. "I guess he and Ethan thought that I would rat them out. That's when Ethan came over that day and we broke up. He had a gun and told me he'd shoot you if I didn't go with his story. I knew what I had to do to keep you safe. It was the hardest day of my life leaving you that way."

Jameson shifts his body as he continues to listen. I run my hands over the bubbly white foam in the bath. This isn't easy to talk about, but I want him to know everything.

"I was really young when my mom became a drug addict. There was a time when we were close but then she just stopped being there for me. My relationship with my dad was okay. He always treated me well and ended up being the one to support me more than my mom. But things changed when I started to realize he wasn't doing anything to get my mom help. He enabled her and things got worse. He wouldn't even get her to rehab when she ended up in the hospital one night. She could've died."

"Shit," James whispers.

"But that wasn't what made me run away." I swallow as I think about what I'm about to tell him next.

Tears start to fall, reliving that night as I tell Jameson everything.

I don't know when he got into the tub, but I lean into him and let him hold me. "I'm so sorry, Scout. That never should have happened to you," he says.

I let out a breath. "It's okay. It *almost* happened."

He holds me tightly. "Don't downplay what happened to you. It clearly hurt you. They hurt you. Including your own mother."

I cry because it feels good to hear someone say that. "I've always felt a little guilty feeling so horrible about it," I say, feeling James hold me tighter. "It could have been so much worse. They could have killed me. And here I am crying."

James tilts my head back to look at him. He leans in close. "Listen to me. They assaulted you. Your feelings are more than fucking earned and valid. Don't ever feel like you shouldn't feel a certain way about it Scout, do you hear me?"

He's right. "I didn't realize how badly I needed to hear those words," I admit.

James sits back again and kisses the side of my face tenderly.

"That night I left and never looked back," I say.

"You're so brave," he says. "And you opening up to me only makes me love you even more, if that's possible."

"I love you too."

James reaches to the side of me to grab the bottle of shampoo. I hear him open the lid behind me before his hands begin rubbing my head. He's washing my hair, even though I know he just watched me do it myself. My heart wants to burst as he slowly massages the shampoo into my scalp. He's taking care of me, more than anyone ever has before.

"I hate to ask this," he says. "But I need to know. That day Ethan hurt you, was JC with him?"

"No. He just sends Ethan to threaten me."

Jameson's breathing is rapid, but he remains calm behind me. "He threatens you?"

I nod.

"Mother fucker," he mumbles. I can feel him trembling as he holds me, so I place my hand on his leg when I realize he's still wearing pants. "You didn't even take off your clothes before getting in the bath?"

"Didn't think about it." He pulls me closer to him and presses his cheek up against my face. "Thank you for telling me."

"Thanks for listening."

My heart rate slows down as he holds me. I've always felt so safe with him. That's what makes him so different from everyone else I've ever been with. I learned the hard way with JC and other relationships in the past. I believe a man should make a woman feel safe, period. If he doesn't, you shouldn't be with him.

Chapter Thirty-Eight

Jameson

Scout wakes me up with a scream. Her face is flushed as I brush a strand of hair off her forehead. "Scout, wake up, you're having a nightmare."

Her breathing is heavy as she opens her eyes. "I got you," I say, grabbing her waist. I can't imagine going through the things she's been through. "It's going to be okay."

She immediately sits up when she's aware of what just happened. "James, I'm so sorry."

"Don't ever be sorry," I tell her.

She looks over her shoulder at me with swollen eyes. "You deserve better. I'm so complicated. You could be with anyone else, and it'd be easier."

"Who ever said I wanted easy?" I ask. She turns away.

"Look at me." Her glossy green eyes land on mine and I say, "Every problem that you have is now mine. You will not do anything alone. Not anymore. Promise me."

A smile forms on her full lips and I never want her to stop smiling. "I promise."

Then she chews on her bottom lip as she swings her leg over and sits up on top of me. She takes off her shirt, her eyes never leaving mine. I'm the luckiest man alive. She's so fucking perfect. The thought of how good she felt last night makes my body ache for more of her. I'll never have enough of her. I flip her over on her back. Anticipation is written all over her flushed face and the way her chest rises and falls when I move up her body is so beautiful.

I want to make love to the woman who shattered my heart and then made it whole again.

Scout

As soon as Jameson's firm body presses me up against the mattress, I moan. He pushes himself off me and holds himself over me with his forearms. He removes my shorts and panties and I arch my back, my hardened nipples pressing to his chest. Grabbing his hair, I feel desperate for all of him again. All at once. But he seems hesitant. Maybe he regrets this.

"Scout, it's taking all my strength to keep myself off you. But I want to savor you this time," he says, his eyes skim down my body, sending shivers down my spine.

I run my hands through his sandy blonde hair and a smile tugs at my lips. "Okay."

His lips brush up against my cheek. "God, you're beautiful."

I smile even wider.

He looks down at my mouth. "Have I ever told you that I love how your bottom lip is slightly bigger on one side?"

I cover my lips with my hand. "I've always hated that."

He smiles at me. "You have an insecurity? That's so hot."

I half laugh. "You can't be serious."

"I'm obsessed. Do you have any more?" he asks.

"Too many," I answer honestly.

"Well now that I know that you have insecurities, I'm going to discover each one. And when I do, I'll make them my favorite parts about you."

Butterflies swarm my stomach. I've never felt more beautiful to someone. He looks down at me with so much care in his eyes. I feel it burn straight through me.

"I missed you," I say.

"I've missed every little thing about you," he whispers in my ear, causing my lips to part. "I've missed that humming sound you make when we first kiss." His lips brush my ear lobe. He kisses right below my ear, right at the crease of my jaw.

"How shaky your breathing gets when I kiss your neck." As soon as his lips hit my neck, I feel my breath tremble.

"How it gets even more shaky, the further my mouth goes down your body." His tongue rolls down to my chest as I feel my whole body shake. He teases my nipples as he circles them with his tongue. "I've missed how you try and hide yourself around everyone but as soon as we're alone in bed, your eagerness comes out to show me all of you." The heat of his hands slides down each side of me as his mouth continues getting lower. The anticipation is causing my head to spin. "How soft your skin feels," he continues, "especially right here." His finger tickles the inside of my thigh before his lips gently touch the sensitive area on my leg. His tongue slides up against my legs and I grip onto the sheets of the bed.

"James," I whimper desperately. I spread my thighs, wanting more. He continues kissing the inside of my legs and I feel myself getting more desperate.

He keeps his head down, shifting his eyes so that he can look up at me when he says, "I missed the way you taste."

My teeth are digging into my bottom lip, and I feel him smile against my thigh. I gasp with a moan when he gently takes his two fingers and pushes them inside me. My moans grow louder as he goes in and out hitting the perfect spot. Just when I'm about to come, he stops. Then he pulls his fingers out and puts them in his mouth. Jameson is sucking my juices off his fingers and I'm pretty sure it's the sexiest thing I've ever seen. My pussy floods when he brings his mouth down between my legs and circles his tongue around my clit. At the same time his fingers go back inside of me and I come hard.

Then he brings his face up to mine and looks at me full of even more hunger than before.

"I'm not done with you," he says as my legs still shake beneath me.

He slides deep inside of me. I feel my eyes roll back with pleasure. His thrusts are hard and fast as he continues to plunge in and out of me, staying in the perfect rhythm.

I come long and hard before he finishes too.

"So much for savoring," he says.

I laugh. "We'll have plenty of time for that."

I can feel Jameson's heart beating fast with mine. His arms are wrapped around me as I lay on top of him. This feels better than the sex. Neither one of us wants to move as we stay cuddled up in my bed.

"What are you thinking about?" James asks.

I sit up and rest my chin on my forearm to look at him. "I'm thinking about how excited my students probably are that Santa came this morning."

He smiles. "Did you believe in Santa as a kid?"

"Of course, I did. Didn't you?"

"I think I did at one point. My aunt would send gifts for my father to put under the tree from Santa. Sometimes my dad would even say a couple were from him although I'm not sure they were. But I loved that he actually bought me a present more than I even cared about Santa bringing any. One year when I was about eight and Will was six, there were no presents under the tree and my dad wasn't home. That's when Will realized Santa wasn't real and he was heartbroken. I was more upset that my dad wasn't there. I couldn't care less about Santa. But Will was so sad that I found two old cookie sheets that morning and quickly wrapped them up and stuck them under the tree. I waited for Will to find them, and he was so happy Santa actually came. When we opened the gifts, I told them they were the fastest sleds that were ever made. We went sledding on those cookie sheets every year after that. And I always made sure Will and I had something from Santa."

I'm pretty sure my heart just grew three sizes, just like the Grinch. "You were Santa at eight years old? That's the sweetest thing I've ever heard."

He blushes and I never want to forget this image of him.

"Did your family have traditions when you were a kid?" he asks.

"My mom would take me ice skating every year until I was twelve. That must've been when she started using. Since my family was wealthy, they always made sure there were plenty of gifts under the tree. And even though my mom wasn't exactly present, that was the only time I ever felt at peace with my family. I guess that's why I let my mom convince me to fly home my first year in college."

James tickles my back with his fingertips. "Wait really? You spent Christmas with your family while you were living in Ohio?"

"Yeah, before I even met you. My mom promised me that Ethan wouldn't be there but when I showed up to Tilly's restaurant, I found my parents sitting at a table with my brother. I immediately turned around and started to walk away but my mom chased me out and said Ethan just wanted to apologize and make things right. I told her I didn't want his apology but agreed to go back inside with her. Ethan kept trying to have a conversation with me and it felt strange being with them again. I was anxious and miserable. As soon as dinner was over, I left and went to the airport to fly back to Ohio."

"That's terrible," James whispers. "I wish I could have been there for you."

"Harper was."

He smiles. "Merry Christmas."

"Merry Christmas," I reply.

He gets up to find his clothes.

"Are you leaving already?" I ask.

"No. I'm going to go make us some breakfast and then I'm going to spend the whole day with my girl doing whatever you want to do," he says.

I quickly sit up in the bed while James throws on his pants.

"I'll go get ready."

After breakfast, James says, "I have something for you. Under the tree."

Feeling confused, since we literally had no time to get each other presents, I stand up and see the tiny box wrapped perfectly underneath the Christmas tree.

"When did you get me a present?"

"It was supposed to be for your birthday in July. I've been holding onto it," he says.

When I open the small box, I gasp at the dainty silver pendant necklace with three engraved hearts.

"James, it's perfect." He comes up behind me to help me put it on.

After we snuggle up and watch another Christmas movie, I talk James into going sledding on cookie sheets.

Chapter Thirty-Nine

Jameson

I t's so hard to leave Scout this morning. After everything she told me on Christmas Eve, I haven't wanted to leave her sight just in case Ethan shows up. Between having an addict for a mother, a father who doesn't care about anything but his business, and an abusive brother, it's no wonder she has a hard time opening up. I'm keeping a lot of emotions in about it since it's time for Scout to let hers out. I'll be pissed about it on my own time, when she can't see me.

"James," Scout says as I hesitate by the door before saying goodbye. "I'm fine. You're going to be late for work. I'll see you tonight."

"Okay, call me if you need me," I tell her.

"I will," she says as I give her a kiss before walking out into the garage and to my truck.

On my way to work I come up with about fifty different ways to kill Ethan and JC and get away with it. If either one of them ever get near Scout again, I'll snap their fucking necks. No, death would be too easy. I want to watch them rot in a prison cell for the rest of their worthless lives. Scout made me promise I wouldn't do anything without talking to her first, but I'll be digging and fighting like hell to put them exactly where I want them. But the most important thing to me right now is keeping Scout safe.

Scout

James shows up at my house right when he says he would. "I'm taking you on a date."

"We can't go on a date. What if someone sees us?" I ask hesitantly.

"You don't need to worry. It's a secret spot hardly anyone knows about. Plus, it will be dark once we get there."

"Okay. Where are you taking me?" I ask.

"It's a surprise. Get some warm clothes and snow boots on."

After an hour drive out of Wood Lake into another secluded town I've never been to before, Jameson parks his truck in a random spot on the side of the road next to thick trees and another vehicle. We climb out of Jameson's truck and step out into the cold winter evening. I look at the white car next to us and notice nobody is inside. "You're right. Nobody will find us in the middle of nowhere."

James laughs. "Yeah, there isn't much here. Except for what I'm about to show you." He swings a backpack over his shoulder.

"And how come you've never taken me here before?" I ask.

"I only heard about it a few months ago. Someone from the gym told me about it and gave me the directions. I've never been here either."

"Cool, I'm excited," I say, as we begin walking up a trail between the trees.

"I think this is the right way," James says.

It's refreshing having a person who loves adventures just as much as me. He holds my hand, and I'm relieved nobody is around to worry about seeing us.

"Wait, did you bring me here to kill me?" I tease.

He turns around to face me with a smile. "You listen to way too many true crime podcasts."

I'm laughing because it's the truth. "It's good to be cautious. But you have to admit, I put you through a lot."

"You are a pain in my ass," he says. I squeal when he throws me over his shoulder. "Here's your punishment." He spanks my ass before plopping me down on my back into the soft snow.

He falls down with me. I love the way Jameson's face lights up when he makes me laugh.

"I needed this," I say, touching the side of his cold, rosy cheek.

"Me too," he says. Then he picks himself up and holds out his hand to help me up. "We better get going. We have three miles to walk."

"Three miles? This place better be worth it," I say as he pulls me up.

"Says the girl who wakes up at five am to run ten miles voluntarily."

We begin walking toward some trees in the distance and the view takes my breath away. The snow fall from last night is coated all over the trees as we walk next to a creek of running water in the field.

"How's your ankle?" he asks. "I can give you a piggyback ride if it's bothering you."

"It really doesn't hurt at all today. I think I can start running again."

"Oh good. You're moody when you don't run."

"I am not!" I laugh.

"You are and you know it," he says looking back at me with a crooked smile.

"Maybe a little," I admit.

Suddenly we hear voices coming toward us in the distance. I contemplate running out into the trees to hide but pull my hood over my head and zip up my coat so it's covering my nose.

It's three women walking toward us and they all wave. One of them says, "Keep going. It's phenomenal."

Excitement overcomes me as we continue walking along a trail of snow from human footprints. I don't mind the view of James' backside in front of me.

"I brought headlamps if we need them, but the moon is so bright, I don't think we will."

The full moon begins coming out as darkness consumes the sky and specks of bright stars appear. It's a clear night and it's absolutely beautiful with all the snow. "Yeah, I can see perfectly."

I'm a little disappointed to see some fog in the distance but maybe it's not so bad to walk through.

"I think we're almost there," James says.

When James stops, I see at least four pools of water covered in fog.

"What is this?" I ask, as I get closer for a better look.

"It's a hot spring. It's all natural. You up for a swim?" he asks as he strips off his warm clothes.

My mouth drops as I look around. "I've always wanted to try this!" I say.

There is so much steam from the heat against the cold that I can't even tell if anyone else is here or not. But it's quiet enough, so I start stripping down with James.

"You could have at least told me to wear a swimsuit," I tell him as I pull down my jeans, trying not to gasp as the cold hits my exposed skin.

Jameson's eyes roam down my legs. "What's the fun of that? We're skinny dipping."

I smile. "Good idea."

I giggle as I strip out of the rest of my clothing, making sure to take off *everything*. I turn away from the hot pools, exposing my back to James as I take off my bra. I turn just in time to see his eyes roam down my body that I'm half covering with my arms since I'm trying to keep warm.

"It's freezing!" I squeal, as the winter chill bites at my raw skin.

I take the hair band from my wrist and wrap my hair up into a messy bun.

"You ready?" Jameson asks.

I nod as we hold hands to walk toward the hot water.

Jameson helps me step down into the pool and the heat tingles my cold toes. "This feels amazing," I tell him before getting all the way into the water. It's not very deep so I'm able to sit down as I feel the dirt and rock beneath me. James sits down next to me as his arm wraps around me to pull me close. We're completely alone. The moon shining down on the water is incredible as the blue creamy color of the water takes in the light.

I float on my back and try to take it all in. "This is beautiful. I can't believe this place."

"It's awesome," James says, "I'm glad we found it."

I look at James across from me. "Me too. As much fun as it is being cooped up with you, it's nice getting out of the house."

"I mean we did go cookie sheet sledding," James reminds me.

I laugh. "That was so much fun."

I should have known Jameson would have done anything for me. "I wish I would've done things differently." I tell him.

He shakes his head. "You have to stop being sorry. I forgive you. And I never said sorry for rubbing Ava in your face or for some of the hurtful things I said."

"It's okay. When Harper told me you and Ava didn't work out, I tried so hard to feel anything but happy, but I definitely was. Even though I knew that I couldn't have you either. I'm so selfish," I admit. "You deserved to be happy, and all I was thinking of was myself."

"Maybe you knew deep down that you're the only one who could truly make me happy. That's why you didn't want me to be happy with her. You knew it wouldn't be real. Not like this. Not like what we have."

I swim closer so that I'm right in front of him.

"Yeah. I like your version of my selfishness better," I say, chewing on my bottom lip. "But I want you to know that I want nothing more in this life than for you to feel happy. Even if that does mean letting me go."

He leans forward and the heat of his hand cups my cold cheek. "Learning to live without you is something I don't ever want to do again. *You* are my happy," he says. The seriousness in his voice takes my breath away.b

]]]]]]]]]

"And you're *my* happy," I say back, realizing how much that means.

James tickles my back with his fingers as he says, "You're also my angry, my sad, my excited, my frustration, my fear, my pride, my love. You're the reason I feel such strong emotions. And it's so powerful that for a while it scared the hell out of me. How I could feel so many emotions for a person. But then I realized how lucky it makes me. I don't know if everyone finds that in life, but I'm glad I did. God, Scout when I thought I lost it, it ripped me apart."

His words bury deep in my heart, the reason it skips a beat but also the reason it pulses harder. Giving it a reason to live. To love.

"If I could physically place you inside my heart, you'd be so overwhelmed with the love I have for you, you wouldn't believe it. I wish I could show you so that you'd know," I say, wishing the words coming out of my mouth sounded as powerful as they felt. They sound so weak, so trivial compared to what I truly want to express. Words can sound so meaningless when our hearts feel everything.

Even after four years, the way James looks at me still makes my stomach flutter. "You may not be able to physically place me inside your heart Scout but you're letting me in it way more than you ever have. And I feel it, believe me."

If words ever mean anything to me, they're the words that come from Jameson.

The moonlight shines bright behind James. I take my ponytail out since my hair is soaking wet now anyway. The water is so hot, I need to stand up for a break. When I get up out of the water, the flare in Jameson's eyes as he looks at my naked body catches my breath.

"Now that's a beautiful view," he says, standing up in front of me.

He pulls me in to hug him and I scrunch my nose against his.

He kisses me passionately before sliding his hands down my back and squeezes my ass. Then lifting me up, James sets me on the edge of the water. We're still kissing as I wrap my legs around him to get closer. But it still doesn't feel close enough. When I feel his erection against my thigh, I slide my hand down to feel the length of him. He lets out a breath before moving his hands up my body. His thumb brushes up against my hardened nipple and my heart rate quickens. He squeezes my breasts and I continue to stroke him. His panting speeds up with the movement of my hand.

"Scout," he whispers. He tilts his head back and groans.

James suddenly grabs my hand that's wrapped around him, stopping me.

"Does that not feel good?" I ask him.

I try and read him when his eyes shoot to mine.

"No Scout, the problem is you're going to get me off. And as good as this feels, I want to feel the clench of your sweet pussy wrapped around my cock."

Turning me on even more, my body reacts to Jameson's filthy mouth and I ache between my legs. And when he guides himself to my sensitive entrance, I moan as he pushes himself inside of me. Catching myself from falling back, I place my elbows behind me. A rock digs into my lower back but I'm too focused on the way Jameson's taking me on the side of the pool. My eyes go over his buff upper body and I brush my finger over a vein that bulges on his shoulder. *This man is gorgeous.* He thrusts harder and faster, watching me closely as he does it.

"James, yes. Oh God!" Our bodies spasm together with the release.

James helps me back down into the warm water and I giggle. "So that's what you brought me here to do?"

He presses his forehead to mine. "It wasn't the plan, but I should've known better considering I can't get enough of you."

My mouth hurts from smiling so much tonight. I squint to help my eyes adjust to the light glimmer I notice in the darkness behind James. *Are those eyes?*

"James!" I scream pointing behind him.

He quickly turns around to what I'm pointing at. "What is it?" he asks.

I look around but the eyes are no longer there. "I saw something. Eyes watching us," I say breathing heavily. James jumps out of the water and grabs his towel.

"Where?" James asks.

"Behind those bushes." After wrapping himself in his towel, James walks over to the bushes and peaks behind them. "There's nothing here," he says. "It could've just been a deer or something." Walking back over to the water James reaches for my hand to help me out. "You're safe."

I nod but still feel my body quivering. "We better get back since you have to work in the morning."

"What happened to your back? You're bleeding," he says wrapping me in my towel.

I touch the spot behind me. "That must've been from the rock digging into my back."

"Shit, why didn't you say anything?" he asks.

"I was a little focused on other things."

James chuckles. "I have a first aid kit in my truck. Let's go get you bandaged up."

He kisses my neck and I smile.

"You'd think by now you'd be sick of me."

"What do you mean?" he asks sternly.

"I just mean because we had sex this morning."

Jameson looks me dead in the eyes when he speaks. "Let's get one thing clear. I will never get sick of you Scout. I knew the night that I met you, from the moment I saw you dancing on that floor alone at that bar that you were mine and that you were always going to leave me wanting more. Now that I have you back, I'm not taking a single moment for granted. So don't you ever question if I'm sick of you, because I've experienced life without you, and I'll do everything in my power to make sure that doesn't happen again."

My bottom lip brushes up against Jameson's jaw. After that beautiful speech, I can't let him see the look on my face. Because then he might be able to tell that I'm terrified if that was someone watching us just now. What if Ethan knows and he had someone follow us?

Chapter Forty

Scout

Harper's house smells like brownies as they bake in the oven and we sit at the kitchen counter, drinking wine.

It's Friday, which means James is out with the guys. Harper and I decided to have a girls' night and paint her kitchen.

"Remember when we always used to do this when we were roommates?" I ask Harper.

"Those were the best days. I miss it so much. I miss you," she says.

"What are you talking about? You see me all the time."

"I know it's just that I can tell you've been weird about coming over here because of you know who. Sorry, I know I said we wouldn't talk about him."

James and I are still keeping our relationship a secret. We've been sneaking around for five days in a row, but he had to work late last night so I didn't get to see him. I'm still sick to my stomach with fear at the thought of Ethan finding out, but I'll hide with James forever if I have to.

"I'll try and stop being weird about coming over, I promise."

Harper smiles. "Good." She takes a big gulp of wine and looks around her kitchen. "Let's get to work."

After changing into some old shirts of Harper's, we begin our mission with our paint brushes.

"The white is going to look amazing in here."

Harper looks pleased when I tell her that. "I think so too."

"You seem happy tonight. Is it that guy from work?" Harper asks.

A smile pulls at my lips, and I can't even hide it. "Something like that."

"Well, whatever it is, I like it." Harper pours us more wine and turns on some music to dance to while we paint the walls. I'm laughing hysterically at Harper as she just fell off the stool she was dancing on, and her butt falls right into the primer.

"Are you okay?" I barely make out the words as I continue to laugh. She stays put and pouts playfully.

Then Harper jumps up when Will walks in with the guys. She wraps her arms around him for a hug.

"What the hell is all over you?" He laughs, inspecting the white paste all over her backside. She just grins and kisses him on the mouth and it's disgusting how adorable they are right now. The buzz from all the wine hits me harder when I see James.

"We're painting the kitchen," Harper tells Will.

"I can see that."

When Jameson sees me, I can tell he wants to smile but refrains. Because according to everyone else, he still hates me.

"How was the game?" I ask nobody specifically.

"It's not over," Will says. "Rafe got us kicked out of there because he wouldn't stop yelling at the Cowboy fans behind us. We're finishing the game here."

"They deserved it. They were assholes," Rafe defends himself.

"I'll never forgive you if Red doesn't let us in again," Bond says.

I'll never understand what they love about that bar and football, but I'm happy they got kicked out so that I get more time with James. Even if we do have to pretend that we aren't together.

Rafe already plopped down on the couch, flipping through the channels to find the game.

"Do you guys want to watch?" Will asks Harper and me.

Harper answers him by saying, "Scout and I have a lot of work to do. You guys have fun."

As we start painting again, I'm trying to ignore the fact that Jameson is in the next room looking good as hell. He's wearing a hoodie, jeans, and his hat is on backwards. I wish I could go sit on his lap.

I'm standing on a stool trying to reach the corner of the wall when Harper asks, "What happened to your back?"

I pull my shirt down as I feel caught off guard that she just noticed the scrape I got at the hot spring. I can't explain where I got that. I look into the living room that connects to the kitchen and James is glancing at us. He's eavesdropping. A smile forms slowly on his mouth as he gives me a sexy smirk.

I look back at Harper. "Must've scratched it somehow."

After finishing the last corner, Harper and I clean up our mess since the primer has to dry before we put on a coat of paint.

"This is going to take a lot longer than just one night to finish. But it's our project, so no doing it without me," I tell Harper.

"I was hoping you'd say that."

"Thanks for your help," she says.

Rafe walks into the kitchen during a commercial break. "Hey, are you guys still planning on coming to my party tomorrow?"

He texted all of us last week, including Bond and Jameson, inviting us to his apartment in the city for New Years' Eve.

Harper says, "We wouldn't miss it."

I smile. "Can't wait." Even though it will be a long night keeping my distance from Jameson, I'm glad we're still going to the same place on New Years'.

"Awesome. See you guys tomorrow," Rafe says.

"I'm going to change out of my mess," I tell Harper.

"Yeah, me too. I need to shower."

I laugh at how much Harper is covered in paint. "You really do. I'll probably head out when I'm done changing."

"Are you okay to drive?" she asks.

"Yeah, the wine wore off."

After retrieving my clothes from Harper's closet, I go to the guest bedroom to change. I strip off the old paint splattered clothes and pull on my jeans when James walks in quickly, shutting the door behind him.

"What are you doing?" I whisper.

But before he answers, he grabs me by the waist and kisses me deeply. His hands roam over my breasts, causing my nipples to swell beneath my padded bra.

His kiss slows down as he bites my bottom lip. I feel my lip glide between his teeth. He knows I love it when he does this so I can't help but smile slowly when he kisses me again.

"Do you want to know what's even better than seeing your smile? Being able to feel it form on my lips and tongue." He mumbles before devouring my mouth again.

I pull away from him and laugh quietly. "You're going to get us caught. You couldn't wait until you came over after the game?"

"No," he says before I let him kiss me again. I can't stop him because I don't really want to wait either and something about the thought of getting caught is exciting.

"James?" We both freeze when we hear the sound of Will's voice coming from outside the door.

I cover my mouth, trying not to laugh. "You need to go," I quietly mouth the words.

When he walks toward the bedroom door to leave, I panic and grab him before he gets us caught in here together. "Don't open the door. Will is out there," I whisper.

"Right. I'll sneak out the window and pretend I went out-side."

"Okay meet you at my place," I say before he opens the window, pops the screen out and climbs through it.

I finish getting dressed when I hear Bond's voice. "Where the hell did you go? You just missed overtime. Cleveland scored the winning touchdown."

The game is over.

Chapter Forty-One

Scout

Jameson has a smoothie ready for me when I get back from my run this morning.

"I can't tell you how amazing it feels to move my legs again."

"Good run?" he asks.

"It was great," I say before taking a drink of my smoothie. He's so good at making them now. "What time will you be at Rafe's tonight?" I ask. "I wish we could ride there together."

"Me too. I'll be there around nine, but I'll swing by with dinner first if you want."

I wrap my arms around his neck. "That sounds perfect."

His eyes devour my sweaty body before he kisses me, brushing his tongue against mine. Then he pushes me against the counter as we make out in the kitchen. If he keeps kissing me this way, I know where we'll end up. "I need to shower," I say, trying not to sound as turned on as I am.

Ignoring me, James pulls my sports bra up over my head and takes one of my breasts in his mouth. I moan. He bites down on his lip and smiles when he can tell how aroused I am.

"James, I'm all sweaty."

Jameson grips the side of my hips, flipping me around to press himself against me from behind as I'm facing the kitchen island. My mouth gapes open with anticipation as his lips brush up against my ear. "Do you think I care?"

Goosebumps rise on my skin as my body aches for more of his touch. I feel him growing hard against my ass and I arch my back, wanting to feel more. He caresses my breasts with his hands as he slowly kisses my neck.

James leans me forward.

He grabs my ass and the way he's sliding my shorts over to the side to touch me instead of pulling them off arouses me even more. "Jesus, Scout... are you not wearing underwear?"

"I never run in underwear." My voice comes out raspy as I'm hunched over the counter while he teases the sides of my entrance with his fingers.

He groans. "Why?"

It's hard for me to concentrate on anything other than how much I want him inside of me. "Umm," I say, the sound coming out more as a moan as his fingers get closer to the spot I desperately need him to touch.

"Tell me why," he demands, gripping my butt cheek with his other hand.

"P- panties slow me down. I hate wedgies."

His breathing is heavy. "Okay, I never want to get that image out of my head."

I gasp when Jameson yanks my shorts up hard, giving me a wedgie that burns but feels good. And somehow, completely turns me on.

Jameson

I get a good look at her from behind as she's bent over the counter with her shorts hiked up her ass.

"Fuck, Scout. That's so hot."

I touch the beautiful, tight, round view in front of me. When my fingers move back up into the front of her shorts, she moans.

My fingers slide against her slick folds from behind as she grips the counter in front of her. I dip just the tip of my finger inside of her, so that she has to roll her hips forward to get more of my finger.

Fuck.

She does it again. And again. "Jameson," she moans my name as she continues moving her hips in a slow, shaky rhythm.

"Keep going Scout. Keep fucking my finger."

The way she humps my hand and I get to watch from behind is an image I'll never be able to forget.

As much as I like watching her doing the work, I really want to make her come. I pull my hand out from underneath her shorts and pull myself toward her as I hug her ass from behind. I'm practically on top of her to get a better hold as my hand slides down the front of her shorts. I pull her up and toward me to get my finger hooked inside of her deeper.

She moans louder as I hit that right spot.

I know exactly how she likes it, and she takes my fingers like a good girl.

She cries out as she finishes.

When I know she can't take anymore, I help pull her back up and kiss her now hot mouth.

She's even more out of breath now than when she came back from her run. It's going to be a long day with blue balls, but totally worth it.

"I'm late for work. I'll see you tonight," I say before kissing her goodbye.

Chapter Forty-Two

Scout

"Will you zip me up?" I ask James as he scrolls through his phone on my couch.

His eyes wander over me with desire as he lazily sits back to watch me. I knew the short, glittery, white dress was a good choice.

He sits up and rests his chin between his index finger and thumb. "You should probably change."

I frown. "You don't like it?"

He half laughs. "No, the problem is that I like it way too much. Every time I look at you tonight, I'll be imagining myself ripping the dress off you."

"And that's a problem because?" I ask mischievously.

"Because how am I supposed to be expected to keep my hands off you?"

I lick my lips. "I think you can manage for a couple hours. Now, zip me up." I turn around.

Chills cover my body as I feel his lips press against my back before he slowly zips me up.

I'm a little nervous about tonight. Pretending not to be with each other as we're around the people we love most.

Normally I would love to go to a New Year's party but not when I have to pretend that I'm not with Jameson. "It's going to be hard, isn't it?"

"I know something will be," Jameson jokes.

I laugh. "I'm not talking about your penis. It's going to be difficult being around you without touching you, without talking to you."

"Who says you can't talk to me?" he asks as his hand rests on my hip.

"I'm worried if I talk to you, I might slip up. What if I accidentally tell you I love you?"

"Maybe we should come up with a code word. When we have a moment when we really want to say, *I love you* we could say something else. Something entirely different so nobody catches on."

"That's a great idea! How about...." I think for a moment before I say, "What's that smell?"

He chuckles. "What's that smell? As the code word? Why?"

"It's random and I'm brilliant. Nobody will catch on to that question."

"You are brilliant." He pulls me onto his lap and groans. "And so damn beautiful. You really are going to torture me wearing this dress, aren't you?"

"Yes," I give him a quick peck before standing up.

"I guess I better go get ready," he says. "I'll meet you there."

Jameson

There are so many cars parked outside Rafe's apartment when I pull up that I sigh just thinking about all the conversation I'll have to make. I'm definitely an introvert. Being around a lot of people exhausts me. Scout is the opposite. She's an extrovert who loves being around people. I guess that's why they say opposites attract.

Rafe opens the door and I try not to make it too obvious as my eyes search for Scout. She drove over with Will and Harper, so I know she's here already, since I saw their car in the parking lot.

Will pats me on the back. "You made it."

I nod my head as I spot Scout across the room. Her long, toned legs, perfectly crossed as she leans forward, talking to—*who the fuck is that?* A man wearing a cowboy hat sits across from her, his hand on his drink and his eyes all over her. He's flirting. He wants her. He can't have her. She's *mine.*

"What do you want to drink?" my brother asks, but I can hardly hear him as the man touches Scout's back as she stands.

"James," Will says as he forces me to look at him. He leans into my ear and grumbles, "Stop looking at her."

I can't help it. "I'll take a water." I know if I drink any sort of alcohol tonight, I'll most likely shake the earth if a man so much as looks Scout's way again.

My mood lifts when Scout smiles slightly at me before she walks up to Harper, leaving the cowboy behind. A couple other guys that went to CHU talk to me and I'm already tired of this party. It's New Year's Eve and the one person I want to spend it with, I can't even talk to tonight. When I get into the kitchen for the water Will never brought me, Rafe says, "Hey man! Glad you could make it." He hands me a beer.

Someone steals Rafe away and I take a gulp of beer before I hear my favorite sound. Scout's laugh. I find her dancing to some pop music, her hips swaying from side to side in her little white dress. I love that she's not afraid to be the only one on the floor dancing. Just like the night I first met her, this woman is like a damn magnet and I can't stay away.

Scout

The sound of a deep masculine voice tickles the back of my neck. "Do you smell that?"

I turn around to find James walking past me with a crooked smile.

Grinning back at the gorgeous man, all I do is plug my nose to let him know I love him too.

He turns his back to me as he walks away. Harper appears with one of her co-workers. "Scout, do you remember Monica from the Christmas party?"

"I do. How are you, Monica?" I ask the tall brunette.

"I'm great! Hey, I noticed Wyatt Holden talking to you earlier." Then she looks over at Harper. "Isn't he a big-time roper?"

"A what?" I ask, stuffing a chip from the snack table into my mouth.

Harper says, "Yeah, he's a cowboy. His mom and my mom are friends. He's single."

"He's really nice. You should go talk to him Monica," I mention.

She looks around for him. "He seemed pretty into you. Aren't you single now? Why are you passing up a sexy cowboy?"

I laugh. *I'm more into sexy police officers. One specifically.* "I'm not interested. Go for it."

Monica looks at me like I'm crazy but takes my advice and talks to Wyatt.

I grab a Jello shot since Will and Harper drove me here tonight. If I can't spend time with Jameson, I might as well get drunk.

James studies me from across the room and I smile at him. At least we can flirt a little.

When it gets close to midnight, Rafe has a huge countdown on the screen TV and flashing lights everywhere. I stand back, wondering where Jameson is.

"Six! Five! Four!" Everyone shouts. Someone pulls me around the corner, behind the wall that leads down the hall. I smile when it's Jameson. He smiles back, his eyes drop to my mouth. "Two! One!" His lips find mine at midnight as we hide from everyone else. I take him in without a care in the world, tasting his cinnamon gum as he presses me against the wall. His hands roll through my hair, tilting my head back to deepen the moment. He pulls away and walks off, leaving me feeling drunk from his kiss.

Chapter Forty-Three

Scout

My anxiety I had at the hot springs is still there. As much fun as it's been sneaking around, I'm really hoping James and I can come up with a plan that stops Ethan and JC from controlling my life. Something that will keep us both safe. I know James will do everything he can to fix it but there is a pit in my stomach that's churning and makes me sick. It's only a matter of time before Ethan shows back up. Whatever the plan ends up being, something tells me it's not going to be pretty. But no matter how hard it gets or how big of a war it becomes, for the first time in my life I have something worth fighting for. I'll fight for myself, for James, and for love. No matter what it takes.

But now that the long break is over, I'm ready to go back to work. Every morning I have each of my students write down an affirmation for themselves on a sticky note and place it on the board in the front of the classroom. Then I read them aloud and have them repeat each of the affirmations after me. It starts our day with positivity, and they love it.

"I am proud of myself," I read aloud before they repeat after me.

"I am a good friend." The class repeats after me.

"I can do anything," I say when I notice a delivery man walking in with flowers and a box.

"We'll finish affirmations in a minute. Practice the spelling worksheet I left on your desk," I tell the class. But they're all just as excited to see flowers as I am.

I tell them to quiet down as the man says, "Scout Addison?"

"That's me," I answer as he hands me the box and flowers. "Thank you."

I smell the pink roses and place them on my desk. When I open the box there's a flip phone and a note inside.

The phone is untraceable with unlimited texting. My number is the only contact in it. I'm sorry I have to leave for work tonight. I'll make it up to you in a few days when I get back.

My cheeks start to ache from smiling so hard.

My students are still concentrating on their worksheet and being surprisingly quiet, so I immediately flip open the phone and text Jameson.

You just want to be able to sext while you're away don't you? Jk. Thanks for the phone and beautiful flowers.

He texts back.

Hey I just wanted to make sure you're okay while I'm away. But I'm not going to lie, imagining you sit at your desk right now being the sexy teacher you are is putting some pretty dirty thoughts in my head. ;) You're welcome for the flowers.

I smile at his text before slipping the phone in my bag.

Chapter Forty-Four

Jameson

Scout: Where did you park your truck at the airport?
I text back, **201 A. Why?**
Scout: Just making sure you don't get lost ;) Miss you
Just boarding the plane. Meet you at your house in about three hours.

When I get to my truck after landing at 9 PM, I'm surprised to find Scout sitting in the passenger seat with a mischievous smile. Before I can say anything, she begins unbuttoning her long overcoat. My pants tighten instantly, feeling myself grow hard at the sight of her black bra and matching lace panties.

"Hi," she says innocently when she's anything but. Getting in, I shut the driver's door and look her over. Her legs are crossed but I can still get a peek through her see-through panties. Her dark hair lays over perky tits covered in black lace that looks perfect on her porcelain skin. I notice her clothes are thrown in the backseat. "You are sexy as fuck."

Then with a smirk on her face she says, "Put your hands on the steering wheel Officer Karter." I do as I'm told, and place my hands on the steering wheel. Then she takes the hand-cuffs off my deputy belt. *Fuck...* She fastens them around my wrists to the wheel as I get a good look at her ass from the side. She starts by rubbing my stiff cock through my pants.

"Just the way I like it," she says before unbuttoning my jeans and pulling me out of my underwear.

Then she leans forward, and I hiss when her red plump lips wrap around my tip. She slides her warm mouth down taking me all in at the back of her throat. The way she looks up at me is beautiful. My hands grip the steering wheel, and I can hardly contain myself at the sounds she's making while she sucks me off. Scout's mouth feels like heaven.

"Such a good girl," I tell her.

The way she flicks her tongue and sucks at the same time causes me to come apart in her mouth.

After wiping her lips, she sits up and says, "Surprise!"

I smile. "That was the best surprise I've ever gotten. How did you get in here anyway?"

She pulls out the handcuff key and sets my hands free. "I found the spare key to your truck, and I was hoping you had your handcuffs on you." She goes to open the door and says, "I better go find my car. Meet at your place?"

I grab her waist, pulling her back into my truck. "Where do you think you're going?"

She giggles. Then I take her in the backseat and return the favor more than once.

"I don't want to go home," Scout says after we get our clothes back on.

"Let's go somewhere then," I say, starting up the truck.

"We can't. What if someone sees us?" she asks.

An idea instantly comes to mind. "Let's pick your car up later. I know where to go."

<hr>

Scout's laugh is contagious as we climb the sketchy ladder up onto the rooftop at Copper Hill, the same rooftop she brought me to the night we met.

"I can't believe you remembered this place," she says.

"I'd never forget this place." We get to the top and sit exactly where we did the last time.

"I remember feeling so nervous around you the last time we were up here," I tell her.

She giggles. "You were nervous?"

"Yeah. You were all long legs, confidence, and mysterious as hell. I loved it. But I'd never felt that way around a girl and it made me nervous that I was going to screw it up."

"Really?"

I nod. "Then you said you were probably going to break my heart and I'm pretty sure I almost fell in love with you right then and there."

"I was right," she says, looking out at the city lights. "I did break your heart."

I bring her face back to mine and press my forehead against hers. "Now look at us."

Scout's breath hits my lips before I kiss her. That's when I hear someone climbing up the ladder and pull away to see a flashlight.

"Shit, it's the police," I tell Scout, pulling her up off the ground.

I'm about to explain to the city police officer that I'm a U.S marshal on the rooftop making sure no college kids are sneaking up here when I see who the officer is.

"James. I knew it," Bond says, looking at both Scout and I like we've been caught. Which we have.

"Did you follow us?" I ask, feeling annoyed by the judgment in his eye when he doesn't know the whole story.

"Yeah. When you never showed up to discuss the Harley case we've been working on for weeks, I figured I'd better go out to the airport to see if you had made it back. I followed you here when I saw your truck pulling out of the parking garage. Figured I'd give you two kids a minute to do whatever the hell it was you were doing up here." He's pissed.

"Bond," I say.

He interrupts, "Do you not remember what she did to you? You're not thinking with your head. She's trouble."

I glare at him. "You don't know the whole story. And climbing up here was my idea. Speak about Scout like that again and there will be trouble."

Scout says, "I'm going to let you guys talk. I'll be in the truck."

"Okay I won't be long," I tell her. She climbs down the ladder, and I feel pissed at Bond for probably making her feel like shit. And I know for a fact she's worried about someone knowing about us.

Bond looks at me with disapproving eyes. "What are you thinking, man?"

I shake my head. "I'm thinking I'm in love with this woman and you don't know the whole story."

His eyes shoot me a questioning look. "What do you mean?"

"I'll explain later but you can't tell anyone."

I can trust Bond. And maybe he can help me with my plan.

"Right now, Scout needs me because she's probably scared." I walk away and Bond follows. Scout is waiting at the bottom of the ladder.

She says, "Bond, we were just going to pick up some food and take it back to Jameson's. Do you want to join us?"

This is her way of making peace. We'll explain everything to Bond together and hopefully she'll know that Bond won't tell anyone. She sees that I trust him, so she does too.

I look at Bond as he scratches his head, looking unsure of what to do. Then he nods. "That sounds good."

⚜ ⚜

"You're fucked," Bond says when I walk him out to his car at my place after our late night of explaining everything to him.

"We're figuring it out," I tell him, leaning up against his vehicle.

"I have a feeling this isn't going to end well. Her family is clearly–"

"Don't call them that," I say. "They're not her family. I am."

"Fine. Her brother and his gang clearly don't want you dating her. What are you going to do when they find out? We work with these kinds of people every day, James. They don't blink an eye if they feel the need to kill someone. What are you going to do when– and I say when and not if, because I know it's only a matter of time– they come after you? Come after Scout? What's your plan then, huh? And how is Scout going to feel if you have to kill the bastards first? Or lock them up? Will she ever forgive you for that? She may act like they don't mean anything to her, but her brother is still her family."

I wish he would stop calling him that. But he's right. "That's why I'm trying to figure out a plan that works for both of us. I have to get it right."

"Damn right you do. I'll do some digging. See what I can come up with, okay? But whatever happens isn't going to be pretty. Are you sure you want to risk that?"

"I'd risk my life for Scout."

Bond opens his door and smirks. "That's exactly what you're already doing."

Chapter Forty-Five

Scout

My eyes feel heavy from getting hardly any sleep last night, knowing Bond knows about James and I getting back together. But someone was bound to catch us at some point and James trusts him. A double shot espresso chai tea with extra whipped cream is calling my name. After picking up two of them after my teacher's meeting, I text Jameson on my non- traceable phone. It's almost dead so I type it out fast.

I'll be home around six.

Harper answers her door and instantly smiles when she sees me. "Hey!"

"Are you busy?" I ask.

"Not too busy for my best friend. Come in," she says, opening the door wider. I step inside and hand her one of the chai teas.

"Thank you," she says, taking a sip. "Ugh you're the best. How did you know I needed this?"

I laugh. "Because you always need it. How's work?" I notice her laptop is open on the coffee table that's also scattered with paperwork. She loves her job, and she goes out of her way to help every child she can as a social worker.

"It's good. Sorry about the mess," she says, closing the laptop and stacking the papers.

"Don't worry about it. Is Will working late?" I sit down next to Harper on the couch.

"Yeah. I figured I'd do the same. I'm glad you stopped by. Everything okay?"

I sigh. "Not really."

Concern floods her face. "Do you want to talk about it?"

I shake my head. I can't burden her with everything until James and I fix it. If we ever can. "I can't talk about it. I just needed you to know I'm not okay and I'm worried I've made a mistake."

She places her hand on mine. "Some mistakes are worth it though." I know deep down, that she knows it has to do with Jameson, but she doesn't say anything. These Karter brothers sure know how to steal our hearts.

"This mistake won't be worth it if it ends badly," I say.

"Then it's up to you to decide if it's worth that risk," she says.

I nod.

"What do you need?" Harper asks.

"A distraction. I've been thinking too hard all day."

"In that case let's bake some cookies," Harper says, standing up.

I follow her to the kitchen. "You just know that sugar is the way to my heart."

Chapter Forty-Six

Jameson

I get to Scout's after work and she's not home but there's a note left on her door. She told me she'd be home at six and it's past seven. My jaw clenches when I read the words. **Final warning. Stay away from him.** They were here. Threatening my girl again. They're done. I call her untraceable phone. It goes to voicemail, and my knees feel weak. Before thinking twice, I make another call.

Harper answers with a laugh. "Hi James."

"Is Scout with you?"

"Um, yeah. Why?" She asks with a suspicious tone. I sigh, letting relief settle. *Thank God.*

Shit. I called Harper.

I try and play it cool. "Oh. Damn, okay. I was going to stop by, but maybe I'll swing by tomorrow."

I can almost see the death glare Harper is giving me through the phone when she says,

"You know what James? Scout is mature enough to get over what happened between you two. When are you going to grow up and do the same?" Click. She hangs up.

Harper is mad at me but all I care about is that I know Scout's okay.

Ten minutes later, Scout shows up. As soon as she walks through the door, I sense something is off. She doesn't smile, she doesn't touch me, she just throws her purse and keys on the counter and stares at the floor, as if she doesn't even know I'm there.

"Hey. Sorry I called Harper. I was worried. This was left on your door." I hand her the note.

I stand in the living area, watching her keep her head down.

I think she might be mad at me like Harper but then lifts her head up to look at me. And when she does, she looks at me with such sad, tired eyes, I go to her.

"Baby, what's wrong?" I wrap her in my arms. Nothing hurts worse than seeing her hurt. When I let her go she takes a deep breath before reading the note. I regret giving it to her knowing she's already scared. But she needs to know.

She throws the note after reading it. "I don't know how much longer I can do this."

No.

Her voice shakes. Making me angry all over again that anyone is making her feel like this. Scout is terrified. "They know James. Don't you realize how bad this is? They told me they'd kill you if—"

"Don't you know who you're with? I'm not worried about me but I'm going to do everything I can to protect you Scout that's a promise. All I need from you is to remember the names of Ethan's friends that were at that party you went to."

She chews on her cheek. "I'll try and remember as many as I can and write them down. But the party I went to was pretty big. I'm not sure who was all involved."

"Try and remember."

She writes down at least four names for me, and I make a call to Seattle's police department.

Turns out, they are holding a partygoer named Jason Rod. And he wants out of prison bad enough to be ready to work with us.

⚜

"This is all happening so fast," Scout says with a concerned look on her face. She's been worried sick for two days straight.

"Honestly, it's not happening fast enough," I say, putting on my coat.

"What if our plan doesn't work?" She asks. "What if something goes terribly wrong?"

My contact person, Walt, is meeting me in Seattle, where we'll be listening to Jason have a conversation with JC and Ethan through the wire. It took Walt some convincing in Washington to get the prison to let Jason out long enough to rat, since he's been convicted of murder. But when Walt told them what Jason told him, they let Walt do whatever he needed to do. Jason is claiming JC gave him the kill order and Ethan is the one who helped him do it. They are the reason Jason is behind bars.They'll be convicted to life in prison for all the crimes they've committed. It also took me some convincing for Scout to let me go to Washington, considering

I have a target on my back there. If JC or Ethan see me, they'll know. That's why I have to be careful. Bond offered to go instead but this is something I have to do myself.

"Everything is going to be okay," I try and convince her. Scout's face is pale, and she's hardly eaten at all today. "You're still planning on going to dinner with Harper and Will?"

She nods.

I press my lips to her forehead. "I'll call you as soon as I'm done."

"James please be safe," she says. She taps three times on my chest.

"I love you," I tell her before walking out the door.

I park my truck in the parking garage at the airport.

My bag is light, considering I'll be flying back home as soon as possible. Anticipation eats at me just thinking about handcuffing them if everything goes well. *This has to work.* The parking garage is pretty empty today, so I park close to the elevator. I smile thinking about the visit Scout made me the last time I was here. I swing my truck door open but just as I step out, gunfire rings my ears and a shooting pain strikes up my right leg.

I've been shot.

Chapter Forty-Seven

Scout

I barely remember getting here. I'm pretty sure Will drove so fast that we got here in thirty minutes. I sprint as fast as I can to the E.R entrance, hoping I don't stop to vomit again. When Bond called and told me James was shot, it threw me into the worst panic attack I've ever had. *He's okay. He was shot in the leg, Bond had said.* Please let him be okay.

I hear Harper and Will come running up behind me as I talk to the lady at the front desk.

"Jameson Karter. Is he okay? He's been shot." Words come flying out and I'm not even sure what I'm saying.

"Are you family?" She asks.

"Yes," Will says, "we're family. I'm his brother."

"I'll send a doctor out to speak with you," she says.

"Please," I say, "Is he okay?"

Her brows furrow but she nods. I'm sick to my stomach. Harper holds me and I feel like I might break.

"Are you Officer Karter's family?" A doctor asks.

"Yes," Will says.

"How is he?" I ask.

"He's stable. Luckily, he was shot in the posterior portion of the lower leg. He will need surgery, but that won't be for a few hours. He's been admitted upstairs. Room 216. Go ahead and see him, he's waiting for you."

I barge into room 216 and run to James, who is sitting up in the hospital bed. I know Will and Harper don't know about us but right now I don't care. I wrap my arms around him.

"Are you okay?" I whisper.

"I'm fine." James looks at Will and Harper behind me.

My eyes stay on James, but I hear Will say, "Happy to see you're okay. We'll give you two a minute."

As soon as they walk out, I kiss Jameson and he grabs my hand. A nurse walks in to check his vitals as I watch with a giant pit in my stomach. Seeing Jameson lying down in a hospital bed because of me causes me so much pain, I can hardly stand it.

The nurse takes off the blood pressure cuff and says, "We'll be back in an hour to prepare you for surgery."

"How long will the surgery take? Is it serious?" I ask.

James shakes his head. "Nothing serious. They just have to go into my calf and repair the damage done to the tissue."

I nod my head and the nurse assures me, "It's a safe surgery. Your husband will be just fine."

"Okay thank you," I answer as James grins at me from ear to ear.

The nurse walks out and he says, "Wife. I like the sound of that," he says.

My breath catches. We've talked about marriage before but after everything that's happened it hasn't come up again.

"What?" I whisper, desperate to hear him say it even though it will crush me, knowing it may never happen.

"I like the sound of you as my wife."

As if he can read my devastated expression he says, "This is not your fault. You know how many times I've almost been shot at with my job? We don't know if it even has any-thing to do with Ethan or JC. It was just my leg. Completely non-lethal. I'm fine."

"We both know it most likely had to do with Ethan," I say.

My lip quivers when I feel like I could cry and James says, "Come here."

After getting into the bed with him, I sob into his chest as he holds me. I feel his fingers in my hair when I say, "I could have lost you today."

"You're not going to lose me," he tries to convince me.

But everything in me knows what I have to do.

James pulls my forehead and presses it to his. When I sit up, a tear falls off my cheek and onto his bare chest.

He pulls the blankets off to let me crawl into bed with him. When I lay my head down on his chest, I feel the sound of his heartbeat. The thing that matters most to me is that Jameson lives as he continues to put more light into the world. I kiss the skin over his heart three times and when I look into his blue eyes, my heart skips a beat. I've figured out what I have to do. I can't tell James because he'd never let me go. I'm going to confront JC and Ethan alone.

James kisses me passionately as I feel the heat of his body close to mine. He groans against my mouth and tries pulling me on top of him.

"I don't want to hurt you," I whisper.

He laughs. "My injury is much lower...."

He pulls my leg over so I'm straddling him, and I smile. He runs his hand through my hair and I lean in to kiss him deeply. He pulls my shirt up and my hips move, gently grinding against him until I'm startled by the sound of a loud beeping noise.

Chapter Forty-Eight

James

I smile thinking about my bad girl sneaking in the sheets with me minutes ago. "Is it dangerous that it went up before surgery?" Now she acts so innocent as the nurse comes in to see why my heart rate went up so high.

"No, just unusual," the nurse answers.

"It's my wife's fault," I say with a grin.

Both the nurse and Scout look at me. But the nurse just looks confused, Scout's eyes are wide and like she could smack me.

"She's always causing my heart to speed up. Have you seen her?"

The nurse smiles. "That makes sense. Let's check your bandage," she says before lifting the sheets at my feet. I close my eyes from the pain in my leg as she lifts the bandage. "It looks good. They'll be prepping you soon. If you still want your other visitors to come in before surgery, you'd better let them now."

"Can you send them in?" Scout asks.

The nurse takes off her gloves and nods before leaving the room.

Will, Harper, and Bond walk in moments later. "Shit man, I knew this would happen," Bond says.

I shake my head to shut him up. I don't want Scout feeling any worse than she already does.

"What's going on?" Will asks.

"Just business, brother," I answer.

"We're just glad you're okay," Harper says.

As much as I like the pity party in my hospital room, I need to talk to Bond.

"I'm glad you guys are here. Will, why don't you guys go find something to eat? Scout was just saying she's hungry." I'm sure Will and Harper know something is going on between the two of us, but they don't ask. We'll explain everything to them later.

They take the hint and say their goodbyes. I don't miss the sadness in Scout's eyes as she turns around and blows me a kiss before walking out with Will and Harper.

"I need you to get to Seattle," I tell Bond at the sound of the door shutting.

Bond scratches his head. "I already talked to Walt Bradshaw. Ethan and JC never showed. Jason is already back at Stanley Correctional prison. Jason is freaking out now, worried that they know."

"Goddammit," I say. *There is no possible way Ethan or JC could have known what we were up to.*

"What are we going to do?" Bond asks.

"I need you to figure out what the hell happened. But first, I need you to get Scout to your house and keep her safe. If there is any chance JC and Ethan did this then they know where I am. I don't want her here or her house." *I trust Bond with her life and I'd hate to put Will and Harper in any danger. Especially since they don't even know what's going on.*

"Got it," Bond says. "Keep us posted with the surgery."

"I'll call and check in as soon as I'm done. Scout is going to try and stay. Make her go." He begins walking out. "And Bond?"

He turns to look at me.

"There's nobody else I'd trust right now besides myself to keep her safe. Thank you."

He walks out just as the nurses come in to move me for surgery.

Scout

I wanted to stay at the hospital until Jameson was at least out of surgery, just to make sure he's okay. But after Bond basically forced me out into his car, I'm hoping this will make things easier.

As we drive away from the hospital, I look back.

"He's going to be okay," Bond says.

"I hope so," I say quietly.

"It's a simple surgery. You'll be back in his arms at the end of the day," he says jokingly.

When I don't say anything, I feel Bond studying me while I keep my head down.

"Wait, you're leaving?" he asks.

Damn these cops are good at reading people.

"It's the only choice I have. If I go back to Washington and talk to Ethan and JC, maybe they'll listen. It's what I have to do, and you know I'm right."

Bond sighs. "He'll never forgive me if I let you leave."

"He may never get a chance to forgive you if you don't let me leave." The heaviness in my chest makes my voice crack.

Bond looks at me. "You're a better person than I thought you were. But I doubt you'll be able to change their minds."

"I know someone who might. My dad. Ethan wants to take over his business so badly he'd do anything he says. I know you said we were going to your place, but I need to get to my house and pack my things. I need to leave as soon as possible. Before James catches on."

"What about your job?" he asks.

"I have a teacher's aide who should be able to take over for a few days. I'll tell my boss it was a family emergency."

Bond nods. "Okay. Let's go get you packed."

Chapter Forty-Nine

James

I've begged every person who has walked into my room for my phone. I'm thankful when a nurse finally brings it to me, giving me a disapproving look as I take it. They want me to rest but I don't have time.

Then the nurse says, "So you're the man the whole hospital is talking about. The one who drove himself here after being shot." As far as I know, nobody heard the gunshot in the empty parking garage, so I picked myself off the ground and drove here. Luckily the shooter only fired at me once.

"That's me," I say, turning on my phone.

"The police want to talk to you as soon as you're ready. Expect them to come into your room for a statement."

"I know the drill, thanks."

I dial quickly and Bond answers on the fourth ring. "Hey man, you're out of surgery already?"

"How's Scout? Did you make it to your place?"

"We made it to Wood Lake. We're at her house, picking up her dog."

I hate that they even stopped there, but of course Scout didn't forget about Sickem. "Okay get to your house. I'll try and be out of here as soon as possible."

"They're letting you out today?" Bond asks.

"I'm persuasive," I answer, winking at the nurse that brought me my phone as she checks my vitals. She leaves the room.

Bond says, "James, you were shot in a parking garage barely six hours ago. You need to relax. Listen to the doctors. I told you I'd keep Scout safe."

Only the shooter would know that I was shot in the parking garage. *Because I haven't told anyone that's where I was shot.*

"How did you know I was in the parking garage?" I ask.

Bond pauses. *He's hesitating.* "From the police report," he lies. *There is no police report.*

My blood runs cold when I hear Scout's laugh in the background. "Oh, right," I lie. "What's Scout doing?"

"She's just getting the dog. Do you want to talk to her?"

"Yes."

The phone ruffles and my instincts kick in. I rip out my IV and struggle to stand.

I fall back down on the bed just when Scout picks up. "Hey. You doing okay?" she asks.

"Scout," I say quietly, "you need to listen carefully, but I need you to act completely normal. In fact, laugh right now."

She pauses for a moment but laughs. Damn. Lucky for both of us, she's a good actress.

"Now, when I hang up, I need you to say that you're going to the store to get dog food. Get out of there. I need you to not make a sound when I tell you this, okay? Bond is working for Ethan. He's the one who shot me. If you understand, say you're planning on watching some chick flick later."

She says, "Yeah, I'm planning on watching *The Notebook* tonight. Don't worry about me." I hope Bond doesn't catch the shake in her voice.

"I love you baby."

"Love you," she says quietly, before hanging up.

Scout

Bond is giving Sickem a belly rub when I quickly hand him back his phone so he can't see my hands shake. *He's working for Ethan. He shot James.*

I let out a silent breath before I say, "I just realized I ran out of dog food. I better go get some at the store before I take Sickem to Harper's. In fact, I can get myself to the airport. You can go. Thanks for your help."

I turn and quickly grab my purse and keys off the counter and start heading toward the garage door in the kitchen. Sickem follows.

"Are you sure? I don't mind giving you a ride. It's probably safer," he says, pretending to care.

My voice comes out shaky when I say, "No it's okay, really."

I can't look at this man that betrayed us any longer. After I swing the door open, I hit the garage door button open and race to my car. But as soon as I see who's standing in the driveway, I stop in my tracks.

"JC?" My body tenses and for some reason I can't move.

"Going somewhere, Della?" he asks, walking toward me.

I finally manage to open my car door when JC lunges toward me, stopping me from getting in. He slams the door shut and leans in close. I shut my eyes, letting fear take control.

"What do you want?" I ask.

"I'm just here to see the look in your eyes when I tell you Ethan is giving your boyfriend a visit in the hospital since Bond here failed to do his job."

I panic. "No. I'm leaving and coming back to Washington. Call Ethan right now and tell him to stop this," my voice races.

He slams his fist into my car, causing a dent in the door. "Too bad you've already opened your mouth to him. We know about Jason and the wire." I look at Bond and the guilt on his face is basically a confession. I glare at him, and JC continues, "Once again, this is all your fault Della." He grabs me by the jaw tightly with his hand. I try and turn my head but he's too strong. "But this time you're going to pay for it."

Bond stands in front of my car watching us, not doing a thing to stop this.

Sickem keeps barking and JC says, "Shut your dog up before I shoot her."

"It's okay girl," I try to calm her down, but she can obviously tell something is wrong because she won't stop growling.

When she nips at JC's feet, he kicks her hard, causing her to yelp.

"Don't!" I scream. "I'll put her in the house."

JC looks around and lets me go. Then they both follow me into the house.

"Lock up the dog," JC orders.

I call Sickem to my room and she freaks out when I shut her in there. I've never heard her bark so uncontrollably but at least the closed door muffles the sound. Thankfully JC lets it go.

I lean up against the wall in the hall before turning to face JC. "What can I do to stop this?"

"You can't stop it. But that doesn't mean I can't have some fun with you in the meantime." JC eyes me up and down before leaning into my ear. "You've gotten even sexier. It's a shame you're such a rat or I'd still want you to be my girl."

Bond steps up to us. "JC, you've come here to say what you needed to say. Scout is willing to come back to Washington with you. Just because Jameson knows things, doesn't mean he has to die. I'll protect anything from happening to you."

JC laughs in Bond's face. "How stupid do you think I am?"

Bond glares at him. "You can still stop this. I can't protect you and Ethan from getting away with murder."

JC says, "So that's why you missed the shot? I should have known better than to hire a shitty ass cop to take care of things. Now, if you want your niece to get the treatment she needs, you'll shut your goddamn mouth and do as I say."

An intense anger rolls through me and I slap Bond across the face.

"How could you be a part of this?" I yell at him. "Jameson is your friend. And you tried to kill him?"

Bond shakes his head. "No, I never meant to kill him. I only agreed to shoot him because I wanted to warn him. To scare you off. And it worked... until now."

JC laughs. "Don't you get it Della? The only reason Bond works in this dumpy small town and pretended to be friends with Jameson is because he was working for us the entire time." He looks at Bond. "Are you just going to let her hit you like that?" JC asks.

"What?" Bond asks.

"Hit her back," JC demands.

"I don't hit women," Bond says.

"Do as I say, if you want to save your niece's life. I said hit her."

"I'm sorry," Bond whispers but before he can hit me, I'm shocked to see James tackle Bond to the ground, his crutches falling next to them. His leg is wrapped in a cast, reminding me that he just had surgery. How did he get here as quickly as he did? Before I have time to blink, he's punching Bond repeatedly. Bond tries to get free and unintentionally kicks Jameson's gun that was hidden in the back of his jeans, and it goes flying across the floor.

"Perfect timing that was," JC says, lowering his gun at James.

I jump in front of James and Bond in their brawl on the floor. "No, don't shoot him!"

James looks at me and throws me out of the way and I stumble forward, my hands catching my fall on the wall. "Stay right there!" James yells at me.

"Awww. Trying to be a hero? How sweet," JC says.

He points the gun back at James as I feel like the earth could crumble beneath me. Jameson's life is in JC's hands right now and I've never felt so afraid. JC looks at me. "I'm going to make you watch me kill your boyfriend," JC tells me before looking at James, "Then I'm going to take you back home with me."

"You don't want to do this," Bond tells JC, walking slowly toward him.

James watches closely as I stay up against the wall, my head tilted to the side, afraid to watch. Gunfire rings my ears.

I slide down to the floor and I'm still afraid to look. But when I do, I realize Bond is the one that shot JC and he's not moving. My ears continue to ring when a whole swat team swarms in. One of the officers cusses at James for coming in when they ordered him to stay back.

They clear us out and put handcuffs on Bond. When we get outside, they put Bond in a police car and carry JC out on a stretcher into the ambulance parked outside. James wraps me in his arms and squeezes me tight. We don't have the energy to speak yet.

A man in uniform walks over to us. "Ma'am, we're going to need your statement as soon as possible," he tells me.

I nod.

"She will take the time she needs," James tells the guy before looking back down at me.

Neither one of us has the energy to talk about this right now.

The same man asking for my statement stands next to us, waiting. "Whenever you're ready," he says.

Then James looks at the man and says, "Give her space Ed! Let her breathe and I'll call you when she's ready. Leave."

The man nods and walks off.

James holds me again. "What do you want to do? Where do you want to go?"

I say, "Anywhere but here."

We drive to Jameson's house and for the first time in a long time, it feels like I can call it home again. We can be together.

"What about Ethan?" I ask when we get inside.

"As soon as I knew Bond worked for them, I knew Ethan would be coming for me. Right after I called a swat team over to your house, I called for backup. Ethan was arrested in the hospital before he could get to me, and I convinced one of the officers to drive me to your house."

My eyes widen. "Are you alright?" I ask, sitting down next to him on the couch. My hand wraps around his arm.

"I'm more than alright."

I smile but it quickly fades. "I was leaving," I admit. "I was headed to the airport to fly out to Washington to try and stop this mess." James pulls me in close. "I'm just glad you're safe."

I sigh. "Bond was only a part of it because he was desperate to help his niece with something."

"Shit," James says. "That's how he was paying for her cancer treatments."

"His niece has cancer?" I ask.

"Yeah. Still, he betrayed us," James says.

"I know what he did was wrong, but he helped us in the end."

The pain is written all over Jameson's face. Bond really hurt him. I touch his cheek.

"I can never forgive him," James says.

I nod. "You don't have to. But we need to tell Harper and Will everything. I'm sure word has spread through town already and they're worried sick. I'm going to call Harper and tell them to come over."

"That's a good idea," James says.

I go step up off the couch, but he gently pulls me back. "I'm proud of you."

"I'm proud of you too." I kiss him softly on the lips.

He smiles and cups the side of my face. "We don't have to hide anymore. We won, baby."

"We did. Even after everything we just went through, I feel really happy."

I feel the weight of it all leave my shoulders. I get to show the world how much I love James.

Chapter Fifty

Scout

Six weeks later...

E than definitely got what he deserved and will be spending the rest of his life in prison for attempted murder. I reached out to my parents over the phone after the sentence and they were both thrilled to hear from me. They hoped that one day I would. Although I know I may never be close with them, it felt good to talk to them. I was happy to hear my mom say she's been clean for over a year. James and I are planning a trip to Washington this summer so he can meet them.

JC died that day in the hospital after Bond shot him.

Bond was sentenced to five years in prison but secretly I'm hoping he gets out sooner so that he'll see his niece is getting the treatment she needs. Maybe she'll even be in remission by the time he gets out.

It took some convincing for me to get James to agree to my plan to host a fundraiser for Bond's niece. We had a huge turnout at the fun run because I got a hold of the Copper Hill University's track coach, and he helped spread the word to the other colleges around the country. Hundreds of runners showed up and even donated extra money. We made more than enough to get her the treatment she needed so we donated the rest to other children at the hospital. James thought it was absurd that I would do anything for Bond. But then I proved to him that it wasn't about Bond when I took him to the children's hospital, and he agreed. No child deserves to suffer, and Bond was doing everything he could to make sure that didn't happen. I've already forgiven him although I don't think James ever will.

"I have a surprise," I tell Jameson at the restaurant for lunch.

"Me too," James says.

"Wait really?" I ask, taking my purse off my shoulder and setting it next to me on the booth seat.

"Yes, you first."

"Well I have to take off my shirt to show you mine, so it will have to wait. You go first."

James arches his eyebrow. He's waiting for me to explain so I just say, "You'll see. Tell me my surprise."

"We have a flight in three hours. To Hawaii."

"What?! Are you serious?"

He smiles. "You said you wanted to go to each island. You've already been to Oahu, so we're headed to Kauai. Harper and Will are coming too."

I stand up and do a happy dance. "We don't have time to eat, let's go pack!"

His crooked smile makes my heart want to explode.

We leave the diner and when we get home I say, "This is literally the best surprise ever." I get my suitcase from the closet and begin packing.

"Speaking of which, take off your shirt so I can see my surprise," he says laying on my bed and throwing his arms behind his head to prop himself up.

I pull my shirt over my head and show him my new tattoo located on my right side on my upper rib.

He sits up to examine it closer. "Wow. I didn't know butterflies could be sexy."

I look over my shoulder and down at him to see him licking his bottom lip as he stares at me. "I like that its wings are kind of beaten up. That it's imperfect. It's so... hot."

I smile. "I knew you'd like it."

He quickly pulls me down onto the bed and rolls over my topless body.

"I love it." He kisses me deeply, causing me to hum.

We pull apart and he looks down at me.

"If you keep kissing me like this, you're going to make us miss our flight," I tell him.

"Marry me," Jameson says with his eyes on mine.

He lights a spark in me. "Are you proposing, Jameson Karter?" I'm smiling so big it hurts.

"Dammit," he whispers with his head down. He looks up at me with his eyes. "I don't have a ring yet. Did I screw this up?"

I run my hand through his hair. "No, I love that this was spontaneous. That you asked in the moment because you felt it. That means way more to me than a ring."

He smiles. "Is that a yes?"

"It's a hell yes."

Our bodies intertwine and our mouths collide. Fireworks are going off somewhere. They have to be. Birds are singing, the earth is spinning, waves are crashing. The hectic world we live in beyond these walls is filled with chaos and I know we'll have to go back out there. But right now I'm where I belong.

"I'd marry you tomorrow if I could," he whispers.

"Let's do it."

Jameson's face lights up. "In Hawaii?"

"Why not? Will and Harper will already be there."

He looks a bit surprised but completely happy. "Don't you want a big wedding?"

I think about it. "No, actually. Not at all. I want to elope in Hawaii. On the beach."

"Holy shit, we're really doing this," he says.

"We're doing this," I say back.

He smiles. "I can't wait to make you my wife."

Chapter Fifty-One

Jameson

Four years later...

"Uncle James! Again, again!" Noel says before I pick him back up and toss him in the air. He makes a big splash when he hits the water. My arms are tired, but my nephew's little giggle makes it all worth it. Being around him makes me even more excited to be a dad.

"Noel, it's time for more sunscreen!" Harper yells from the beach.

Noel grumbles, "Okay, mom." We both climb out of the water, and I look up at my beautiful wife laying on her towel in her red bikini. She looks really relaxed with her sunglasses resting over her eyes. Harper and Will can't seem to rest as they sit next to her, never taking their eyes off their son even though I would never let anything happen to him. They're overprotective and I guess I'll understand soon enough. I plop down next to Scout and kiss the side of her forehead before kissing her round, pregnant belly.

She drops her head to the side when she looks at me. "Is it normal for pregnancy to make me feel this exhausted?"

"You're growing our daughter inside of you, it's a lot of work."

"I know I said I would keep running until the day I give birth but this morning I had to walk most of the way."

"Walking's good."

She looks down at her feet and frowns. "And my shoes are feeling tighter. Do my feet look swollen? I knew I'd have to buy bigger clothes, but nobody told me anything about bigger shoes."

I smile at how adorable she is.

"Not to mention I feel like a beached whale."

She looks at me. "Sorry. I know I'm complaining a lot. It's probably so unattractive."

I grab her chin. "You're perfect."

She scrunches her nose and tries not to smile. "I love you Jameson Karter."

I kiss her again. "I love you too."

I rub her belly. "How is Charly doing?"

She rolls her eyes at me. "She's good and I told you, I still haven't decided if that's her name yet."

I laugh. "You love it, and you know it."

She just shakes her head with a smile.

"Are your parents still planning on flying to Ohio to meet the baby when she's born?" I ask. We've met up with them a handful of times. Scout still feels a little guarded around them but the relationship between the three of them seems to be getting better each time they get together.

"They already have their bags packed," she says.

Harper is drenching Noel in sunscreen when I look over at them. The poor boy looks miserable.

"Uncle James when I get as big as you, do I still have to wear sunscreen?"

"Little dude when you get as big as me you can do whatever you want and don't want. So no, you don't have to wear sunscreen."

Harper pulls her sunglasses down to glare at me as Scout hits my arm. Will laughs.

"Yeah, dude. You still have to wear sunscreen," I say.

He frowns. "Ah, man. Why?"

"Because it protects your skin from the UV rays," Will says.

I lean back on my elbows, close to Scout.

"Really?" Noel says. "Well, I'll make sure Charly wears it then."

Everyone is laughing at the fact that he just called the baby Charly. I love that he's already being protective of his cousin.

Scout

"I'm going to put my feet in the water to bring down the swelling," I tell James.

"That's a good idea," James says and helps me stand up.

I turn around to see him watching me walk away, like he always does. Even still. I'm not sure that everyone gets to experience this kind of love, but I hope our daughter finds it one day. James and I will take down any JC that ever tries to step a foot in her life. I don't even know her yet and I already love her so much. I'll never understand why my parents didn't show me the love I deserved when I was young but I'll go to the ends of the earth to make sure she never feels that way. The water feels amazing when I step in. I take a deep breath when I feel James wrap his arms around from behind me. It's terrifying growing a child, knowing she'll arrive any day now. But one thing I know is that I'm happy I get to have James by my side through it all.

"What are you thinking?" he asks.

"I'm thinking Charly is going to have the best dad in the world."

I don't have to look at James to know he has a shit eating grin on his face that I finally accepted the name he came up with.

"I don't know about that but we'll both have you and that's everything," he says in my ear.

I turn around to face him. He's always making sure I feel like I'm enough.

"How do you always know exactly what I need to hear?" I ask.

"I only speak the truth," he says.

After years of being together, James still looks at me like I'm the most beautiful woman in the world. Our daughter will know what true love looks like because of us. Jameson Karter walked into my life and filled the empty spaces of my heart that were broken in me as a child. And I will never have to let him go again. "I'm yours and you're mine *forever*," I say.

He kisses me once more, "Forever."

The End

———————————————————

We hope you enjoyed Out of Love! It would mean the world to us if you left a review on Amazon and Goodreads. Thank you!

Follow us on social media:
Instagram and TikTok- @twicethe_spice

www.ingramcontent.com/pod-product-compliance
Lightning Source LLC
Chambersburg PA
CBHW021225310726
48971CB00006B/1684